RAZOR SHARP

Also by Ashwin Sanghi

RAZOR SHARP

ASHWIN SANGHI

HarperCollins *Publishers* India

First published in India by HarperCollins *Publishers* 2024
4th Floor, Tower A, Building No. 10, DLF Cyber City,
DLF Phase II, Gurugram, Haryana – 122002
www.harpercollins.co.in

2 4 6 8 10 9 7 5 3 1

P-ISBN: 978-93-5699-721-9
E-ISBN: 978-93-5699-984-8

Typeset in 11.5/15.2 Arno Pro at
Manipal Technologies Limited, Manipal

Printed and bound at
Replika Press Pvt. Ltd.

This book is produced from independently certified FSC˚ paper to ensure
responsible forest management.

1

'Come on, Ravi, open the damn door!'

Khushi Mehra hopped from one foot to the other restlessly and pressed the doorbell for the third time. She heard the bell ringing inside the flat where she lived with her husband, Ravi. She stilled, desperately hoping to hear approaching footsteps, but there were none.

'Dammit, Ravi, my bladder's going to burst. If I pee in my pants, I'll kill you,' she muttered. 'Bloody hell! The one day I forget to take my keys with me … THIS happens!' She slammed her palm on the door in frustration.

It swung open with an eerie creak. Taken by surprise, Khushi almost fell forward. She hastily recovered her balance and peered inside. The house was pitch dark.

'Ravi?' she called out as she entered. 'Where are you?'

There was no response. Only the sound of her own breathing—and the thumping of her heart.

'He must have fallen asleep after a few extra beers,' Khushi grumbled. 'And here I am, slaving away on a Sunday night. This damn job. It's no way to live.'

She groped her way to the switches on the wall and pressed them together. All the lights came on simultaneously, illuminating the room. Khushi blinked, the sudden brightness momentarily blinding her, and shielded her eyes with her hand. She waited for a few seconds, allowing her vision to adjust, then lowered her hand and looked around the living room.

Seconds later, loud screams rent the quiet night.

2

Senior Police Inspector Vishnu Tawde sighed and stretched his aching back, wincing at the cracking sound. It was Monday morning, just a little past midnight, and he had hoped to be home and comfortably tucked into bed by now. Instead, he had got that damned call telling him to rush to a flat where a body had been discovered. He had quickly assembled a team consisting of a forensic pathologist, a sub-inspector and a few constables, and deputed them before rushing to the spot himself.

Tawde looked around the flat now. It was a typical middle-class apartment, small, but organized and clean. The only anomaly was the body lying on the floor of the living room. The pathologist was busy examining it. The victim's hands were tied behind his back.

The sub-inspector walked up to him. Tawde yawned, vigorously stomped his feet to get some blood circulation going.

'You've finished speaking to the wife?' he asked her.

'Yes, sir. She was the one who called it in.'

'What's her story?'

'Works at a call centre in Jogeshwari. She got home at around 11.30 p.m. after finishing her shift. The door was unlocked. Found her husband lying dead on the floor. Then she called us.'

'Hmm, make sure to get the details of the place where she works. We'll check if her story holds up. What did the husband do for a living?'

'Day trader in stocks. Not a wizard or anything. Seems he did well enough, from what she says.'

'A punter. Run a check on his finances tomorrow … today. Shit!' Tawde scowled.

He cautiously walked up to the body, taking care not to disturb any potential evidence, and bent down to look at the knife handle sticking out of the victim's chest. A brand was engraved on the handle. Finek.

'Anything interesting?' he asked the pathologist.

'Well, he didn't die of a heart attack,' came the sarcastic reply.

'Saala chutiya,' mumbled Tawde under his breath. Aloud, he asked, 'Got a fix on the time of death?'

'Around 6 p.m. But that's an estimate. Wait for the autopsy.' He prised open the victim's mouth with his gloved fingers. 'Hain? Yeh kya hai?'

'What is it?' asked Tawde.

'There's still some food in his mouth. It hasn't been chewed. Almost raw. Who eats food like that?'

'Was he eating it or was it placed there?'

'You're the investigator,' shot back the pathologist. 'I can't do your job for you.'

Tawde sighed. The pathologist was a pain in the ass. Alas, he was the only one available in a force that was woefully understaffed. 'Let me know if you find anything else.' Tawde cut short the discussion.

He signalled to the rest of the team to assemble near the entrance. A few curious neighbours were trying to peer into the flat. 'Pudhe chala … Move along please. Let the police do its work,' he instructed. As they reluctantly shuffled away, he shut the door firmly and turned to the team.

'Report,' he growled.

'A few fingerprints,' said one. 'Final report awaited, but preliminary results show that they match with those of the couple. No signs of a break-in, either.'

'CCTV?'

'The building doesn't have a video surveillance system.'

'Foolish,' muttered Tawde. 'Any problems between husband and wife?'

'Not according to the neighbours,' said the constable who had been assigned to conduct those interviews. 'They would have the odd screaming match, but after that the neighbours would usually hear moaning and furniture creaking.' He smirked knowingly as he spoke. Tawde glared at him and his smile faded.

'Still at the furniture-creaking stage? How old were they?' asked Tawde.

'The husband was in his late thirties. The wife is a few years younger,' said the SI.

'Any domestic staff? A maid or a cook or anyone who might have access to the house?'

'None. They used all the modern-day appliances—dishwasher, vacuum cleaner. Didn't bother with any domestic help. Meals were mostly take-away, though they sometimes took turns cooking over the weekend.'

Tawde shook his head. 'I just don't get this lifestyle. Kiti murkh aahey. To each his own, I guess.' He turned to the cop who was taking photographs. 'Have we got all the photos we need?'

The photographer nodded. Tawde stretched his back once again and the cracking sound was even more pronounced.

'Okay, doesn't look like we'll be getting anything more here tonight. I assume the wife will be staying with relatives?'

The SI nodded.

'Fine,' said Tawde. 'Bag the body, seal the premises, and let's get out of here.'

3

A few hours earlier, there had been a minor incident at the Trimbakeshwar temple near Nashik.

The queue that had formed outside the imposing black stone edifice on Sunday afternoon was a long one. Devotees were eagerly waiting to view the unique jyotirlinga with its three faces embodying the holy trinity of Brahma, Vishnu and Shiva. All of a sudden, a short, wiry man, with long hair and a saffron bandana tied around his forehead, became impatient and began pushing the people in front of him.

'Chalo, move. I haven't got all day,' he snapped as others in the queue glared at him.

'We're all awaiting our turn,' said an elderly gentleman. 'What's your problem?'

'Why don't you move instead of standing around, zavnya?' asked the man with the bandana. 'There's a long line behind you.'

'The line hasn't moved. I'll move when it does,' retorted the elderly gentleman. 'And talk politely, please. There's no need to use bad language.'

'Now you'll teach me manners? Are you a schoolmaster or what?' The younger man took a step towards the old man aggressively.

Others in the crowd immediately rushed to the old man's defence. Some yelled at the uncouth youngster for his aggressive behaviour. Others begged everyone to calm down.

'Kaay chalu aahey?' bellowed a constable, brandishing a lathi. On duty near the entrance, he had walked down on hearing the commotion. 'Shanta vha! Everyone, quiet down! Otherwise, I'll send you all to the back of the line. And don't think troublemakers will get away. God is seeing everything!' He gestured with his lathi at the strategically placed CCTV cameras. Security—if not God—was certainly watching.

Everyone immediately calmed down. The constable gave the man who had started the ruckus a long, hard stare. 'Tujha naav kaay, hero?' he asked, suspiciously.

'Raju, saheb,' replied the troublemaker with exaggerated politeness.

'Well, Raju, stand quietly and wait for your turn. Otherwise, I'll give you a taste of this,' said the cop, swinging his lathi.

Raju Dabhade smiled at the cop submissively. Then, with a loud 'Har har Shambho!' and a namaskar, he settled down with a wounded sigh, realizing that any pickpocketing would have to wait.

4

'I am a killer.'

Prakash Kadam waited for a reaction from his psychiatrist, Sandra Gomes. When he realized none was forthcoming, he shifted uncomfortably in his chair. Then he bent to adjust its height. Satisfied, he leaned back and tried to focus on his doctor, but failed hopelessly. His attempt to supress a sudden yawn was similarly ineffective and he hastily covered his mouth with his right hand.

Sandra's office in Prabhadevi was in an old building adorned by electric cables and water pipes running haphazardly alongside, a creaking wooden staircase. Thankfully, the clinic itself was clean, modern and air-conditioned—an oasis of organization within a messy landscape.

Sandra tried not to stare at the missing index finger on Kadam's left hand. He had lost it many years ago while fighting a criminal, but refused to share details of the encounter with her. It was just one of many things he had boxed up. She had tried her best to coax him to talk, but her patience was wearing thin. Equally futile had been her attempts to get him to discuss his career in the police force—one that had seen him become the deputy commissioner of police—and the circumstances leading to his suspension.

Kadam shifted again and scratched irritably at his almost entirely grey stubble. Then he puffed out a cheek. Next, he ran his finger along a prominent scar under his left ear. He was a bundle of tics, a man who simply could not sit still. It was barely 10 a.m. on Monday morning, but his eyes were bloodshot. He looked haggard and exhausted. His clothes were unkempt and creased. His broad shoulders and barrel chest suggested that he had once had a powerful frame, but he had added many kilograms and inches since. He had heavy jowls and his trousers struggled to contain his belly. His appearance made him seem at least a decade older than he was.

'No comment?' Kadam asked Sandra, looking pointedly at his watch. It was a wonder that she had not turned him out yet.

Sandra sighed in exasperation. 'Prakash, there's a pattern here. You always begin our sessions by confessing to being a killer. Then you resolutely refuse to elaborate on it. Is today going to be any different?'

'I was responsible for that young man losing his life,' said Kadam bitterly.

'The one you keep having nightmares about?'

Kadam nodded, but remained silent. He puffed a cheek out again, creating a noticeable bulge, then allowed it to deflate.

'And you had the nightmare again last night?' asked Sandra, making notes on a thick yellow pad.

'That obvious?'

'Yes. Most days, you just look terrible …'

'Thanks!' said Kadam caustically.

'I mean that you look terrible after your nightmares,' explained Sandra hastily. 'If I wasn't aware that you are off alcohol, I would attribute it to whisky. On those mornings, you look like you've been to hell and back. Was it the same dream as always?'

'Yes.'

'Describe it please.'

'You already know what it is. I've described it many times before.'

'Humour me.'

Kadam sighed. 'There's a young man,' he said slowly, 'drenched in blood and tied up in a chair. He's screaming for mercy. I'm standing there with a meat cleaver—dripping blood—in my hand, laughing like a mad man.'

'Go on.'

'That's usually the part where I wake up.'

'You knew this man?'

Kadam shrugged and looked away, staring outside the window.

'Did you kill him?' asked Sandra. 'Is that why you keep repeating that opening line?'

'I'm responsible, okay?' snapped Kadam. 'I'm the chutiya responsible.'

Sandra remained silent. She counted to ten and then spoke. 'Are you sure? Could it be your imagination? Are you blaming yourself for something you never did?'

'Save your breath.' He reached for his Wills Navy Cut cigarettes and put one in between his lips.

'You know the smoking policy here.'

It's a fucking stupid policy, thought Kadam. He put the cigarette back in the pack and puffed his cheek out once again.

The two lapsed into a strained silence. After a while, Sandra spoke again, gently but firmly. 'Prakash, do you think my sessions are of any benefit to you?'

Kadam responded with a shrug that spoke more eloquently than any words could have.

'I see. I suspect you could find better uses for your time.' *And I for mine.*

'I'm a suspended cop. Finding time is the least of my problems. If I don't come here, my daughter—Ketul—makes my life miserable. It's better to sit through these sessions with you than suffer her endless nagging.'

'That's flattering indeed. Well, looks like our time's up for today. I'll see you again, same time, two weeks from now?'

'Whatever,' said Kadam, hauling himself to his feet with the first sign of enthusiasm he had displayed during the entire session.

'You must be running low on your medicines. Do you want me to write out a prescription?' asked Sandra.

Kadam responded with a non-committal grunt.

'I'll take that as a yes.' Sandra wrote down a list of medicines. 'I've increased some dosages, especially the anti-depressant and the insomnia pills. I don't think they'll clash with the meds you're on for your heart condition, but you might want to check with your doctor anyway.'

Kadam gave the paper a cursory glance, folded it and put it into his shirt pocket. 'Thanks, doc. A pleasure, as always.' He smirked as he left the room.

Sandra shut her eyes and took several deep breaths to calm down, then applied pressure on both sides of the bridge of her nose with her index fingers. Her assistant opened the door and wordlessly handed her a cup of steaming black coffee.

'Thanks. That might just help ward off the headache I can feel coming on,' muttered Sandra.

'Why do you persist with these sessions? Maybe you should save yourself the grief.'

'Part of it is professional pride. He's a challenge that I'm determined to overcome.'

'And?'

'And then there's pure curiosity,' said Sandra. 'This man was supposed to be the finest investigator in the Mumbai Police. The cases he cracked regularly made front-page headlines. How did he manage to fall so low, so fast? And then …'

'Yes?'

'There's pure human concern. If he tips over, he could be extremely dangerous. To himself … and to everyone around him.'

Kadam exited the building in which Sandra's office was located. He quickly looked up in the direction of her office window to make sure that she wasn't watching, then took out the prescription, tore it into tiny pieces and tossed them into a garbage bin. Then he pulled out a Navy Cut. For a moment, his daughter's reproachful face appeared before his eyes. He shook his head, irritated. 'Get out of my head, Ketul,' he growled. Then, with a defiant shrug, he lit up a cigarette, put it between his lips and took a long drag.

An expression of intense relief appeared on his face. He looked at his watch. 'Good, I can still make the poker game,' he muttered.

'Matunga Circle,' he said a few minutes later as he got into one of the taxis at the stand. The taxi took off as soon as Kadam shut the door. He pulled out his kerchief to mop his brow, and gasped when he saw the blood on his hands and on the cloth.

'Which side of the circle?' asked the driver.

Kadam stared at the bloodstains as if in a daze.

'Which side?' asked the driver again.

Kadam snapped back to the moment. 'Drop me near Café Mysore.'

When he looked down at his hands and the kerchief, the blood had disappeared.

It was around 1 p.m. when Tawde and his team arrived at Patel Corporate Park and made their way to the call centre where Khushi worked. The area was booming, owing to frenzied growth driven by businesses, SEZs, IT parks and industrial zones.

The manager, a potbellied man called something-Sharma, came hurrying up and ushered them into a conference room.

'Welcome, sir. You must be here about Ravi Mehra's death?' he asked. 'So shocking! What's the world coming to?'

News travels fast, thought Tawde, arching his back to relax the tightness in his spine. 'Yes. We just want to ask a few questions. Do you have an official record of how long Khushi Mehra was in office yesterday?'

'You're not seriously thinking of her as a suspect, are you? Khushi is one of the nicest people you'll ever meet. She couldn't hurt a fly.'

'Just answer the question please. We need to explore all possible angles.'

'Yes, yes, of course,' said Sharma hastily. 'Well, I'll just ask HR. We have biometric attendance records, you know. They can't be fudged.' He made a quick call on the intercom and spoke briefly. A couple of minutes later, he looked up at Tawde. 'She was here from 2 p.m. to 11 p.m.,' he said. 'We arrange transportation for all employees on the night shift. She took the office cab, along with some other people. I can put you in touch with them—and with the cab driver—if you like.'

'Not necessary,' said Tawde. 'Would it have been possible for her to leave the office sometime in between and return without being noticed?'

Sharma shook his head. 'It would show up in our records if she did. In any case, we have CCTV cameras always tracking the work area. We can share the footage for that period with you if you like.'

'Thank you, Sharma ji,' said Tawde. 'You've been very helpful. We'll just collect the CCTV feed and be on our way.'

Sharma nodded proudly. Tawde turned to leave, then he remembered something. 'One last question. Would you know what sort of relationship Khushi and her husband had?'

'Like any married couple, I would assume,' said Sharma. 'I think her only concern was that they had been unable to start a family. She spoke about it to her friends in office sometimes.'

Tawde nodded to Sharma as he opened the door.

Could Khushi have been depressed about being childless, he wondered. *Saala, not everyone named Khushi is happy. Could unhappiness be the trigger for murdering a spouse?*

6

In Matunga, in the sweltering heat of the afternoon, a chai shop stood as a refuge for weary souls seeking respite. The air was thick with the aroma of freshly brewed tea and fried samosas. Inside, worn-out tables and mismatched chairs occupied the cramped space, showcasing years of use and character. Creaking ceiling fans spun lazily overhead, their rhythmic groans punctuating the chatter of customers and merging with the cacophony of traffic and horns outside.

Kadam's opponent stared hard at him, as though trying to penetrate his mind with his gaze. Kadam looked back casually, regarding him with as much interest as he had shown in Sandra Gomes. Then, very slightly, his right eye quivered. It was a tiny motion, almost imperceptible, but Kadam's opponent caught it immediately.

I've got you, he thought exultantly. Kadam's right eye had quivered earlier too. And his cards had turned out to be lousy. 'Show,' he declared, opening his cards. Three jacks, a five and a seven.

'Three of a kind. That's good,' Kadam acknowledged ruefully. Then, just as his grinning opponent was reaching for the chips on the table, he gestured to him to wait. 'Unfortunately not good enough,' he said, laying his cards on the table. Five of hearts, six of clubs, seven of diamonds, eight of spades and a nine of hearts.

'What! How, wait ...' his opponent spluttered. Then his shoulders slumped as he realized that Kadam had double bluffed him.

My tics are all my own, gloated Kadam. *You really think I would be that obvious?*

'Another hand?' he asked nonchalantly.

'Enough, Kadam,' said one of the group members. 'Saala, you've cleaned us out already.' He counted the chips stacked before Kadam, opened the calculator app on his mobile and began entering numbers. 'Let's see how much damage you've done to us today.'

Kadam had already worked out the figure in his mind. But he waited patiently for the man to finish. 'Chottu, aur chai de,' he yelled.

A teen who worked in the small shop came scurrying up with a kettle and poured tea into Kadam's glass. 'Here, sa'ab,' he said. 'Garam aur cheeni-maar ke, jaise you like.'

'Good boy,' said Kadam. 'You're still going for your evening classes, aren't you? Better not drop out or I'll tell Ketul didi.'

'No, sa'ab, I go, I go,' said the boy hastily.

Kadam's friend, meanwhile, had finished his calculations and showed the figure on the screen. 'I hope this is okay,' he said.

Kadam shrugged. It was a few rupees less than what he had calculated. 'Whatever,' he said, feeling magnanimous.

As the cash was handed over to him, he gestured to Chottu. 'Yeh le, hero. Buy samosas for yourself and your friends.'

The boy grinned and enthusiastically saluted Kadam. 'Thenkoo, sa'ab,' he said, his eyes shining with hero-worship. He ran off with the money, whistling jauntily.

'Chutiya, why the fuck do you keep taking our money if you're just going to give it away?' asked one of the men sourly.

'You know this is chicken feed for me.' Kadam chuckled. 'I make my money online. I play with you gaandus just for the pleasure of seeing your faces when I beat you.'

If looks could kill ...

'Well, enjoy your afternoon, boys!' Kadam drained his glass in a gulp, then strode towards the exit, stopping to pay the owner.

The remaining players exchanged glances. 'He's a harami,' said the newest member of the group. 'Rude, arrogant bastard ... but also damn generous. I wonder if anyone understands him, including his wife.'

The others hastily looked around. They heaved a sigh of relief when they realized that Kadam was safely out of earshot. 'Never bring up the topic of his wife, especially when he's around,' warned one of them.

'Why, what's the story?' asked the newcomer.

'She walked out on him some years ago,' the oldest member of the group informed him. 'Nobody knows why or what happened to her. We've all heard the rumours. She's locked up in an asylum. She married some NRI and shifted to Dubai. She jumped off a bridge. Hell, at one point of time, it was even said that Kadam might have killed her.'

'Really?' asked the newcomer, his eyes wide. 'Do you think that's possible?'

The old-timer shook his head. 'That rumour ended when Sunny spotted her in Gorai, but then she vanished again. It's a very touchy topic with Kadam. A couple of years ago, some of us had had been drinking during a late-night session. Kadam was an alcoholic at the time. One guy got irritated with him and said, "No wonder your wife left you." Kadam got so mad that he beat up the guy … Made keema out of him. Since then, we play early in the day and stick to tea. That poor lauda hasn't been back for another session since.'

'Did Kadam ever try to find his wife?' asked the newcomer.

The older man shrugged. 'Only he can answer that. All I can say for sure is that he hasn't been the same man since she left. He's turned dark and bitter. His career tanked. God knows what happened between them and where that bitch is now.'

But Kadam knew exactly what had happened that day. He could never forget it, no matter how hard he tried.

7

Tawde found the SI on the Ravi Mehra murder case waiting for him when he got back into office around 3 p.m. The police station in Goregaon West was a drab yellow structure with a mustiness that was typical of government buildings. Cracked ceilings, paan stains and cobwebs were ubiquitous.

'So, did her alibi check out?' she asked.

'Seems like it, though we still have to go through some CCTV footage to be absolutely certain,' said Tawde. 'Did you check the husband's finances?'

She nodded. 'I went through the records of his trades online. Got himself in a jam. The bewakoof tried to conceal it from his wife. She didn't know about it when I spoke to her just now.'

'What sort of jam?' Tawde's interest was piqued.

'He was heavily in debt. Several bets had not paid off. But then it seems he was suddenly able to settle some of his liabilities, though he was still in deep. Then he doubled down on some riskier bets.'

'Where did the money come from?' Tawde placed his hands on his hips.

'There's nothing on the books. But I also got hold of his call records. Around the time he got the cash, he made many calls to one Deva Ingale.'

'If it's who I think it is then Mehra was tatti. The man's a shark. Nasty piece of work. They call him Ekahata.'

'Why?'

'He's one-handed,' replied Tawde. 'His right hand was chopped off below the wrist some years ago. That's not stopped him though. If there's a stink, Deva is usually involved.'

'So, do we bring him in for questioning?'

Tawde shook his head. 'We must tread carefully. He's well connected. They say he's Bhau Patil's pilla.'

'Don-turned-MLA? *That* Bhau Patil?' came the surprised response.

Tawde confirmed with a nod. 'Calling Deva here will tip him off. I think it would be better if I paid him a visit. If Bhau Patil is involved, it could be my career on the line.'

Deva Ingale—alias Ekahata—grunted as he finished a set of curls and swapped the heavy dumbbell for a towel to mop his sweaty face. The air-conditioned gym was insulated from the noise and dust of Mumbai Central, the city's busiest railway station. Around 80 lakh passengers used Mumbai's local train network daily. The rumble of each train that passed through the station was felt as a mild tremor at the gym, located just a few metres away.

Deva flexed his left bicep in front of a mirror and nodded in approval at the bulging muscle and swollen veins. His body was almost like that of a bodybuilder's, except for his right arm with the missing hand. His asymmetrical build made it virtually impossible for him to get ready-made shirts that fit well, forcing him to rely on a local tailor for his needs. His shaven pate and bulbous eyes gave him a threatening appearance—very useful in his line of work.

'Keeping in shape, I see.'

Deva swivelled around and saw a vaguely familiar man standing in front of him. He frowned as he tried to place the fellow. Alas, he was slightly cockeyed, so the frown resulted in his eyes diverging.

'I've seen you somewhere. Tu poliss aahes! Which police station?' Deva asked.

Tawde had come in plain clothes. He nodded. 'Namaskar. Senior Police Inspector Vishnu Tawde. Goregaon police station.'

'Arrey wah!' said Deva. 'The big man himself has come to meet me. How can I be of assistance to you, saheb?'

It was hard to tell whether Deva was being sincere or sarcastic, though Tawde suspected it was the latter. 'Did you know someone called Ravi Mehra?' he asked, arching his back to relieve the persistent stiffness.

'Of course. I heard the pilla is dead. It's a shame. Seemed nice.'

'You loaned him a large sum of money recently?'

Deva picked up a water bottle and sipped from it briefly before replying. 'Usski phat gayi thi. Came pleading for a loan. I was moved by his plight and gave him some money.'

'Arrey, what a generous man you are!'

Anger flashed in Deva's eyes, but he reined it in. 'Yes, I like to help people whenever I can. Mehra was not the first person to turn to me in his hour of need, nor will he be the last. I'm very active in public service—samaj seva.' He delivered the last sentence with a grin that revealed his smoker's teeth. As he walked over to the bench press, he glanced over his shoulder and asked, 'More questions? Majhi kasrat … Need to finish my workout. You should try it for your back.'

Tawde nodded. 'Thanks for the advice. Just one more thing. Any thoughts on who might have killed him?'

'Not me, for sure,' Deva grimaced. 'His death means I'll have to write off his loan.'

'Samajale,' said Tawde. 'Carry on. Apologies for interrupting your workout.'

Deva smiled with his yellowed teeth as Tawde walked out of there.

Back in his office, Tawde quickly read through an email on the Ravi Mehra autopsy from the medical examiner. Most of it was stuff he already knew, but something caught his eye. He re-read the line and made a note of it. He scanned the rest of the report, then phoned the examiner.

'What's this jhamela about blue fibre?'

'We found it under the victim's fingernails,' Shirodkar, the examiner, replied in his trademark raspy voice.

'You think the victim was clawing at the killer and got some fibre from the killer's clothes?'

'Possible,' came the cautious response.

'Hmm. Could be a crucial clue. Possible to identify the source of fibre?'

'Not from my shithole of a lab. We'll have to send it to the Directorate of Forensic Laboratories.'

'Theek aahey, do whatever you have to,' said Tawde impatiently. 'How soon can they let us know?'

'Slow down ... Halu kara! They're understaffed and overloaded. I'll pull whatever strings I can, but it may take a few days before they give us any answers.'

'Barobar, try to speed it up as much as you can.'

Nestled between dense mangrove forests and the Arabian Sea, the Mumbai suburb of Gorai offers a picturesque escape and welcome respite from the hectic pace of Mumbai. On a humid Tuesday evening, just a short bus-ride away from the serene Global Vipassana Pagoda, hundreds of men and women dressed in white had gathered under a massive canopy set up on a grassy field. Large planter pots with tall shrubs lined the perimeter to prevent outsiders from peering in.

'Salaam, Momuma! Show us the light,' the group chanted as a slender man with shoulder-length hair and a neatly trimmed beard stepped onto the carpeted platform covered by a white sheet at one end of the field.

The man gestured for silence and sat down. His voice was a soft whisper, but his words carried clearly across the enormous tent, helped by the state-of-the-art sound system designed by the acoustic engineers among his disciples. His name, Momuma, was merely an acronym for three 'avatars' of the preacher—a Hindu one called Mohan, a Muslim one called Mustafa and a Christian one called Matthew. Little did the gullible souls know that he had picked up the idea from the 1977 hit Bollywood film *Amar Akbar Anthony*.

'Look within yourself,' instructed Momuma. 'Understand your limitless potential. You are the stuff stars are made of. Your souls are timeless ... eternal.'

The crowd listened, mesmerized by his words. No one knew what religion he had been born into because most of his childhood story was a fabrication.

'I am neither a Muslim fakir nor a Hindu rishi,' Momuma said softly. 'I am neither Christian preacher nor Sikh granthi. I am simply the light in your darkness.' Neutrality ensured that all communities felt comfortable joining Momuma's bandwagon.

'Look beyond the artificial boundaries created by humanity,' he continued. 'They have power over you only if you allow it. Listen to the birds that surround us. Do they need passports to go from one country to another? Don't let age, gender, caste, sexual orientation, nationality, race or religion define you ...'

Momuma paused and looked around at the assembly, his disciples gazing up at him adoringly. Their eyes were glazed, the result of a cocktail of drugs.

'You are not your name. That is just a label stuck on you. You are not a son or daughter, father or mother. Those are the bonds that cage you. You are pure, unfettered energy. You are the light. Break the chains that bind you. Cleanse the world, O enlightened souls! Free yourselves! Liberate society!'

'Salaam, Momuma!' the crowd roared again in unison, like a savage beast coming to life. Many whipped off their clothes and began to copulate right there, on the grass. In the front row, a woman on all fours moaned as a stranger took her.

The man grunted in pleasure, but the woman didn't seem to notice him.

Her eyes were fixed on Momuma, tears of ecstasy running down her face.

9

Ketul Kadam finished her morning yoga session in the cramped bedroom of the 1BHK flat in Matunga that she shared with her father. The open window, however, brought the entire neighbourhood into her room. A symphony of sounds and smells evoked the vibrant spirit of Matunga. The rhythmic clatter of local trains, the laughter of children awaiting their school bus, fragrant aromas of freshly made coffee and spices being roasted. There wasn't much space in the room, so Ketul slept on a folding bed that she would put away in a corner whenever she needed to stretch.

She hopped into the bathroom for a quick shower, and emerged looking fresh and energized. A petite girl in her mid twenties, Ketul had wavy, shoulder-length hair, an olive complexion and large, almond-shaped eyes. A close look at her revealed a striking resemblance to Kadam—he must have been an attractive man in his youth, before he put on weight and allowed his careless lifestyle to ravage his features.

Ketul had grown up in that tiny flat. As had Kadam, who had inherited the tenancy from his father. This was the very house into which Kadam had brought his wife—Sarla—after their marriage and where Ketul was born. But it was also the place from where Sarla had walked out in a fit of rage around five years ago, leaving father and daughter to pick up the pieces of their lives with occasional help from Kadam's mother. The brokenness of their lives was visible in the flat. It had an uncared-for vibe: the walls needed paint, damp patches remained unattended and the electrical fittings were outdated. Still, Ketul loved the house deeply. It was the only home she had ever known and she had no desire to find another.

From the bedroom, Ketul walked over to a shelf in the living room where small figurines of Lakshmi and Ganesha sat. She lit an incense stick and placed it in a holder in front of the deities. There was a hint of melancholy in her eyes, probably a consequence of having been abandoned by her mother. The rejection had made her turn to the divine for solace.

Then she tiptoed across the room to the portion that Kadam had curtained off to create sleeping quarters for himself. She smiled indulgently as she heard him snoring, and gently adjusted his head to allow him to breathe freely. By his side was the Caravan radio, which Ketul had presented to him with her first salary. She turned it off.

Kadam muttered something in his sleep and rolled back to his original position. She shook her head in exasperation, then frowned at the cigarette packet and lighter lying on a low table next to him. She quietly scooped up the offending articles and hid them in the kitchen.

Ketul made tea and transferred most of it into a thermos. She poured the rest into a cup and sipped from it, occasionally dunking a piece of kadak pav in it. From time to time, she habitually fiddled with a pendant around her neck—a simple coral given to her by her grandmother to neutralize the negativity of Mars in her birth chart. Ketul was 'manglik'— someone whose birth chart is strongly influenced by the planet Mars—and, astrologically speaking, could bring harm upon her mate if their stars were not aligned. Though Kadam believed this was rubbish, Ketul took the notion seriously, influenced as she was by her grandmother.

She finished her tea and left the thermos on the table beside her snoring father before leaving for work. At the entrance, she reached up and replaced the old nimboo-mirchi string with a fresh one left by the vendor. Ketul firmly believed that it warded off the evil eye, another notion instilled in her by her grandmother. Stroking the back of her neck absently, she took a step backwards to check if the lemon-chilli dangler was straight and bumped into someone. She let out a startled yelp.

'I'm so sorry, I didn't mean to scare you, Ketul,' said their neighbour, Dr Ravikant Desai. A tall and thin man with receding grey hair, Desai was wearing a blue Nehru jacket and had a stethoscope slung around his neck—his uniform of sorts.

'No, I'm sorry, doc,' said Ketul. 'My fault entirely. I was lost in my own world.' With a smile, she asked, 'Off to visit a patient?'

'A lady complaining of kidney pain,' said Desai in clipped tones. The good doctor had graduated from London's Imperial College decades ago, but had retained the accent acquired in England. 'I couldn't help noticing you were massaging your neck. Do you have a back or neck problem?'

'No, doc, just the after-effects of a hurried yoga session.' Ketul smiled.

'How's your father doing? I hope he's taking his heart medication regularly?'

Ketul shrugged with an air of helplessness. 'You know how he is. For a super-intelligent person, he can be remarkably dumb at times.'

'I think that after a certain age, daughters end up parenting their fathers,' said Desai with a wink. 'Well, I had better be off. Work beckons.'

Ketul nodded politely. 'Please come and have a cup of tea with us soon. And try to talk some sense into my father.'

Desai laughed and bustled off, taking the stairs two at a time.

He's fit for his age, thought Ketul admiringly. *I wish Baba would take inspiration from him.* She shook her head at her wishful thinking, then followed him out of the building at a more sedate pace and hailed a taxi.

10

Ketul's office was near the Small Causes Court on Picket Road in Kalbadevi, one of the most congested areas of Mumbai. But Ketul quite liked the vibrant and chaotic atmosphere. She was adept at navigating the crowds and ignoring the incessant honking of car horns. A bonus was that the office was located just a couple of floors above a Hanuman temple, so Ketul was able to stop and seek the blessings of Bajrang Bali before starting each day. Moreover, Shree Thaker Bhojanalay, Mumbai's finest purveyor of Gujarati thaalis, was just a four-minute walk away at lunchtime.

Ketul had barely slung her bag on her chair when a peon appeared. 'Trivedi sahib tumhala bolavat aahet,' he informed her. Ketul nodded and walked to the cabin where Sandeep Trivedi, managing partner of the law firm, sat. At her knock, Trivedi looked up from the file he was reading and gestured to her to enter.

'Shabaash, Ketul! You're starting to make quite a name for yourself!'

'I'm sorry, sir, I don't understand,' she replied.

Trivedi pointed to the file he had been reading. 'A potential client specifically asked for you. A charitable trust called the Shri Haripriya Aid and Kindness Trust of India.'

'That's quite a mouthful,' observed Ketul, toying with her coral pendant.

'Try the acronym,' said Trivedi.

'Oh, S.H.A.K.T.I. That's neat. Haripriya is a name for Durga. This is something to do with women, I presume?'

'You assume correctly,' said Trivedi. 'Shakti is active in combating the trafficking of women.' He grimaced. 'There are some sickening photographs included in this file. You can look at them later. But here's the rundown. Shakti has filed criminal complaints against two men, accusing them of facilitating the abduction of very young girls from villages. Girls as young as nine were being abducted and sold off.'

Trivedi passed the file to her. Ketul quickly scanned the summary on the first page. The younger girls had been sold for Rs 3 lakh each, while older women had fetched a price of Rs 1 lakh each. Most of them had been abducted, but there were some who had been sold off to the brokers by their own families. The girls were then transported to the city and placed in dormitories in Sonapur, the red-light district in north Mumbai, where they were starved and beaten until they obeyed. Often, these dormitories were nothing more than glorified cubbyholes, called pinjaras.

'Depressing stuff,' said Ketul. 'But what is required from us?'

'Shakti has rescued hundreds of young women from Sonapur,' said Trivedi. 'They've rehabilitated and trained these women as taxi drivers and parcel couriers. Providing an occupation means economic independence. But now they want to bust the ring entirely.'

'How?'

'They want the police to bring charges against two known culprits. But the authorities are dragging their feet. They need a lawyer to speed things up.'

'Why me?' asked Ketul.

'They read that *Mid-Day* news report about your case involving the domestic worker. You're famous. Have a look and decide if you want to take it.'

Ketul nodded and returned to her desk with the file. She supressed a yawn as she opened it and began looking through a bunch of photographs attached to the first page with a clip. She was jolted out of her drowsiness almost instantly. Shock was followed by pity, then rage. She shut her eyes and took a couple of deep breaths. After a while, she rose to her feet and walked back to Trivedi's cabin.

'I'll take the case,' she said.

Ninety minutes later, Ketul was outside Vikhroli police station. As with most government buildings, the walls were grimy and stained. A strange smell that was a combination of phenyl floor cleaner, body odour and open tiffin boxes pervaded the interiors. The confrontation that followed with the SI was unpleasant, to say the least.

'Can you explain to me why exactly you won't file these FIRs?' asked Ketul, frustrated.

'Not enough evidence for FIRs,' mumbled the SI.

'Rubbish! You have sworn statements by more than fifteen women who were purchased. How much more evidence do you need?'

'Maaf kara, but I don't think this case falls under our jurisdiction,' said the SI, looking visibly uncomfortable.

'Please don't teach me about jurisdiction,' retorted Ketul. 'I am a lawyer. My father's a policeman. Even if a crime is out of jurisdiction, an FIR can still be filed. It can always be transferred later.'

'Yes, but there is no emergency, no? Mala samajate, these women have already been rescued.'

'Many more women could be getting abducted, beaten, raped or killed while you argue with me.'

'Tell the complainant to come here, maidam.'

'This NGO came to your station with the complaint many days ago.' Ketul glared at the SI. 'Has anyone even looked at their complaint in all these days or was it just tossed into the bin?'

'Kshama kara, we've been very busy. Lots of crime in the locality,' said the SI defensively.

Ketul looked around. Several policemen were sitting idle. A few pretended to be filling out paperwork, but it was obvious that their attention was on the conversation between Ketul and the SI. She gave him a pointed look.

He tried to bluster his way out. 'We're slightly relaxed today after a very long time. Anyway, no jurisdiction. Maidam, you should try the Crimes Against Women Unit.'

'Fine, I'll go there,' said Ketul. 'And they'll send me right back like a tennis ball.' She stood up and started to leave. Then something else struck her. 'There are only two reasons for not registering FIRs. Either the station wants to keep the crime statistics low or there is pressure from the top. Which is it?'

The SI made a show of looking at a file, refusing to meet her gaze.

Ketul nodded scornfully. 'I'll be back,' she said as she swept out of the station.

The SI waited for a couple of minutes, then rose from his chair and went to the men's toilet. Entering one of the cubicles, he farted loudly before peeing. That vada-pav for breakfast had not agreed with him. He zipped up and—without bothering to wash his hands—took out his mobile phone and sent a message.

Mee khup kaam kele, he thought with a grin. *Bhau will be happy.*

11

The office of the ethical hacking firm SafeWebber at Nariman Point was a messy affair: a bunch of mismatched desks overloaded with hardware and untidy cables running all over the place. Files and cartons of takeout food jostled for space. The clutter did not seem to bother those working there though—least of all Nirmal.

His fingers flew across his keyboard effortlessly. Every now and then, he would glance at the two extra monitors placed on his desk. As lines of code rolled on the three screens, his excitement increased. 'C'mon, baby,' he muttered. 'Open up for me.' His breathing was shallow, all his attention was focused on the task at hand, like a hunter moving in for the kill. The tension was palpable.

Suddenly, he punched the air in triumph and chortled, 'Yes! Fuck, I'm in!' Three of his colleagues came rushing up. Nirmal exchanged high fives with them, then gestured contemptuously at the screen with his thumb. 'Tell those pussies at the client's IT department to patch those codes.'

One of his co-workers shook his head. 'Doesn't help. Their IT is handled by a bunch of morons who've probably not even realized that their system has been breached.'

'Well, I'm done for the day, guys. That went faster than I'd expected.'

Nirmal picked up his satchel, slung it around his shoulders and walked out. He paused momentarily to check his reflection in the glass door of the empty office next to theirs. Several corporate offices in the area had relocated to the newer Bandra–Kurla Complex and left behind vacant premises. *No Hrithik Roshan, but not so bad either,* he thought, appraising himself. He had a wiry frame with surprisingly broad shoulders, thanks to a regimen of taekwondo that he had taken up in school. It had helped ease the incessant bullying. Nirmal had been a geek in school. Even now, in his late twenties, he was still one, with his floppy hair, John Lennon–style glasses and oddly fashionable scruffy beard. He patted a stray lock of hair into place, then dug out his phone and pressed a number on speed dial. 'Want to meet for coffee?' he asked.

'I've just reached Haji Ali on my way back from Vikhroli. I'm not really getting much done anyway. Coffee sounds good,' replied Ketul, sounding thoroughly disgruntled.

'Tough day, huh? The usual place in half an hour?'

'See you,' said Ketul, cutting the call.

Oh Ketul, Ketul … always so abrupt, thought Nirmal, pushing the fingertips of his left hand against those of his right. The gesture resembled the movement of a spider extending and retracting its legs on a mirror. Spider push-ups.

For the umpteenth time, he wondered whether to confess his feelings to her. But the same voice of caution that always stopped him emerged once again. What if she just thought of him as a friend? Why risk ruining such a beautiful friendship? He shook his head, irritated by the dilemma. *Some other day, maybe.*

Having put off the difficult decision, he relaxed. He began thinking about Ketul and her beautiful smile; the way her eyes lit up when she saw something exciting; the way her face became animated when she spoke passionately about something; how her lips turned moist when she licked off the latte foam; the way sweat trickled down her cleavage …

Fuck! Why am I such a perv?

12

'Who's this kutti? Ketul something?' Bhau Patil growled into his phone. He was seated in an expensive recliner in his plush bungalow in Malabar Hill, the windows providing breathtaking views of the Arabian Sea.

Patil was a short, stocky man with close-cropped salt-and-pepper hair and a thick moustache. His teeth were stained red from the paan that he chewed continuously. Despite his unimpressive stature—or perhaps to compensate for it—he had a brusque manner and an aggressive attitude. Who he was addressing made little difference to him. In this case, it happened to be Gopal Chavan, Mumbai's Commissioner of Police.

'Namaskar, saheb,' said Chavan, politely, swallowing his anger at Patil's rudeness. 'I'm not sure who exactly you're referring to.' He toyed with the pack of pink and blue antacid tablets on his table.

'She's some bhosdiki lawyer ... Trying to file an FIR in Vikhroli. Luckily, the duty cop told Deva about it right away.' Patil cleared his throat and spat out the phlegm.

Chavan fought his revulsion at the sound.

'A lawyer named Ketul?' asked Chavan. 'That name sounds familiar. It'll come to me ... Wait a minute... Oh teri ... Dhikkaar!' he exclaimed loudly as the penny dropped.

'What? Have you figured out who she is?'

'Yes. Ketul Kadam, daughter of that gaandu, Kutta Kadam,' said Chavan with a scowl. Kadam's uncanny ability to latch on to a scent had earned him the pejorative nickname during his time on the police force.

'That madarchod has a grown-up daughter? And now she's sniffing around my business? What is it with this family?' grumbled Patil.

'Both father and daughter are troublemakers. Constantly poking their noses into other people's affairs. It must run in the genes.'

'Well, make sure nothing comes of this Shakti business. Or we may have to teach the daughter a lesson like we taught that bastard Kadam. I knew he was a son of a bitch. I didn't know he was also the father of one.' He sniggered at his own coarse humour.

'Yes, saheb. I'll pass on the word,' said Chavan. He cleared his throat. 'About Deva ...'

'What about him?' Patil demanded impatiently.

'His name has cropped up in a murder case,' said Chavan. 'He'd given a hefty loan to the victim—Ravi Mehra.'

'So? Is he in any trouble?'

'No, the investigating officer spoke to him, but Deva was able to manage. There's nothing to link him to the murder.'

'Theek. Let's keep it that way. Who's the investigating officer?'

'Vishnu Tawde. Goregaon station. Solid officer.'

'Is he cooperative?' asked Patil, stressing on the last word just enough to leave no doubt about his meaning.

'Not very. But he follows orders.'

'Good enough,' said Patil. 'Whom does he report to?'

'My deputy. Special Commissioner of Police Sharad Rane,' said Chavan tightly.

Mumbai had never had a 'Special Commissioner' until recently. The post had been especially created to accommodate Rane.

'Arrey, that might be a problem. Rane is close to your boss, isn't he? Deputy Home Minister Jayant Gaikwad? He will be difficult to control.'

It was well known that Chavan had a good equation with Bhau Patil, but Rane had a cosier one with Gaikwad.

'Don't worry, saheb. I'll have someone keep an eye on Rane,' said Chavan.

'Do that. Rane is too close to Kutta Kadam for my liking. Saala, the work Deva does is important to me. Make sure nothing disturbs it.' He spat out the remnants of his masticated paan into the spittoon with another guttural sound and ended the call abruptly.

Chavan glared at his phone with loathing. He wondered why he had succumbed to his greed and partnered with Patil. Well … he knew why … He could feel the acid bubbling up. It always did after a conversation with Bhau Patil. He quickly took out an antacid from the packet and chewed on it. Resignedly, he picked up the intercom and dialled a number. 'Shinde? Meet me for a minute,' he said.

Assistant Commissioner of Police Vasant Shinde walked into Chavan's office a little while later. Shinde was a thin, fair-skinned man with a sly and obsequious manner that Chavan found intensely irritating. But he put up with him because the man had his uses.

Chavan got to the point immediately. 'Shinde, I want you to keep me posted on everything SCP Rane does from now.'

Shinde's eyes widened slightly, but he quickly assumed a neutral expression. 'Anything the matter, sir?' he asked, the corner of his mouth twitching. There was something intensely slimy—almost snake-like—about him.

'I don't trust Rane. I get the feeling that he is angling for my job.'

'Samajale, saheb, I'll keep an eye on him. Is there anything specific that I need to watch out for?'

Chavan shook his head, suddenly anxious to end the conversation. 'Just observe your boss, nothing else. Rane is a headache, but his friendship with Kutta Kadam is like a bullet in the head.'

13

Kadam yawned and stretched leisurely, then reached for his pack of cigarettes. His hand encountered … nothing. Irritated, he opened his eyes and looked around. Sure enough, the packet was missing.

Ketul. She had straightened his reading glasses that were lying on the small table next to him. Mutinously, he set them at an angle. She had buttoned and folded his shirt, and left it neatly on a chair. He unbuttoned it and draped it over the chair so he could put it on quickly. He fervently wished Ketul would stop trying to organize things around the flat. Kadam could find his way around his mess, but not around her tidiness.

His little acts of rebellion over, he spotted the thermos of tea that she had left for him. He scratched his stubble as he tried to figure out the sequence of events. 'I left my cigarettes here on the table. Then she brought the tea thermos and left it here. The kitchen ...'

He walked into the kitchen, opened the cupboard where the tea jar was stored and found his cigarettes and lighter inside the jar. He smiled to himself triumphantly. *Never try to outwit your dad*, he admonished Ketul mentally. He settled down in a chair in the living room and took his first puff. He was about to reach for the Caravan radio when there was a perfunctory knock on the door and SCP Sharad Rane entered.

'Your daughter still hiding stuff from you?' joked Rane. His voice carried a distinct nasal quality, its timbre resonating with a subtle yet noticeable twang.

Kadam shrugged. 'She keeps hiding it and I keep finding it.'

'Stubborn girl. I wonder where she gets it from,' Rane deadpanned.

Kadam ignored the jibe and took another puff. He offered the cigarette to Rane, who waved it away.

'You know I quit years ago. Just like you gave up the bottle. Why do you keep trying to tempt me, chutiya?'

'Maybe because I'm jealous of your youthful good looks, gaandu,' growled Kadam.

'The secret is clean living. You should try it sometime.'

Though Rane and Kadam were around the same age, the physical contrast was incredible. Rane had a runner's whipcord lean physique and wore simple but immaculately pressed clothes. His hair, dyed jet black, was always neatly combed.

Kadam was ... well ... Kadam.

When the two men had started their careers together, Kadam was considered the future star, but he had ended up in exile. Meanwhile, Rane had emerged from Kadam's shadow and risen steadily within the system. The two had remained friends and made it a point to lunch together once a fortnight.

Kadam took a few more puffs, then stubbed out the cigarette. Pulling on his shirt, he nodded. 'Let's go.'

Located exactly opposite Matunga Central Station, the Ram Ashray restaurant was always busy, owing to their outstanding south Indian fare and famed Udupi efficiency. The walls adorned with garlanded pictures of deities and photographs of the founders, the simple chessboard floor and the squeaking ceiling fans captured the timeless essence of the place. The aroma of hot sambar, frying dosas and filter coffee wafted through the air as they sat down.

The waiter, who had known Kadam and Rane for years, didn't even bother placing a menu before them. He just asked, 'The usual?' On getting an affirmative nod, he scurried off to get their butter idlis and filter kaapi.

'So, when are you planning to enter and win *Kaun Banega Crorepati*?' asked Rane.

'I could win it easily, where's the challenge in that? In any case, my online poker brings me more than enough,' Kadam retorted cockily.

When the waiter placed their meals before them, Kadam rearranged the katoris on his plate before taking a bite.

Rane watched, intrigued. 'Why do you always do that?'

'I use my spoon to take a chunk off the idli, then dunk it in the sambar and then coat it with coconut chutney. The operation must run clockwise and in that order. If you use the chutney first, then it comes off during the sambar dunking!' replied Kadam earnestly.

A Tamil patron sitting at the next table piped up, 'Now, you will teach south Indians how to have sambar?'

Kadam gave the man a withering look, puffing up one of his cheeks. Then he asked, 'Why do you think it is called sambar?'

'Ennai manniyungal, what sort of question is that?' asked the patron, confused.

'Well, for your information, sambar was first made— accidentally—by the Maratha ruler Sambhaji, when he added imli to his dal. Which makes sambar Maharashtrian, not south Indian. So yes, I can certainly teach you how to eat it!'

Rane burst out laughing. 'Trust you to know stuff like that.'

The two men tucked into their meal, chatting about everything that they had done since they last met. Rane had considerably more to say than Kadam.

'So, how's Ketul doing?' he asked eventually.

'Same as usual. Terrorizing me—and all the stray kids trying to skip school.'

'Shouldn't you be looking for a match for her marriage?'

'Seriously? Can you see me hunting for a groom for Ketul? In any case, an arranged marriage is out of the question given all that manglik nonsense her grandmother drilled into her. Hopefully, she'll find someone who doesn't believe in this bakwaas … Oh wait, I forgot. You're a believer yourself.' Kadam glowered.

Rane made a placatory gesture. 'Isn't there some puja or something that can be done for her? I could make inquiries … The deputy home minister has a guru who is supposedly very powerful.'

Kadam shook his head stubbornly. 'I'm happy to have her at home. Besides, marriage is highly overrated. Just look at the mess I made of mine with Sarla. The only good thing that emerged from it was Ketul.'

Rane pursed his lips thoughtfully, then turned back to his food.

'What is it?' asked Kadam, scratching his stubble. 'That expression on your face means there's something that you want to say. But you aren't sure if you should. Jaldi bol.'

Rane nodded. 'Vedna aahes. It's about Sarla.'

Kadam looked up sharply. 'Is she still alive? Not that I care.'

'Of course, you care, saala. I've known you for too long.'

'Chalo, as long as she's alive and well, I'm not too bothered. Where is she, anyway?' He tried very hard to keep his tone nonchalant.

Rane was about to answer when his phone rang. 'Sorry, I'll have to take this,' he said. He shielded the phone with his hand so that his voice would not be audible to others nearby. 'Hello?'

Deputy Home Minister Jayant Gaikwad's voice crackled into Rane's ear. 'How are you, Rane?' he asked.

Kadam strained to hear the conversation without making it obvious.

'I'm fine, saheb, thank you. I hope you and your family are well.'

Kadam rolled his eyes at Rane's ingratiating tone.

'Arrey naahin, baba, which is why I'm calling you,' said Gaikwad, getting straight to the point. 'I think Pankaj is back on that powder.'

'So sorry, sir,' said Rane.

'Don't be sorry! Kuchh karo. You had helped with his rehab last time. Talk some sense into the chutiya.'

'Ho, saheb, I'll do my best.'

'I'm counting on you, Rane,' Gaikwad growled, abruptly ending the call.

Kadam, meanwhile, had signalled to the waiter to bring the bill. When it arrived, he pushed it towards Rane, who paid via the UPI app on his phone. Kadam took out exactly half the amount in cash and handed it over to Rane.

'So, what are you? His pet pilla?' asked Kadam as they left the restaurant.

'What are you talking about?' Rane's voice became even more shrill and nasal when he was being defensive.

'That's a randi's tone you assume when you're talking to Gaikwad. It's almost like you're bending over so he can fuck you. What did he want to talk about?' asked Kadam, pulling a cigarette out of the pack, and holding it between the middle finger and thumb of his left hand. It had been a while since his brain had bypassed his missing index finger and begun using his middle finger instead.

'His son.'

'Hmm, he needed you when that ghanta was caught at Bangalore airport with coke in his luggage. Then he needed you to put the boy in rehab in Thailand. What does he need you for now? Why don't you just tell him to fuck off and stop making you the father?'

Rane knew that Gaikwad expected such favours because he had pushed for creating the position of special commissioner of police. And it was Gaikwad who had ensured that Rane occupied the post. Rane waved his hand before his face to blow away the smoke from the cigarette. 'Fuck, Prakash, you are a genius when it comes to know-how. But what really matters in this system is know-who. That's why I'm still in the field, while you're on the bench.'

Kadam shrugged, not letting Rane see how much his words had stung. 'Theek. I suppose if Commissioner Chavan can serve that prick Bhau Patil, you may as well lick Gaikwad's ass.'

'You can't compare an underworld thug with a deputy home minister,' replied Rane hotly. 'I'm told that Gaikwad is unhappy being Omkar Lokhande's deputy. He wants to be made home minister.'

'If he becomes home minister, he will make you commissioner.' Kadam ran a finger along his scar thoughtfully.

'No point in too much vichaar,' said Rane, but it was obvious from his expression that he liked the idea very much.

'I hope it happens—just so I can see the look on Chavan's face!' Kadam laughed as the two men parted.

As he slowly walked back towards his flat, Kadam reflected on Rane's words. He wondered whether he should have compromised with the system. He would have been a joint commissioner by now, probably commissioner in a few years. He puffed a cheek as he contemplated what might have been. Then he shook his head. *Never.* He would have had to lick the boots of bastards like Chavan and Gaikwad. It was better to live alone as a lion than in a pack of hyenas.

Besides, if Rane runs into a case he can't solve, he'll come running to me as usual.

14

Bhau Patil looked up from his iPad as his secretary ushered Deva into his study. Ekahata had been discreetly admitted into Patil's lavish Malabar Hill bungalow through a small rear gate.

Deva gave a clumsy half-salute to Patil with the stub of his right arm. 'You called, saheb?' Even though there were a couple of chairs in front of him, Deva remained standing. Nor did Patil invite him to take a seat.

Patil spat into a spittoon. 'Saavadh raha. At least for a few days until things settle down,' he said. 'That Mehra murder has got the police investigating the loan angle. Tu tyala dhamki dilaas ka? One of your famous threats?'

Deva laughed, his eyes darting in opposite directions. 'All of them need threatening at some time or the other. That gaandu Mehra too. They start taking us for granted. We can't have that.'

'It's not a joke,' snapped Patil. 'Listen to me. Lie low.'

'Ho, saheb. Of course.' Deva's smile vanished in the face of Patil's anger.

Patil stared hard at Deva, then nodded, satisfied that he had made his point. 'Any information about that new consignment coming from Kathmandu?'

Deva nodded. 'Seventeen of them. Good quality maal. I have informed Sonapur. One of the randis died on the way. Too much heat in the truck, the others complained. What to do? Fly the bitches business class?'

Patil laughed, baring his stained, red teeth. 'Send me samples.'

'Of course, saheb. Only the best for you,' said Deva, relaxing visibly at Patil's changed demeanour.

'Okay, go now. And remember what I said about the Ravi Mehra case.'

Deva saluted with the stub again. 'Don't worry about it, saheb. Those madarchod cops can't find their own arseholes, how will they solve murders?'

15

Monday, 10 February, around 1 p.m., Lower Parel, Mumbai

Lower Parel, located in the heart of Mumbai, is a bustling neighbourhood that epitomizes the city's rapid transformation and modernization. Once a predominantly industrial area, it has evolved into a vibrant hub of commercial activity and urban living. The streets of Lower Parel are lined with sleek skyscrapers, trendy cafes, upscale restaurants, fashionable boutiques and residential buildings.

Poonam rang the apartment bell in one such building repeatedly. When there was no reply, she pounded on the door. There was still no response. She frowned and scratched her head. *Where is didi?* Her employer always let her know if she was going to be out. The door was the kind that automatically locked shut even without a key. Still, she pressed down on the handle on the off chance that it might open, but the door didn't budge.

'Stupid lock,' Poonam cursed.

Eventually she concluded that Suchi madam was not at home. She then had the happy thought that she could go home early. As she was exiting the building, she passed the guard sitting at the entrance. 'Did Suchi madam leave a message for me?' she asked.

The Bihari guard shook his head. 'Not seen her aakhaa din,' he said.

'How long have you been on duty aaj?'

'Subah se. She hasn't stepped out since I came.'

Poonam began to worry. Suchi madam lived alone. Maybe she was sick and needed help? 'Come with me and break open the door,' she told the guard.

'Kyaa boli? I'm not breaking into her house. I could get into trouble.'

'Arrey, kuchh to karo! What if she's had a heart attack?'

'Go to the RWA office and tell them,' said the guard. 'They're having a meeting. They can decide what to do.'

The office-bearers at the Residents' Welfare Association didn't take the maid too seriously. 'Your madam may have spent the night out,' said the president. 'She's a single woman.' He winked at the other members. Most of them tittered. Poonam flushed.

The secretary, a grey-haired woman, was not amused. 'Let me call her,' she said. 'Number hai?'

Poonam nodded and read it out from her mobile. The call went unanswered. The secretary tried again, but with the same result. She looked at the others. 'This could be serious. I think we should force the door open.'

'What if she's with a ... *friend*? She could get upset if they're ... umm ... busy. She could just be out too, you know,' said the president.

Poonam interjected. 'Sa'ab, I've known her for years. Suchi madam never disappears. She ekdum calls and tells me.'

The president sighed reluctantly. 'Chalo, but if it turns out to be a false alarm, the two of you can deal with her,' he said. 'Tell the guard to force the lock.'

'Didi? Didi, aap kahaan ho?' Poonam called out a few minutes later as she entered the apartment. Her eyes widened at the sight before her. She sank to her knees with a gasp, shaking all over.

Suchandra Agarwal lay dead on the floor. Her hands were tied behind her with a rope. Her mouth was stuffed with food. A knife was embedded in her chest. The brand, engraved on the handle, read 'Finek'.

16

The plush new police headquarters opposite Crawford Market had been inaugurated just a few months ago. The offices within the building were shielded from the heat, dust and noise of the surrounding area by double-glazed windows and the hum of air-conditioning.

SCP Sharad Rane frowned as he looked at the document in front of him. It was a summary of all the cases filed by the police in the past fortnight. One of the cases mentioned in it seemed vaguely familiar. He read the report again, carefully, then rang the bell placed on his desk.

A constable opened the door and peered in. 'Saheb?'

'Majhyasathi kahitari kara,' said Rane in his nasal voice. 'Get me the file on the Goregaon West murder—man by the name of Ravi something. And the one for the Suchandra Agarwal murder.'

The constable returned a few minutes later with the files. Rane dismissed him with a nod and began reading the Ravi Mehra file, occasionally scribbling some notes in a pad in front of him. Next, he started on the Suchandra Agarwal file, continuing to jot down points alongside. When he was done, he looked at his notes, checking for the name of the person who had signed off on the cases. His expression darkened. 'Vasant Shinde,' he scowled. He should have known.

He dialled Shinde's extension on the intercom. 'Can you come to my cabin?' he asked, keeping his tone neutral. 'Make it quick. I'm waiting.' After he hung up, he drummed his fingernails on the table impatiently.

Shinde walked in after a few minutes, an ingratiating smile on his face, and saluted. 'Namaskar, saheb,' he said in his slithery tone.

Something about the man's demeanour reminded Rane of a snake. 'Sit down, Shinde,' he said, his voice menacingly soft. 'As ACP, Crime Branch, you review all violent crimes cases that have taken place in the city through the day. Right?'

Shinde nodded. 'Ho, saheb. Standard operating procedure.' One corner of his mouth twitched.

'Right, right. So, tell me a little about the Ravi Mehra case.' Rane's tone was matter-of-fact.

'Ravi … Mehra? Yes, of course. Well, er …' Shinde's voice trailed off. 'Actually, sir, there are so many cases every day, it's hard to keep track. If I could just … umm … see the file …' His tone was defensive.

'No problem, Shinde. Let me refresh your memory,' said Rane nasally. 'Vishnu Tawde's case. The victim was found dead in his house in Goregaon West. His hands were tied and there was food in his mouth. He had been killed with a Finek knife, which was still in his chest when the body was discovered.'

'Ho nakkeech, saheb. I remember. But why are you asking about the case?'

'I'll tell you in a minute. What about the Suchandra Agarwal murder? Remember that?' When Shinde shook his head, Rane continued, 'This one was in Lower Parel. Found dead in her house. Hands tied, food in mouth, knife in chest. Want to guess the brand?'

Shinde's eyes widened as Rane recounted the details of Suchandra's murder. He opened his mouth to speak, but no words came out.

Rane had been making a conscious effort to remain calm so far, but the sight of Shinde's bewildered expression made his self-control evaporate. 'Bekkar, Shinde! Doka satkavu nako. Are you fucking blind? Or do you mooth-maro while signing off on files? Do you even read what's written in them?' For a moment, he was tempted to punch Shinde, but he settled for slamming his palm on the desk ... hard.

Shinde flinched and his face turned bright red, but he wisely kept his mouth shut. He could always go to Commissioner Gopal Chavan if things got out of hand.

'The two murders happened in different parts of the city. They fall under different police stations. Both investigation teams are working independently—so no sharing of information. But both files came to you, benchod. You should have spotted the pattern!' Anger had made Rane's nasal twang even more pronounced.

'Mala maaf kara, saheb. I'm ekdum careful. I must have been unwell the day the second file came,' stammered Shinde.

Rane gave him a disgusted look. *To do your job properly, you'll first have to remove your lips from around the commissioner's gaand, where they are permanently stuck,* thought Rane. But he left the uncouth thought unsaid.

Instead, he looked at the file again. 'The investigating officer from Lower Parel is Satyadev Deshmukh. Get him in. Let me hear what he has found so far.'

'Now, sir?' asked Shinde, his eyes straying towards the clock.

Rane's temper flared again. 'Chutiya! We're going to have to work extra to make up for lost time. I just hope we're not too late to prevent another murder.'

17

'So, this case comes under the N.M. Joshi Marg police station?' asked Rane.

'Yes, sir,' replied Inspector Satyadev Deshmukh. He was tall and lean, with a luxuriant waxed moustache that seemed incongruous on his wiry frame. Deshmukh twisted a handkerchief between his perpetually sweaty palms. ACP Shinde had called him an hour ago and ordered him to drop everything and come to the headquarters right away. 'Is there a problem, saheb?' he asked nervously.

Rane shook his head. 'I don't know ... yet. Tell me everything about the investigation so far.'

'Yes, sir. We got the call in the afternoon, around 1.30 p.m.—'

'This was Monday?' interrupted Rane.

'Yes, sir. Monday, 10 February.'

Rane was seething. *Three days ago—and I am finding out about this only now!* 'Go on.'

'Ho, saheb. The body was found by the victim's part-time maid, who used to cook for her,' said Deshmukh, dabbing his hands on his kerchief. 'She was worried when her employer didn't answer the door and created a scene in the building. The RWA called us after they forced the door open and found the body.'

'Do we know what time the death took place?'

'The examiner said she died—andaaje—around 10 a.m., sir.'

'I see. Then she would have been dead for at least three hours when she was discovered. Any signs of a break-in?'

Deshmukh shook his head. 'There was no sign of any forced entry or a struggle.'

'So, it was someone she let inside herself. Any record of visitors?'

'There's a single CCTV camera—black and white—in the lift lobby. But the lens was dirty, so the picture quality is poor. There are over a hundred flats in the building, so it will take time to eliminate everyone who went through that lobby. Aani, no idea where they were going or coming from.'

'Don't the security guards check with the visitors which flat they're going to?'

Deshmukh nodded. 'They maintain a visitors' register, saheb, but according to that the victim did not have any visitors. Besides, there is no way to confirm if people have written correct details.'

Rane frowned. 'Locha zhala. Why do residential societies— even the ones in upmarket localities—not follow basic safety measures? Anyway, what do we know about the victim?'

'She used to work as an executive at an ad agency, sir. Single woman, thirty-two,' said Deshmukh, looking at his notes.

'Boyfriend?'

'No, sir. Umm … more of a girlfriend,' said Deshmukh, grasping his kerchief tighter.

'Ho kaa? Batting for both teams or only for the ladies' side?'

Deshmukh shrugged. 'Not sure, sir. But for the last two years, the only person she was seen with was this woman called'—he scanned his notebook—'Nidhi. Nidhi Khanna. Not a steady relationship, though. Kadhi chalu, kadhi banda. On–off.'

'Theek aahey. What does this Nidhi do?'

'She used to work at the same ad agency. She quit only a few months ago.'

'Have you spoken to her? Where was she at the time of the murder?'

'At a doctor's clinic, sir. He confirmed she was there. One GP by the name of Dr Ravikant Desai.'

Rane looked up sharply. 'Kay mhanta? What did you say the doctor's name was?'

'Desai, sir. Ravikant Desai. Do you know him?'

Rane shook his head slowly. 'I know someone who knows him. Desai is the neighbour of a friend.'

'Atrangi,' said Shinde. It was the first time he had spoken since Deshmukh entered the room. 'What a small world!'

'Indeed,' said Rane curtly. He turned his attention back to Deshmukh. 'Go on.'

'Yes, sir. Well, Dr Desai confirmed that Nidhi had come to his clinic for a sinus infection. His receptionist saw her too. So did people in the waiting area.'

'I see. Looks like she has a kadak alibi,' said Rane. 'What about the maid? Could she have killed the victim? And then done drama about discovering the body to avoid suspicion?'

'Poonam. We asked around about her. The other employers spoke very highly of her—honest, reliable, etcetera. No complaints or crime record either.'

'Nakki ka? Where does this model of virtue live? Maybe I should introduce her to my wife who keeps cribbing about our maid,' said Rane sarcastically.

'The story of every household, saheb,' Shinde said with an oily smile. He was trying very hard to worm his way back into Rane's good graces.

Rane ignored him. 'The victim's hands were tied, right? Could it have been a sexual encounter gone wrong?' he asked Deshmukh.

'The examiner didn't find any signs of sexual activity, sir.'

Rane grunted in frustration. 'So we're stuck with no leads.' He paused as the inspector, who had been sniffling for a while, used his handkerchief to wipe his nose. 'You're not feeling well?' he asked.

'I've had a cold for the past few days, sir,' Deshmukh replied, stashing the handkerchief in his pocket. 'Ever since I went to Suchandra Agarwal's flat. The AC was on full blast.'

'An AC at maximum power in early February. What would she have done in peak summer?' Rane shook his head. Then a thought suddenly struck him. 'Fuck!'

'Sir?' asked Deshmukh.

'Was the AC on when the body was discovered or did someone switch it on later?' asked Rane.

'I think it was on the whole time, saheb. We definitely didn't switch it on. Why—'

Rane slapped his forehead. 'Doesn't anybody use their bheja in this department? Think! If the AC had been on for a long time, it could have slowed down body decay. She might have died a lot earlier. Was the examiner smoking charas?'

Deshmukh looked crestfallen. 'You're right, sir. We must rethink.'

Rane nodded grimly. 'First, let me show you something.' He handed over the file on Ravi Mehra's murder to Deshmukh.

The inspector looked at the photographs on the first page. His expression changed to one of shock and surprise. He quickly flipped through the file. 'It's the same MO, saheb!' he exclaimed, looking at Rane. 'It must be the same killer. It would be too much of a coincidence otherwise. The details of the first murder were never shared, so it can't be a copycat.'

'Which means we have a serial killer in Mumbai. Someone who's already killed twice and may be planning another murder as we speak.'

The three men fell silent as they absorbed this information.

'Right, well,' Rane said abruptly, 'this investigation will have to be handled by someone senior, someone who can work across jurisdictions. Shinde, I'm putting you in charge. Have all the files and evidence transferred to the Crime Branch, and let this other fellow'—he looked at the file—'Inspector Tawde know.'

Shinde beamed and puffed out his chest. 'Thank you, saheb. I'm honoured by the faith—'

'Kadam will assist you,' said Rane, interrupting Shinde mid-sentence.

Shinde's face fell. 'What? But why, sir? There's really no need—'

'Do you have a problem with my decision, Shinde?' Rane snapped.

The special commissioner's nasal twang was the object of many a joke among Shinde and his cohorts, but, coupled with the challenge in Rane's eyes and grim set of his mouth, it left the ACP fumbling for words.

'Sir, Kutta … er … Kadam saheb has been on suspension for a long time. How can we involve him in a murder investigation?' Shinde protested weakly.

'Kadam may be on suspension. His brain isn't. I have used him as an advisor on many tough cases, and he's never failed.'

Kutta Kadam is going to be a royal pain in my gaand, thought Shinde bitterly. Worse, Kadam was Rane's buddy … This was Rane's way of controlling the whole investigation.

Rane glared at Shinde. There was simply no way the incompetent jerk in front of him would ever solve the case. Kadam was his only hope.

Shinde was the first to blink. 'As you wish, sir,' he said, his voice surly.

'Excellent,' said Rane briskly, dismissing both men. Once they left, he phoned Kadam. 'Are you busy?'

'Well, I've got video conferences with Joe Biden and Narendra Modi lined up. But I can try to squeeze you in,' retorted Kadam. 'What's up?'

'Two linked cases—'

'Ravi Mehra and Suchandra Agarwal, is it? What took you so long!'

'What!' sputtered Rane. 'You know … But how?'

'I still have sources in every station,' chortled Kadam. 'And I keep my eyes and ears open. Chalo, I'll be happy to help. Which ghanta will I have to deal with?'

'Technically, you will only be consulting … er … assisting. ACP Shinde will be leading the investigation,' said Rane formally, mindful that Shinde may well be outside his door.

Kadam sighed. 'That chutiya? No wonder you need me.'

18

The music in O!Maria, the upscale Bandra nightclub, was deafening. It was complemented by occasional whoops and cheers from the dance floor. Dozens of sweaty bodies heaved and swayed in the dark, congested space meant for far fewer people.

Nidhi Khanna determinedly headed towards the small VIP enclosure at one end of the club, pushing her way through the crowd. There were loud protests as she stepped on several toes along the way.

'What the fuck, bitch? Watch where you're going,' said one man, shoving Nidhi angrily. She stumbled and clutched at the wall for support. The soundwaves bouncing off the walls vibrated through her fingers. She giggled at the sensation, then started walking again.

Upon reaching the enclosure, she rapped on the partition and peered in. 'What's up, Punky?' she said in her sweetest voice.

'You again? Haven't I told you to stop bothering me?' the young man slurred irritably. He had thick curly hair and a scruffy beard. There was a glazed look in his eyes.

Nidhi stepped inside. 'Oh, come on. If you keep having the good stuff yourself, what are you going to give your loyal customers?'

'No money, no stuff.'

'Don't be like that, Punky. I'll get you the money. I always have in the past, no? Just one fix, please. Please?'

Pankaj suddenly reached out and grabbed Nidhi's right breast. She gasped in agony as he pinched her nipple hard. Tears sprang to her eyes. 'You still owe me for the last few times,' he hissed.

Nidhi pulled away, rubbing her breast, trying to soothe the pain. 'I'll get it, I promise.' A thought suddenly struck her. 'I could pay in other ways,' she suggested. She deliberately brought her gaze down towards his groin.

'Shut your fucking mouth, cunt. I don't do dykes,' said Pankaj. 'Besides, what would your girlfriend say if she found out? Oh wait, she's dead. She was too good for a worthless whore like you.'

Nidhi fell to the floor with a whimper and grabbed his leg. The young man looked at her pleading expression with disgust. Then he gave a tiny nod. 'I don't know why I keep doing this. I just have a soft heart, I guess. Fine, you can have one fix.'

'Oh, thank you, Punky!' Nidhi gabbled pathetically. 'I'll pay you for all of it, I promise.' She wiped her eyes, smearing her already ruined eyeliner further across her face.

'See that you do. Though how you're going to is beyond me, now that your girlfriend isn't around to act as your ATM.' He threw a small plastic pouch at her. 'Fix your goddamn face and get out. You look like a fucking racoon.'

Pankaj shook his head angrily. He had a bad headache coming on. *Better get some air*, he thought. Avoiding the crowd on the dance floor, he took a small exit meant for VIPs and emerged into the lane behind the club. The stillness and quiet were a relief. He leaned against the wall, lit a cigarette and took a deep drag.

A figure materialized from the shadows. Pankaj started to tense, but then relaxed as he saw it was the beat constable.

'Tu kasa aahes, Pankaj baba?' asked the constable deferentially.

Punky tried to recall the man's name, but couldn't. 'What's up, pandu?' he said instead.

'Rane saheb wants to see you,' said the cop, jerking his thumb towards a police vehicle parked at the end of the lane.

'Fuck. That madarchod is here? What does he want?'

'No idea, baba,' said the constable. 'Maybe you should ask him yourself?'

'Don't take that tone with me, pandu. It'll take me just a couple of minutes to have you posted to some Naxal-infested district for the rest of your fucking life,' snapped Pankaj. He took a couple of quick puffs, then threw away the cigarette and walked down the road unhurriedly.

Rane was standing by the car, waiting.

'Long time, SCP saheb,' said Pankaj in a surly tone, stressing on the 'SCP' ever so slightly to remind Rane that his position was due to his father.

'I hear you're up to your old tricks again,' snapped Rane. 'I could shut down that nightclub, you know. All the powder that you consume and sell from there would be khallaas.'

Pankaj laughed out loud. 'Really? We both know that Omkar Lokhande is the real owner of the place. The guys who run it are just a front for him. Try shutting it down and your ass will be fired within an hour.'

The mention of the home minister annoyed Rane. He cocked his head to one side thoughtfully, his gaze on Pankaj.

'Run along,' said Pankaj mockingly. 'Your big-bad-cop act doesn't scare me one bit.'

'Tu barobar aahes,' Rane twanged in his nasal tone. 'But Lokhande can't stop me from doing this.' With lightning speed, he caught Pankaj by the neck with one hand. Just as a startled Pankaj reached up to free himself, he promptly used his other hand to grab the young man's testicles. When Pankaj opened his mouth to protest, Rane squeezed hard.

Pankaj screamed in agony and sank to his knees the moment Rane released him. He lay curled up on the road in a foetal position, cupping his throbbing privates and moaning in pain. Rane squatted next to the prone Pankaj and reached out with his hand yet again. The young man flinched, his eyes wide with fear. Rane smirked and put his hand under Pankaj's chin, forcing him to make eye contact.

'Listen to me very carefully, benchod—or is it Punky?' said Rane. His soft and gentle tone somehow made his words even more menacing. 'Your father is my friend. I helped with your rehab earlier. For his sake, I'm not going to arrest you. But no more using or dealing drugs. If you do, your father will never experience the joy of playing with his grandkids … because I'll crush your gotay with my bare hands. Samjha?'

Pankaj nodded feebly, not daring to speak. Rane smiled and patted his shoulder, then rose to his feet. He got into the car and drove away.

The constable walked up to Pankaj and pulled him up. Pankaj winced as the abrupt jerk sent another wave of excruciating pain between his legs. Abruptly, he lurched towards the wall and threw up all over it. In the darkness, the constable smiled, enjoying the sight. *It's high time this benchod was taught a lesson,* he thought.

19

'I've kept all the evidence files ready. When would you like to come and review it all?' asked Shinde over the phone sullenly.

'Arrey baba, Shinde. That's not how it's going to work. Just bring it all to my place,' replied Kadam.

'Everything? All the files and evidence bags to your house? But there are rules …' said Shinde, the corner of his mouth quivering.

'And I am all about ignoring them,' said Kadam. 'Now, are you bringing me the files or do I have to call Rane and tell him that you're getting all bureaucratic with me?'

'I'll be there soon,' said Shinde hastily. He swore under his breath as he hung up. Then he looked around and summoned a constable. 'Load this stuff in the jeep and let's go. We have an appointment with the great Kutta Kadam himself.'

Less than an hour later, all the material was deposited in the living room of the tiny Matunga flat. Kadam stood to one side and watched the constable at work. When it was finally done, Shinde nodded to the constable. 'Go down and wait for me,' he said dismissively.

'Kshanabhara thaamba, Namdeo,' said Kadam. 'Ketul, get him a glass of water and some tea, please.'

The constable nodded gratefully and withdrew, shutting the door behind him.

'So, this is why the rank and file adored you so much,' said Shinde scornfully.

Kadam shrugged. 'They're human. And they work a lot harder than most officers.' He rubbed his hands as he looked at the boxes on the floor. 'Now, what masala have you brought for me?'

Shinde looked around at the cluttered living room. Before he could comment, Kadam had shoved all the furniture up against the walls and created space. Then he pulled out everything from the boxes and began reviewing the material.

'Saheb, mee kaahi vichaaru ka? Wouldn't it have been easier to simply come to the station?' asked Shinde.

Kadam didn't bother looking up from the file in his hand. 'Understand something, Shinde. An investigation is not just a job for me. Saala, I live and breathe a case every minute. If something comes to my mind, I want to check it taabadtob.'

Shinde raised his hand in a conciliatory gesture. 'Whatever works for you.'

'Now, tell me about the murders,' said Kadam. 'There was no break-in at either crime scene?'

'No sign of any forced entry. No windows pried open or picked door locks.'

'Only someone who had access could have got in—a spouse, lover, family member or part-time staff who had a key. Or, it could have been someone admitted willingly—a friend, neighbour, doctor, delivery guy or repairman.'

'That really narrows the range of suspects,' said Shinde. His tone was casual and slimy as usual. The jibe was unmistakeable though.

'One step at a time, Shinde,' said Kadam.

Ketul took the tea for the constable outside, and then brought some for Kadam and Shinde. Chores done, she began assembling the photographs and other material on an information board. On one side, she scribbled: Who? Where? When? How? Why?

'Wait a minute. She's going to be working this case too?' asked Shinde.

Kadam laughed. 'Ketul has been assisting me for years. When kids her age were reading mystery novels, she was helping me crack real-life cases. She's the only one who can organize things properly for me.'

He looked approvingly at the board. Every little detail about the two cases was being systematically listed: victims' names, the dates of the murders, estimated times of death, geographical locations, the murder weapons, crime scene clues … It was all coming together.

Shinde nodded, impressed despite his dislike for Kadam.

Kadam ran his finger along the scar under his left ear as he stared at the board. 'We have the obvious patterns. But what about the patterns that are not obvious?'

20

Ambernath is a quiet Mumbai suburb about an hour's drive from the hustle and bustle of the city. Its most famous landmark is an ancient stone temple dedicated to Lord Shiva, built in the eleventh century. The twenty-first century Finek plant is located a few kilometres away from the temple. Thousands of gleaming knives are produced daily by computer-controlled machining tools and grinding units. The only way to escape the noise is to be inside one of the numerous soundproof cabins.

In one such room, Akash Awasthi, the logistics manager, frowned as he pointed at a chart. Sanjay Bhargava, Awasthi's assistant, peered obediently at the chart. Everyone in the building—including these two—was dressed in the same blue bush shirts, with 'Finek' embroidered on them. The company's egalitarian culture made it mandatory for employees in the factory and office to dress alike, with no exceptions.

'The error rate on missing parcels is just unacceptable,' said Awasthi. 'Five per cent when our target is one. The sales director will chop my balls off if we keep this up.' He quickly took a puff from his bronchodilator. His asthma was acting up these days.

'Let me drill down into the data, sir,' Bhargava said. 'We'll find a solution.'

Awasthi nodded. 'Do that. And get back to me.'

Bhargava rotated his head in an effort to loosen his neck and shoulders. Though short, he was a powerfully built man with muscular shoulders.

'Still a regular at the gym?' asked Awasthi.

Bhargava smiled. 'It's a lifelong habit, sir. Not much else for a single man to do in this place anyway.'

Awasthi sighed and patted his stomach where the first signs of a paunch were starting to appear. 'I wish all of us had your willpower. Especially since the wife thinks you're insulting her cooking if you say no.' He pointed at the chart. 'Get that done.'

'Of course, sir,' said Bhargava with a smile.

The smile only lasted till Awasthi left the room. Bhargava whipped out his phone and dialled a number. A short conversation followed during which he got more and more agitated. 'We need to do something, fast,' he said. 'Otherwise, the bhosada will ruin our side operation.'

21

There was a soft knock on the door. His Holiness Momuma looked up from his laptop and shut it. He was working on a sermon for the following day, but that could wait. He got up from his desk and padded over to a large, throne-like chair in the centre of the reception room. The floor was covered with thick wall-to-wall carpeting and heavy drapes were drawn across the windows. Momuma sat on the chair and fussed with his hair and robes—everything had to be just right. The chamber was mostly kept dark, with a sole powerful focus light directly above the chair. It had the dramatic effect of putting Momuma in the spotlight.

'Come in,' he called out when he was satisfied.

A woman entered, her eyes widening as she took in the opulent room. Most of the devotees in the Gorai commune lived in dormitories. A few of the privileged ones were allowed sparsely furnished private rooms. Momuma, in contrast, had a luxurious and massive chamber. Apart from his reception room and study, he also had a huge bedroom with an oversized bathroom.

Momuma gazed at her, remembering the last time he had seen her. She had been on all fours, screaming in pleasure, tears of ecstasy streaming down her face as she gazed adoringly at him. Their eyes had met briefly.

Momuma felt a stirring in his loins. The woman was well into middle age, but her body was well preserved and there was a raw, earthy sensuality to her. He smiled to himself. He had had a special task in mind for her, but there was no harm mixing business with pleasure. And this one promised to be an exquisite diversion.

'Salaam, Momuma! Show me the light.'

He motioned to the woman to kneel before him. The thick carpets ensured the position was not uncomfortable for her as she knelt.

'Have you been paying attention in the lecture sessions, my child?' he whispered.

She replied enthusiastically, 'Oh yes, Momuma. I'm very good.' She realized how arrogant that sounded and nervously chewed a fingernail.

'Let me see what you have learned, Sarla. Should one be afraid of dying?'

The woman began to shake her head, then abruptly stopped as Momuma frowned. She nodded as she replied, 'No, Momuma.'

'I see that you have still not broken old habits completely.'

'I'm sorry, Momuma. It won't happen again,' said Sarla, contrite.

'In this commune, why do we nod when we mean no and shake our heads when we mean yes?' asked Momuma, a hint of sternness in his voice.

'To break out of old habits and mindsets. To look at the world with new eyes,' rattled off Sarla, continuing to eye her fingernails.

'Good. I see you have at least understood that much. Now tell me, should one be afraid of letting others die?'

Sarla nodded fervently to indicate a negative response.

'Should one be afraid of loving or being loved?'

Sarla was momentarily startled. Then understanding dawned in her eyes. She nodded very slowly to say no. Her pupils dilated and her breathing turned ragged.

'Then do your duty, my child,' said Momuma, his voice quivering. He lifted his robes and gestured for her to pleasure him.

22

Mantralaya is the headquarters of the Government of Maharashtra. Built in 1955, the cream-coloured structure overlooking the Oval Maidan houses the offices of the chief minister and his cabinet.

Everyone in the sixth-floor conference room rose to their feet as Chief Minister Girish Joshi walked in. He greeted everybody with a brisk namaste, then raised his eyebrows. 'Home Minister Lokhande isn't coming?' he asked.

'Bad case of food poisoning,' said the deputy home minister. Jayant Gaikwad was a clean-shaven man with bushy eyebrows. Only a discerning individual would notice that his simple white kurta-pyjama had been stitched by an excellent tailor using the world's best linen. His simple but elegant spectacles cost well over a lakh. His soft leather shoes were custom-made in Italy. The pen in his pocket was made of white gold and his watch, one of many, was worth a small fortune.

Joshi frowned. 'Oh. Something he ate?'

'Seafood, saheb,' said Gaikwad. *The fat bastard was probably up all night drinking at one of his hotels. No wonder he is puking his guts out.*

'Should we postpone the meeting then?'

'No need, saheb. Lokhande ji has seen and approved the entire presentation. You can always take a decision later,' said Gaikwad, not wanting to give up the chance to have the chief minister's attention.

Joshi nodded as he sat down. 'Fine. Proceed.'

'Yes, sir,' began Gaikwad as the first slide came up. 'As you know, the condition of the home department is completely unacceptable for a state of our size and stature. We need to modernize the police force, get better equipment, database management and forensics. The bail-granting system is a mess ...'

Over the next thirty minutes, Gaikwad made a thoroughly impressive presentation, packed with facts and figures. When it was over, the chief minister nodded appreciatively. 'Good job, Jayant,' he said. 'But where are we going to find the money for all of this?'

Gaikwad smiled. 'With respect, sir, can we put a value on human life? Think of the number of unsolved cases that are clogging the system right now.'

Joshi grunted, then looked at his watch. 'I must get back to my office. Walk with me.' The two men walked down the corridor together. The others accompanying them fell behind, giving them some space for a private chat.

'I've been hearing about some serial killer.'

Gaikwad masked his surprise. Only a handful of people even knew the two murders were connected. The wily chief minister obviously had his ears close to the ground. 'We're looking into the cases, sir. But this illustrates what I was talking about. In any decent system, red flags should have gone up immediately. Thankfully, we created the position of special commissioner for Sharad Rane. He's the one who noticed the link.'

Girish Joshi nodded, but didn't say anything. Gaikwad looked around to make sure he wouldn't be overheard, then spoke in an urgent tone. 'Saheb, kripya maajhe aikaa. The home minister—Lokhande ji—is a good man ... But the kind of revamp we need ... Sir, he may not be the best person to make it happen. Crimes are becoming more complex and we need to be capable of handling them. The home minister has so many business interests …'

'I see. And who would be the right person? You?' asked Joshi bluntly.

Gaikwad smiled politely. 'You've known me for so many years. You know I would work tirelessly. And, most importantly, I will be loyal.' The last word was spoken with subtle emphasis.

The chief minister gave Gaikwad a long, appraising look. Gaikwad could almost see the wheels turning in his brain. Finally, Joshi nodded. 'You've given me much to think about, Jayant. Let me ponder on it. I hope Pankaj is doing well.' He patted Gaikwad on the shoulder, then walked into his office.

Gaikwad smiled. The chief minister hadn't given a direct answer, but he hadn't said an outright no either. *It's just a matter of time*, thought Gaikwad as he strolled back towards his office. *Soon, the home minister's chair will have the right person in it— me, instead of Lokhande. Bhairavadas has promised me this. And hopefully that bastard, Bhau Patil, can also be set right.*

23

The Mazagaon docks district lies in the heart of Mumbai. This industrial enclave, once a thriving hub of maritime activity, now wears the scars of time. The red-brick structures, remnants of a bygone era, stand in stark contrast to the towering skyscrapers that now surround them. Faded signs and peeling paint whisper stories of a vibrant past when ships of all sizes crowded the harbour.

Inside a grimy warehouse, Raju grunted as he rubbed his aching back. His friends and he had been busy since his return from Trimbakeshwar. He was proud of how productive they had been. The space was filled with an assortment of goods, including jewellery, electronic items and antiques. He carefully placed a laptop inside a cardboard box and began knotting a piece of nylon rope around it. Suddenly, there was a knock at the entrance.

'Kon aahey?' he called out, his hand instinctively reaching for the knife in his back pocket.

'Katrina Kaif. Tere secretary ne appointment diya,' said a gruff male voice sarcastically.

Raju relaxed. 'Ho, Aslam bhai,' he said, as he walked over to the shutters, unlocked them and rolled them up halfway. He quickly looked around to make sure Aslam was alone, then gestured to him to enter.

'Chutiya, you could pull up the shutters more,' complained Aslam. He stood well over six feet and had to stoop almost to waist level to enter.

'Maaf kara, Aslam bhai. Just being careful.'

'You could also have informed me when you got out of Arthur Road jail,' said Aslam.

'I would have had nothing to show you then,' said Raju. He made a sweeping motion with his arm to indicate the goods piled up inside the dusty depot. 'Now I do.'

Aslam looked around and let out a low whistle. 'Achcha, Ali Baba aur chaalees chor. Khoob maal hai.'

'You can have it all for ten lakh,' said Raju.

'Gaandu, steal from other people, not from me,' Aslam retorted, examining a television. 'I'll give you five.'

'Arrey, Aslam bhai. This is top-quality stuff. You know I'm not being unreasonable,' Raju wheedled. The two men went back and forth on the price for a few minutes, and shook hands at seven lakhs.

'I'll be back in an hour with a truck and the cash,' said Aslam. 'Have the stuff packed.'

'One more thing, bhai,' said Raju.

'Bol.'

'You know that lawyer, na … Keswani?'

'The best crook to represent other crooks,' laughed Aslam.

'Could you introduce me?' asked Raju.

'Chalo, ho jaayega,' said Aslam.

As Aslam left, Raju's face settled into a grin. *Not bad for a few days' work. Maybe it's time to scale up.*

He tossed a spool of nylon rope in the air and caught it.

24

Kadam removed his spectacles and rubbed his eyes wearily. He glanced at Shinde, who looked equally tired. The two men had meticulously gone over all the material that Shinde had brought, including the autopsy results, forensics reports, crime scene photographs and field interviews.

'Anything from the blood reports?' Kadam asked.

Shinde shook his head. 'The blood at both sites was the victims'. No blood from anybody else.'

Another thought struck Kadam. 'Do we have the victims' mobile phones?'

'Of course,' said Shinde.

'Review call histories. Any common numbers in their address books? Any calls made between them?'

Shinde nodded and made a note.

'Check their online browser histories too. Anything that may open up a lead,' said Kadam.

'Sure. By the way, the families are asking for the bodies for the last rites. Can we release them?' he asked.

'Not yet,' said Kadam sharply. 'Hold on.'

'They're insisting. It's a sensitive matter, you know.'

'Buy time. Make up some story,' said Kadam, scratching his stubble. 'We may need to revisit the autopsies. Ask the coroner to check for the exact location of each stab—are they the same in both cases?'

Shinde shrugged. 'Whatever you say. I think I'll be on my way now, if that's fine with you?'

Kadam nodded. Shinde heaved himself out of the chair with a sigh, then paused. 'A couple of reporters have been nosing around. They haven't spotted the pattern yet, but it's a matter of time. Should we consider a press briefing?'

Kadam knew that all Shinde wanted was his own name in the papers. 'And let the killer know that we're on to him?' He shook his head. 'Naahin. In case anybody asks you, just say we're exploring the theft angle.'

Kadam walked Shinde to the door, then shut it. He frowned at the files lying on the floor; they seemed to be taunting his inability to find any leads. After changing his shirt, he switched on the Caravan radio and made himself a fresh cup of tea. As Lata Mangeshkar sang '*Ajeeb dastan hai yeh*' in the background, he settled down again with the crime scene photos.

Kadam squinted and peered at one particular photo, but couldn't discern the detail. He pulled out a magnifying glass and peered at the image. Then he called Shinde. It had barely been twenty minutes since they had parted. Kadam did not bother with the pleasantries. 'There may be a drugs angle. Check it out.'

'What makes you say that?' asked Shinde.

Kadam sensed an odd note in his voice, but he ignored it. 'There was an expired credit card lying on Suchandra Agarwal's table.'

'Barobar, so?'

'Sometimes, users hang on to old credit cards to make coke lines for their fix. Search the apartment again and get that card examined closely. Find out if there are any traces of cocaine anywhere.'

'Will do,' said Shinde. He ended the call, took a deep breath and then dialled Commissioner Chavan's private line. 'Sir, there's some bad news. Kutta Kadam is sniffing around the serial killings case. He's getting suspicious about a drugs angle.'

'Ho, kaa? Why is Kutta involved?'

'Rane brought him on board as a consultant. He's done that in the past also.'

'Rane's too smart for his own good. Gaikwad has placed him as special commissioner only to put a mirchi up my ass. We need to fix this. Come to my office abhi.' Chavan set down the phone and reached for his pack of pink and blue antacid chews. He needed relief.

'Ah, Shinde, come in. Have a seat,' Chavan said a short while later as Shinde was ushered into his office. He acknowledged Shinde's salute with a nod.

'Thank you, sir,' said Shinde, settling in the chair opposite Chavan.

'I was about to ask for green tea. Would you like something?'

Shinde looked surprised at this unexpected courtesy from Chavan, but hastily concealed his expression. 'A coffee would be very nice, saheb. Thank you.'

Chavan nodded at the constable who had escorted Shinde and he withdrew.

'I'm glad you came directly to me with this Kadam problem,' said Chavan. 'How deeply is he involved in the case?'

'He has access to all the material … Rane ordered me to give him full cooperation,' said Shinde, a corner of his mouth twitching as he revealed this nugget of information.

Chavan swore under his breath. 'Arrey baap re … If there's anything there, Kadam will find it sooner or later. To eka kutra aahey. Won't let go of the scent.'

'You sound like you admire him, saheb,' said Shinde, emboldened by Chavan's genial attitude.

Chavan looked up sharply. 'Kadam's a great investigator, Shinde. One of the best. But he's too stubborn. There's no place for a Harishchandra like him in today's kalyug.'

'Barobar, sir. You are right.'

'So how do we get rid of him?' mused Chavan, eyeing the pack of antacids on his desk.

'Can't you order Rane to take him off the case? Rane is your junior, saheb.'

Chavan shook his head irritably. 'Rane might go to Gaikwad and complain. The two are very close. I am Rane's boss, yes, but Gaikwad is mine.'

'Even Gaikwad has a boss,' Shinde said softly.

'Home Minister Lokhande? He's not interested in running the department. Too many business interests to launder his cash. Saala, we must find some other way to remove Kadam.'

There was a knock on the door, and an attendant walked in with their tea and coffee. Chavan skipped his green tea and chewed an antacid instead. Suddenly, he slapped the table with his hand. 'Leak it to the press that Kadam is involved in this investigation. Let there be reports about how a suspended cop is doing official work. That haramkhor Rane will be in trouble then.'

'But the press will find out it's a serial killer case then.'

Chavan laughed. 'That may be a good thing, Shinde. Someone may come forward with useful information ... or not. But Rane and Kadam will be khallaas.'

25

'So, how's the Shakti case going?' Nirmal asked Ketul.

The two were at their usual haunt, Blue Tokai Roasters, for coffee. The warm lighting cast a soft glow on the wooden furniture and rough plaster walls, while the aromas of freshly brewed coffee and delicious pastries and savouries perfumed the air. The gentle hum of conversation and the clinking of cups and saucers, punctuated by occasional laughter, was comforting. As Ketul took a sip of her coffee, a spot of foam settled on the right corner of her mouth. Nirmal felt his heart race as he saw it. *I could reach out with my hand and wipe it*, he thought. *Better still, I could just lick it off her lips …*

'Nirmal! Have you been listening to a word I've said?' asked Ketul, irritated.

Nirmal snapped back to the present guiltily. 'Sorry, my bad, client issue. What were you saying?'

'I said that the case doesn't seem to be going anywhere. Even after several visits, those rascal cops just won't cooperate. I wonder if it's a conspiracy or if they're just like that.' Ketul took another sip of her coffee and sat back in her chair. 'How's your hacking business doing?'

'Ethical hacking,' Nirmal corrected her, tenting his fingers together.

'Yeah, yeah … *ethical* hacking,' said Ketul. 'Who's this client?'

Nirmal shrugged. 'Some guy who's splurged big time on setting up security systems for his website. I must break it to him that he's paid a ton of money for utter crap.'

'At least you're getting something done,' said Ketul. 'This damn case isn't moving at all. And each time I talk to those poor girls, it breaks my heart. I just wish I could get them justice.' Her large, beautiful eyes welled up as she toyed with her coral pendant.

Nirmal reached across the table and put his hand on hers. 'If there's anything I can do, just say the word. You know that.'

There was a long pause. Nirmal tried to act casual, though he could feel his heart pounding. Would Ketul withdraw her hand? To his delight, she let it remain there. The silence became ever more intense. Ketul broke it. 'I do … I will,' she said softly. Then she looked at her watch. 'It's getting late. Drop me home?'

Nirmal removed his hand reluctantly. *Damn, things had been going so well. Never mind. One step at a time.* 'I'll drop you at your society's gate, if you don't mind.'

'Why not to my flat?'

'Your dad has this habit of staring at me like I'm a murderer.'

Ketul burst out laughing. 'Oh, Baba is like that with everybody. He's a pussycat at heart.'

'Whatever. Your pussycat gives me the creeps,' confessed Nirmal.

Ketul shook her head, still smiling. 'Don't worry. Only two kinds of people need to fear Baba. Criminals and those with devious intentions.' She playfully poked Nirmal in the arm. 'You don't fall in either category, do you?'

Nirmal's answering smile didn't quite reach his eyes.

I'm not sure.

26

'Ek minute thamba,' Kadam called out as he stretched his arms and walked stiffly to the door to open it. He found Dr Ravikant Desai standing outside.

'Namaskar, doctor sa'ab! I'm seeing you after a long time. May I get you a drink?'

Desai shook his head. 'I'm here on work, not pleasure, Prakash,' he said in his clipped university English. 'Ketul asked me to drop by and check up on your health.'

Kadam sighed. 'Ketul should mind her own business.'

'Well, you are her business, are you not?' said Desai, stepping inside. His eyes widened as he looked at the material piled up in the living room. 'You seem to have brought the whole police station home,' he commented, his eyes darting to the notations on the board.

'Just helping a friend,' said Kadam hastily as he cleared space on the sofa.

Desai removed his blue Nehru jacket and draped it over a chair. Then he brought out his BP monitor and checked Kadam's blood pressure. He frowned when he saw the reading. 'Deep breaths,' he instructed as he listened to Kadam's chest using his stethoscope. Kadam complied.

Desai sighed as he put his instruments into his bag.

'Here comes the lecture,' muttered Kadam.

Desai ignored the barb. 'Not been sleeping too well, have you?'

'You can figure that out with your toys?'

'You have dark circles the size of craters under your eyes,' was the blunt response. 'Nightmares?' When Kadam nodded, Desai continued, 'The wheezing in your chest tells me that you're still puffing away like a chimney. Each cigarette you light up is one more nail in your coffin.'

'Good thing I'm Hindu,' said Kadam, sniggering. 'I'll be cremated, not buried. No coffin, no nails.'

'Have you written your will or should I ask my friend Keswani to help you?' asked Desai. 'Trust me, you need to prepare, given the way you're going. Prakash, this is not a laughing matter. You *will* collapse one day … It's only a matter of time.'

'Doctor sa'ab, please understand, this conversation will cause me to collapse *today*,' retorted Kadam, running his left middle finger along his scar.

'Bloody hell, Prakash! You've already had one heart attack and another one could be around the corner. Thank heavens the whisky is out. Are you at least seeing your psychiatrist?'

Kadam grimaced. 'Ketul makes sure of that.'

'Good for her. Have you been prescribed medication? Are you taking it regularly?' At Kadam's silence Desai threw up his hands in frustration. 'Prakash, you're a smart man. Why are you doing this to yourself?'

'It's the shrink who needs to get her head examined, not me,' said Kadam mutinously. He paused. 'I have nothing much to live for—except Ketul. If I die, fine. But as long as I am alive, I'm going to live my way, not cower in fear and die a little every day.' He took a deep breath to calm himself. 'Now, if you'll excuse me, I have a case to get back to.'

27

'Please have a seat. Bhau will be with you shortly,' said Patil's assistant. 'Some tea or coffee meanwhile, saheb?'

'Plain water is fine,' replied Commissioner Chavan, chewing on an antacid. He looked around. He had been asked to wait in the lounge area outside Bhau Patil's bedroom. The space was luxurious, in an ornate, garish sort of way. Expensive curios and decorations were packed together with scant regard for cost. *Money can buy a lot of things, but clearly, taste isn't one of them*, Chavan thought as he looked around. The only saving grace was the beautiful sea view from the window.

The bedroom door opened and Bhau Patil emerged, knotting the belt of a silk robe. Chavan heard someone giggle in the room, but the sound was cut off as soon as Patil shut the door. 'Namaskar, Chavan,' he said and sat in his favourite recliner next to the window. Immediately, a servant entered the room, carrying a tray with two glasses of water. He offered one to Chavan and then walked over to Patil. The minister took a big gulp of water, gargled noisily and then spat the reddish, paan-residue-filled water into a spittoon the servant brought over.

Chavan felt a wave of disgust wash over him at the sight. Very carefully, he put his glass down on a side table, suddenly nauseated by the thought of drinking from it. Patil repeated the process of gargling and spitting a couple of more times, then dabbed his mouth with a towel the servant silently handed to him.

'Want a drink?' Patil asked Chavan.

'Naahin, dhanyavad, Bhau. Still on duty.'

Patil shrugged. 'Suit yourself.' He gestured for the servant to get his usual, then settled back comfortably. 'Kaay prakaran aahey?' he asked, scratching his groin.

Chavan made sure that the servant had left the room before he spoke. 'Something has come up. I didn't want to discuss it over the phone.' He quickly briefed Patil about Kadam's involvement in the twin murders and his new-found suspicion of a drug angle.

The servant returned just then, and placed a tray with a glass containing Scotch on the rocks and an assortment of snacks in front of Patil. The minister grunted as he took a swig and waved a hand to dismiss the servant.

'That madarchod Kadam. He just keeps popping up.'

Chavan nodded. 'He still has a lot of well-wishers in the department, including that over-smart gaandu Sharad Rane. SCP my foot! I still can't understand why he has been thrust on me as second-in-command.'

'Don't worry about Rane,' said Patil. 'My friends are as powerful as Gaikwad, his protector. Is Kadam's daughter still sniffing around that Shakti matter?'

'Yes, but we've blocked her. That case isn't going anywhere.'

Patil nodded as he slurped some Scotch and stuffed his mouth with a kebab. He let out a satisfied belch, then held up his hand. 'Two things, Chavan. Get that bitch off the Shakti matter … Whatever it takes. Second, find a way to screw Kadam.'

'I thought we could arrange a press leak,' said Chavan. 'I discussed the idea with Shinde.'

'Whom will Shinde brief?'

'The reporters who cover the crime beat, I suppose.'

Patil shook his head. 'Too low down the chain.' He picked up his phone and made a call. 'Tumhi kase aahat, editor saheb?' he asked. 'How is your daughter liking medical college? ... Arrey, don't mention it. I was happy to help with admission. Do you need anything to make her comfortable there? ... Is that all? I'll get it done. No problem. Now listen, I need a favour. I'll have a photo sent to you soon ... Front page only, understood? Okay, good. My regards to your family.'

Patil hung up and nodded at Chavan. 'All in control. Now here's what you need to do.'

Chavan listened intently as Patil outlined the plan. When the conversation was over, he stood up. 'With your permission, I'll leave now, Bhau.'

Patil took another swig of Scotch and waved his hand, dismissing Chavan the same way he had dismissed his servant earlier. The commissioner felt a rush of fury and humiliation. As he walked out, he noticed that the bedroom door was slightly ajar. Out of the corner of his eye, he saw two young girls in their underwear perched on the bed. Neither looked a day older than fourteen. Chavan felt sick knowing he was aligned with an illiterate, paedophile goon.

'Commissioner,' Patil called out.

Chavan turned, wondering if Patil had read his mind. 'Ho, Bhau?'

'You're doing mast work. Keep it up and I'll take very good care of you. Just never forget that I can be the best of friends, but also the worst of enemies. Kutta knows this well. He's seen both sides of me.'

28

The room was freezing cold, but Kadam could feel sweat running down his face and stinging his eyes. He blinked furiously and looked around. His heart tightened in dread. He was inside an abattoir. The distinctive smell of frozen meat filled the air. It seemed to pervade Kadam's lungs and he found himself struggling to breathe. He coughed and tried to take a couple of deep breaths.

'Please, please,' a voice whimpered in the corner.

Kadam turned slowly. A young man, entirely naked, was tied to a wooden chair. His slim, tightly muscled body had dark bruises. He had curly hair and a chiselled jawline, but the rest of his features had been obliterated by the beating. His eyes were swollen shut. Blood trickled down the side of his mouth. His body and hair were caked in a mixture of sweat and blood. Every now and then, he winced as he breathed—perhaps a few ribs were broken too.

'Please,' he whispered. 'Save me.'

Kadam grinned. Then he sniggered. Then he began laughing—loudly and maniacally. The sound of his demonic laughter bounced off the walls. He lifted his hand to wipe away his sweat and found he was holding a meat cleaver. Light glinted off the sinister-looking blade as Kadam slowly walked towards the weeping young man.

'Please, don't …' the youth begged through broken teeth and split lips, his speech sounding garbled.

But Kadam understood him. He continued laughing as he advanced, cleaver in hand.

Kadam could feel his body moving, as though it was being violently shaken.

'Baba, Baba!'

Kadam snapped awake with a gasp. Ketul was holding him by his shoulders, looking anxious. His heart was pounding and his throat felt parched. He ran his hand through his hair and found it soaking wet.

'Water,' he croaked.

Ketul quickly poured some into the glass kept by his side. Kadam emptied it in one gulp and held it out for more. Ketul refilled it. He drank a little slower this time, feeling his heartbeat settle to a more normal rhythm.

'Was I laughing in my sleep?' he asked.

'Yes, but you didn't sound very happy.'

'I wasn't.'

'The same nightmare?'

Kadam nodded wordlessly and fumbled for his cigarettes, his hand shaking. Ketul gently removed the pack from his hands.

'Why don't you have some tea instead?' she suggested softly. 'I'll put some jaggery instead of sugar.'

Kadam decided not to argue. Ketul usually became extra considerate when she was trying not to fly into a rage. He got up, took a fresh vest from the drawer and walked into the tiny bathroom. He splashed some water on his face, patted down his hair and took off his sweat-drenched vest. As he wiped down his body with a wet towel, he frowned at the sight of his protruding belly. Peering into the mirror, he sucked in his stomach, but to no avail. He shook his head ruefully and pulled on the fresh vest.

'Theek, time for some music therapy,' he said, stepping out of the bathroom.

Ketul had a cup of tea ready. Kadam took it with a grateful nod, then walked across to his prized possession, his Caravan radio. Apart from its sentimental value—it was a gift from Ketul—he loved it because it came with five thousand pre-loaded songs, including many of his favourites. Soon Kishore Kumar's voice singing '*Neele neele ambar par*' filled the room. Ketul smiled affectionately when she saw Kadam humming along with the music.

'Heard the remix? It's quite peppy,' she said.

Kadam scratched his stubbly chin. 'Why does your generation mess with perfection?'

'My old-fashioned father,' Ketul said, chuckling. 'Well, I'd better get ready for work.'

'Oh, I wanted to brainstorm with you.' Talking to Ketul often yielded crucial insights in investigations.

Ketul looked at her watch. 'Sure. I have about half an hour.'

The two walked over to the information board.

'What's common to the deaths?' Kadam mused aloud, absently tracing the scar under his ear. 'Is there some message or pattern that we're missing?'

He pointed to the pictures of the victims' tied hands. 'Why use nylon rope? Why not jute or cotton or any other material?' he asked, looking at Ketul expectantly. She shrugged. Kadam wracked his brain for a possible answer, but couldn't come up with anything either. He decided to move on.

'Food was stuffed in the mouth of both victims. What could that mean?'

'Maybe they were eating when they were killed?' suggested Ketul.

'There was no food next to them.'

'Could there be symbolism here?'

'You mean it's the killer's way of saying the victims were greedy? Some twisted form of punishment? Hmmm.' He puffed his cheek out, then allowed it to deflate. 'In both cases, the victims were stabbed through the heart with a Finek kitchen knife—no fingerprints. The killer must have worn gloves. But the other knives in their homes were not of the same brand. So why is the killer using Finek?'

'Could be a coincidence. It's a popular brand,' said Ketul, fiddling with her pendant.

Kadam shook his head. 'Ekdum improbable coincidence,' he said. 'Shinde is looking into the drug angle. I'll follow up on that. What else—'

'I remembered something,' Ketul interrupted. 'That blue fibre? We still don't have any details about it. Was the killer wearing blue? Or did the fibre get under the victim's nails some other way?'

'Good point. Must remind the examiner. One thought: Could these be sex crimes?'

Ketul rolled her eyes. 'How, Baba? One victim was male, the other was female. One was heterosexual, the other was homosexual. Even the examiner's reports showed that neither had been sexually assaulted.'

'Arrey, murders are often about sexual fantasies rather than the act itself,' said Kadam. 'Sexuality works in strange ways.'

Ketul nodded. If a third person heard them now, they'd be horrified—not quite a normal father-daughter conversation. As if telepathically, father and daughter looked at each other and laughed.

Kadam smiled ruefully. 'You didn't exactly have a regular childhood. I'm sorry about that.'

Ketul hugged him. 'You've been a great dad … in your own way. And I've seen more of life than my friends and classmates.' Her eyes widened when she noticed the time on the clock. 'Okay, now I really need to get going.'

'Theek. Good talk.'

'Was it? We seem to have lots of questions, but no answers.'

'All we need is one answer. That loose thread in a sweater. You pull it once and the whole thing unravels.'

Like the blue fibre.

29

'Welcome, didi! We are so happy you have come to visit us.'

Ketul gave an embarrassed smile to the little reception committee waiting at the gate of the Shakti campus in the Vasai-Virar area. 'Oho, I don't deserve such a VIP welcome,' she said.

'You fighting for us … Aap humari hero hain,' said one of them in a mixture of Hindi and halting English.

'Come and see the facilities,' said the girl who had greeted her in fluent English. She had a stocky, muscular frame and strong, calloused hands. 'Mera naam Heena hai.' She was wearing a simple white cotton kurta over denims and her hair was tied back in a short ponytail.

'Quite a space you have here,' Ketul said, looking around admiringly.

The twin city of Vasai-Virar is located in Palghar district and lies north of Vasai Creek, in close proximity to Mumbai, making it almost a suburb of the metropolis. Within the complex, the low-rise buildings were connected by tree-lined paths.

'Haan, didi, the deputy home minister—Jayant Gaikwad ji—has helped a lot,' replied Heena. 'He got land allotted to Shakti at special rates. His friends gave big donations. That's how all this came up.'

They walked into one of the buildings and peeked into an airy, well-lit room. A woman was writing on a blackboard, while a mixed group of students listened attentively. 'This is our school building. Students of all ages study here,' explained Heena. Ketul noticed that the classroom contained little girls as well as adult women. 'Some older rescued women cannot read or write. We start them off in the junior classes.'

'Don't they feel awkward?' asked Ketul.

Heena shrugged. 'Kabhi-kabhi. But everyone must become literate—how else to become financially independent, no?'

They walked to another building: the dispensary. Heena explained that basic medicines and routine first aid could be obtained here. This was often needed when girls were rescued. Shakti had also partnered with a few hospitals and, on weekends, volunteer doctors would visit to conduct medical check-ups.

They exited the dispensary and strolled to an open area cordoned off by a low wall. Within it was a paved concrete track with old tyres placed at various spots for safety. A small building stood in one corner, with an attached garage. 'Driving school,' said Heena proudly. She explained that they had a driving simulator too. The trust ran two all-women services—Shakti Cabs and Shakti Couriers, both fully staffed by the women who lived there. Shakti Couriers had a nifty motorbike logo, while the one for the cab company had a pink band to reinforce the women-oriented nature of the service.

Ketul suddenly realized that it had become quite warm. She took out a handkerchief from her bag and mopped her face. 'You are tired,' said Heena. 'Let's go to the hostel.' They walked to a dull pink low-rise building in the complex. Much of the ground floor was taken up by the reception area. There was a large hall to the right. 'That's the gym. Want to have a look?'

Before Ketul could respond, Heena pushed open the door. The large area was broken up into different sections. In one, some women were lifting weights; in another, a group of girls was practising martial arts; and yet another had gymnastics and cardio equipment. Many of the girls and women who were working out smiled and waved at Heena. She waved back.

'You seem to be a regular here,' observed Ketul.

'She is,' said a young girl standing nearby. 'Heena didi, show her your move, na.'

'Arrey nahin,' argued Heena, but eventually gave in when coaxed further.

She tightened her ponytail and tucked her kurta into her jeans. A few quick stretches and squats followed, and then she effortlessly executed a handstand on both hands and 'walked' around for a bit. Next she lifted her right hand off the ground, so that she was balanced only on her left hand. She hopped about on her left hand as the other girls and Ketul cheered, and even changed hands in the middle. Everyone in the gym applauded as she stood up. Heena winked and bowed, then sauntered over to Ketul.

'Shabash, Heena! You should be in the Olympics,' said an awestruck Ketul.

'Too old, didi,' said Heena. 'If Shakti had found me earlier, who knows.' Briefly, her face clouded over. Then she gave her head a determined shake; she was not going to wallow in the past. She led Ketul out of the gym and into the reception area. One of the girls brought water, tea and biscuits for them. Tea in hand, Ketul strolled over to a wall with several photo frames. She recognized a few faces. Deputy Home Minister Jayant Gaikwad was cutting a ribbon in one photograph. In another, a team of doctors that included their neighbour Dr Desai, was conducting a health camp.

'Okay, I'm ready and recharged,' said Ketul, a few minutes later. 'What's next?'

Heena showed Ketul around the hostel—the dining hall, kitchen and the rooms. There were two kinds of accommodation: dormitories and triple sharing. Heena explained that the dormitories were for the younger girls. One of the older women would stay with them as a guardian. Many of the girls were terrified initially—nightmares and bed-wetting were common—so it helped to have a maternal figure around. The triple-sharing rooms were for the older residents. All the rooms were simple, but clean. Even the lavatories sparkled. Hostel gates shut at 9 p.m. sharp and everyone had to be in by then.

'There's a Sonapur visit for you after lunch,' said Heena. 'One of our girls, Rani, will meet you there.'

'Thank you, Heena,' said Ketul, absently toying with her pendant. 'Amazing how one place can change the destinies of so many.'

'Bhaagya badaltey hain yeh harami taare,' said Heena sadly. It is the damn planets that determine destinies.

30

Located within the bustling neighbourhood of Bhandup, Sonapur, with its labyrinthine network of narrow lanes, dilapidated shanties and dimly lit establishments, is one of the largest red-light districts of the city. Ketul stepped out of the cab and looked around warily. The surroundings were squalid and depressing. A small woman and a big burly man stepped up to her. 'Main hoon Rani,' said the woman. 'You must be Ketul.'

Ketul gave a hesitant smile.

'Chandu is here for our protection,' explained Rani.

Chandu nodded at Ketul and patted a bulge under his shirt to indicate that he was armed. 'Don't make eye contact with the madams and pimps,' he explained in a low voice. 'Don't appear too shocked by anything you see. If someone asks, aap health

NGO se aaye hain. No mention of who you actually are. Safe nahin hai.'

'Theek hai,' replied Ketul in an equally low tone.

Despite the air of despondency that hung over the area, it was teeming with life. Children played in the lanes. Vegetable sellers had set up pavement stalls, which were doing slow business. Bedding was being aired on the roofs of several structures. Women leaned out of windows, gossiping. Men with phones lingered in doorways, keeping an eye on the street. They gave Ketul appraising looks, as though they were stripping off her clothes with their eyes—it made her skin crawl.

'Watchers,' explained Chandu. 'Their job is to make sure none of the girls try to escape.'

None of the buildings had any windows open at the ground level, or even on the first few floors. Ketul felt claustrophobic just looking at them. She tried to imagine living cooped up inside and shuddered.

Rani stopped outside one of the buildings. A fair-complexioned woman in a low-cut blouse and garish sari, who might have been attractive in her youth, was standing outside. Rani slipped her some currency notes and the woman led them in. 'Five-star maal only,' she said. 'Doston ko yahaan bhej diya karo.' The look that she gave Ketul was one of appreciation. She winked at her and walked back to the exit.

'Who is she?' asked Ketul.

'The madam,' replied Chandu. 'She said she'd only let us in if we paid an entry fee.'

Rani led Ketul towards a dilapidated staircase. A jolt of horror went through Ketul as she saw a cage near the base of the stairs. A young girl lay inside, wearing only a filthy shift. Her face was buried in her hands and she was whimpering in misery, oblivious to the world. Ketul felt like throwing up.

'New girls are broken in like this,' said Rani. Her tone was matter-of-fact, but there was sadness in her eyes.

'They are only let out when a customer comes,' explained Chandu, 'and even then, they are drugged so that they don't make a fuss. This cage becomes home for as long as it takes— sometimes weeks, even months. She'll be freed from the cage only when she no longer tries to run.'

'No escape?' asked Ketul, with desperation in her voice. She was finding it very difficult to maintain her composure.

'Yeh one-way road hai,' replied Rani.

'You saw the watchers,' said Chandu. 'They roam the streets, looking for girls who are trying to escape. The local cops are on the take—so they bring back girls who managed to run away. They get cash rewards and even get to use the girl as a bonus.'

Ketul felt bile rising in her throat. 'What happens to the girls who are caught?'

'An example is made of them,' said Chandu. 'They're thrashed severely, just short of permanent disfigurement, then tossed into the cage and starved. These people know how to take a person right to the brink of death without pushing them over.'

They climbed the stairs and Rani opened a door on the first floor. They stepped into a dormitory-like hall. Clothes were scattered all over the floor. The odour of sweat and cheap perfume hung in the air. Women lay listlessly on the bunk beds and stared at the visitors with blank, dispirited eyes.

Ketul saw some movement in one of the top bunks. Her eyes widened as she realized that a man and woman were having sex with a thin curtain drawn around them. The others in the hall didn't even seem to notice.

'I think I've seen enough,' said Ketul, her voice trembling. 'Let's get out of here, please.'

'Itni jaldi?' called out the madam cheerfully as they exited the building.

Once Ketul was outside, she bent over, supporting herself with her hands on her knees, and took several deep breaths until the urge to retch subsided. Rani hesitantly reached out and patted her back. The watchers were observing them so they had to move. Ketul straightened up. Rani and Chandu escorted her to the car, which had been parked some distance away.

'Thank you. Today has been a real eye-opener.'

'Never forget what you saw here today,' said Rani. 'Once the girls are here, it's usually too late. But if we can stop the trafficking, we can save so many lives.'

Ketul got into the car and drove off. As Sonapur faded away from sight, she let the tears she had been holding back fall freely. She angrily dabbed at them, vowing silently that she would never forget.

31

'That crook won't listen to me. He just keeps giving me the run-around.' Ketul slammed the table hard in frustration.

Nirmal, who had been leaning forward to hear her, started at the violent gesture. Other patrons in the café turned to look at them. 'Easy there,' said Nirmal. 'Other customers might think I just made an indecent proposal to you.'

'It's not funny, Nirmal,' scowled Ketul. But she lowered her voice. 'I took two showers within an hour after I reached home yesterday and I still felt dirty. I can't imagine what those poor women live through every day. Today, I went to the police station determined to get results, but the SI is still unwilling to file an FIR.'

'What did he say?' asked Nirmal, fiddling with the coaster to keep his hands from clasping hers.

Ketul shook her head in disgust. 'He threw some bureaucratic nonsense at me. I just don't understand. The deputy home minister is one of the main supporters of Shakti. How can the police stall such a case?'

'Maybe people even more powerful than Gaikwad want it blocked?' said Nirmal.

'It's possible,' conceded Ketul, instinctively reaching for her coral pendant. 'In fact, that's the only explanation that makes sense. When I pushed him for results, the jerk just gave me a smug grin and said, "Madam, tumhi tumcha kaam kara, and let me do my work." I wanted to punch him.'

'Achcha, I'm not a lawyer like you, but I'm quite sure punching a cop inside a police station isn't a good idea,' deadpanned Nirmal.

'Nirmal, there must be something I can do! I just feel so helpless and useless.' She slouched in her chair, lapsing into a depressed silence.

Nirmal gazed at her with concern, but before he could say something, his phone pinged. Ketul gave him an irritated look and he raised his hand apologetically. He glanced at the phone, then put it away.

'Just an Insta notification,' he said. 'Let me put my phone on silent.'

Ketul sat up abruptly. 'That's it!'

'What's what?' asked Nirmal, puzzled.

'Social media! Your talents go way beyond hacking ... Sorry, ethical hacking,' she corrected herself just as Nirmal opened his mouth. 'Whatever ... You're a champ at making stuff go viral!' Her voice rose in excitement.

Nirmal looked around. 'Softly,' he pleaded. 'I like to do this stuff from the shadows.'

'But you can do it, right?' asked Ketul. 'You can make this issue trend ... The police will be thoroughly embarrassed. It will force them to act.'

'Umm, sure, I guess,' said Nirmal. 'I could engineer an X storm for you, but ...'

'Please do it. It will make a huge difference to so many lives,' pleaded Ketul. She saw Nirmal hesitate and put her hand over his. 'Do it for me,' she said, looking deep into his eyes.

Nirmal gulped, feeling as though an electric charge had passed through his hand. Her skin touching his own was driving him insane. 'Okay, Ketul,' he said finally, in a strangled voice. 'You know there's nothing I wouldn't do for you.'

32

The Chambal river flows through Madhya Pradesh, then through Rajasthan before turning southeast to join the Yamuna in Uttar Pradesh. Nestled within the Mukundara Hills, lies an ancient temple with weathered stone walls on which are etched enigmatic symbols of devotion. The temple's once-vibrant colours have faded, but bright vermilion and sandal paste can still be seen on the ferocious face of Bhairava, who rests within.

In an open field, a group of men sat around a fire. It crackled, casting a sinister glow on the faces of the men gathered around it. Although it was a few hours before dawn, a sheen of sweat coated their bodies. The gentle breeze blowing along the riverbank gave only partial relief from the heat of the fire.

Bhairavadas, a tall, bearded man with open, waist-length hair was chanting a mantra, with his working eye shut; the other one had been plucked out a long time ago. In what seemed like another lifetime, he had been Abdul Gujjar, one of the more fearsome bandits to thrive in Chambal's treacherous terrain. Despite being born a Muslim, his devotion to Bhairava was unparalleled. Dacoits seemed to have fewer religious hang-ups than ordinary folk. Gujjar had eventually morphed to Bhairavadas—the servant of Bhairava. For him, the fierce Bhairava with his garland of skulls was simply the most powerful form of Shiva.

When he finished chanting, he opened his good eye and addressed the gathering. 'Daan ka samay aa gaya hai. Let us begin.'

'Ji, Bhairavadas,' chorused the men obediently.

Each man had a large bottle gourd next to him. They also had small baskets containing lemons, yellow rice, mustard seeds, and some other herbs and grass. Upon the signal, the men picked handfuls of the mixture and tossed it into the fire, all the while chanting a strange mantra along with Bhairavadas.

The fire hissed and sizzled with every offering. The flames danced, their colour becoming increasingly psychedelic. Odd-smelling vapours rose from the fire. The men inhaled them. Their eyes glazed over and their chanting became louder.

Their guru picked up the gourd next to him and guillotined it with a sharp-looking knife. Then he tossed both halves into the fire. The flames leapt up hungrily, racing to devour the offering. Moments later, each of the men followed suit: gourd, knife, fire.

Every single knife had the same brand name. Finek.

33

'I am a killer.'

Here we go again. Sandra Gomes fought the urge to roll her eyes. Once she was sure her irritation wasn't showing, she looked at Kadam. He was fidgeting in his chair, scratching his stubble and puffing his cheeks. *The usual bundle of tics.*

Sandra realized that she needed to try a new approach. 'Tell me about this young man you keep seeing in the nightmare. Did you know him?' she asked.

'Obviously.'

'How? Was he a friend or colleague?'

'Both,' replied Kadam.

Sandra waited for an elaboration. None came. 'When you see him in the nightmare, what's he doing?'

'He's begging for mercy. He's been beaten black and blue. There are cigarette burns on his body. His face is a bloody mess. Both his eyes are swollen shut. His body and hair are covered in sweat and blood. His ribs are broken. He's struggling to breathe.' Kadam rattled off the injuries emotionlessly, as though he were reciting a menu.

Sandra raised her eyebrows. 'Sounds like he's been tortured.'

'Yes. Badly.'

Sandra made a note in her thick yellow pad. 'Were you the one who tortured him?'

Kadam clammed up at that and turned his face away, refusing to make eye contact.

'I won't judge you. If I am to help you, I need to know.'

For a moment, it seemed as though he wanted to say something. Sandra wondered if he would finally open up. Then he shook his head firmly.

A few minutes later, he said, 'I was responsible.'

'How?'

Kadam pursed his lips and looked away again. His body language was unmistakeable. He was telling her that he was done with this particular line of conversation.

Damn, thought Sandra bitterly. They had been on the verge of a breakthrough. *At least we have made some progress.*

'Fine, we'll talk about something else,' she said. 'So, what's new in your life these days?'

'Same old, same old,' muttered Kadam.

'Sure you don't have something else going on?'

Kadam looked at her curiously. 'Why do you say that?'

Because you don't look like a complete wreck today, Sandra wanted to say. Instead, she settled for: 'You're in a slightly better mood. It appears someone or something has engaged your interest.'

'You can tell that just by talking to me?' asked Kadam. There was a glimmer of new-found respect for Sandra in his eyes.

'It's what I do for a living.'

Kadam hesitated, then said, 'Well, I'm working on a case. Purely as a consultant, of course.'

'Oh! That's great,' said Sandra. 'Can you talk about it? Something very important, I'm sure?'

'Can't tell you.'

'I understand. Well, that must be exciting for you?'

Kadam shrugged. 'It helps pass the time.'

Sandra raised her eyebrows. Given Kadam's obsessiveness, no case could ever be purely timepass. 'You know, for an instant, I thought a woman might have come into your life,' she said.

'If you really thought that, then you're the one who needs the shrink, not me.'

'But we're talking about you, not me. So, you've never had someone in your life after your wife?'

Kadam's face darkened. 'How does it matter?' he asked, rubbing his hand over his face.

'It matters very much. Have you ever tried to get in touch with her?'

'Kaay karat? Why are you picking at my scabs?' snapped Kadam.

The intercom rang just then. 'Well, looks like we've overshot the time for today's session,' said Sandra. 'We'll continue this thread next time.'

'Whatever,' said Kadam grouchily, rising to his feet.

'Prakash, I'm glad that you have something new and interesting in your life,' Sandra said as he was leaving. 'But please understand something. New challenges can also add stress. It's very, very important that you take your medicines regularly.'

34

Tuesday, 18 February, around 3 p.m., Thane, Mumbai

'Mangala ben, are you there?'

Chetna Shirke rang the doorbell again and checked her watch. She had been waiting for eighteen minutes now. They were supposed to have afternoon tea at 3 p.m. and she had turned up outside her neighbour's door right on time. Irritated, she contemplated returning to her apartment. Pity though. There had been so much gossip to share. She quickly composed a message and sent it to Mangala. Immediately, she heard the distinctive ping of a message being delivered on a phone. Clearly, Mangala's phone was inside the apartment. What the hell was going on? Was Mangala avoiding her?

She rang the doorbell once more. Then she knocked, practically hammering at the door. Still no response. There was a slot in the door for letters and parcels to be pushed through. Ignoring her husband's frequently offered advice to 'mind her own business', Chetna Shirke decided to stoop and peer through the slot.

'Mangala Shah, forty-four. Homemaker. Wife of a garment exporter. The husband was in his office at the time of the murder. Lots of people there vouched for his presence. Two kids. Both were in school. A neighbour was supposed to have dhokla and tea with her. She is the one who found her lying there and called us.'

Shinde nodded curtly at the inspector from the Thane division who was briefing him at the crime scene. 'Any signs of a break-in?' he asked.

The inspector shook his head. 'Naahin, saheb.'

Shinde glanced at Kadam. The two men had rushed to the site as soon as they were informed of the murder. 'Shall we?' he asked, gesturing towards the body lying on the floor.

'Any servant working in the house?' asked Kadam, pulling on a pair of gloves.

'There's a full-time bai, sir. Pana aaj tichi sutti aahey— weekly off. She's gone to meet her family in Bhiwandi,' said the inspector.

'Barobar. Just make sure she actually went there, theek?' said Kadam. He stepped over to the body, Shinde following.

'Hands tied with nylon rope, check. Food stuffed in mouth, check. Finek knife left in heart, check. I guess there's no doubt we're dealing with the same killer,' said Shinde in a low voice.

Kadam nodded grimly, staring at the corpse. Suddenly he bent down and sniffed hard. Shinde was amused. *Kutta indeed*, he thought.

'What's that smell?' asked Kadam.

'I don't smell anything,' said Shinde.

Kadam inhaled deeply twice more. 'It's some sort of chemical,' he said. 'Like the stuff pest-control people use. Check if any pest-control services were provided in this house.' He walked around the body, then stopped. 'Look.' There was an arc of blood on the floor. 'The body has been rotated. But why move it at all? Why not just leave it lying how it was?'

Shinde was still trying to process Kadam's questions when the latter spoke up again. 'Look at that knot,' he said, pointing to the way the rope was tied.

'What about it?'

'Arrey saala, it's a special knot,' said Kadam.

'A knot is a knot. Tyaat special kaay?'

Kadam gave an exasperated sigh, pained at having to explain himself to an idiot. 'All knots are not the same, Shinde. This is called a packer's knot. It's a binding knot which can be easily pulled taut and locked in position. See that figure-eight? Pulling at the ends tightens the binding.'

'I missed the class on knots in the academy,' said Shinde, irritated by Kadam's condescending tone.

'Not everyone knows how to do these knots. Let's take another look at the photographs in the previous cases. They may have followed the same pattern,' said Kadam.

'And if they did?'

'Then we will know a little more about the killer than we did at the start of the day. And every bit of information brings us closer to our murderer.'

'Theek.'

'Also check the dustbin. Sometimes what people throw away is more important than what they keep.'

35

Kadam peered through a magnifying glass at the photographs pinned up on the information board and grunted in satisfaction. The same knot had been used in the other two cases as well. More importantly, an arc of blood was clearly visible on the floor near Ravi Mehra's body, just like the one beside Mangala Shah. He looked again at the crime scene photo from the Suchandra Agarwal case. A partial arc of blood could be seen here too; the rest was obscured by the carpet. No wonder he had missed the pattern the first time he had seen the photos.

Satisfied, he picked up his mobile phone and called Shinde. 'Do we have floor plans of each of the flats in which the bodies were found?'

'No, but I can easily arrange them,' said Shinde.

'Do that taabadtob. And email them to me as soon as you get them,' Kadam instructed, and ended the call.

Shinde wondered what that was about, but he knew better than to ask. He asked one of his juniors to obtain copies of the floor plans from the housing societies. 'Send them on to Kadam.'

Shinde's phone rang again an hour later. He looked at the screen and frowned. Kadam again. *What does the chutiya want this time?*

'The floor plan of Mangala Shah's flat doesn't indicate the compass direction,' said Kadam when Shinde answered the phone.

'Yes, so?' asked Shinde irritably.

'I need to know the orientation of each flat. And mark where the bodies were found and in what position.' He disconnected the call as soon as he'd finished speaking. Not a word was extra.

Kadam was pacing restlessly up and down his small flat when his phone pinged announcing an email. He opened the mail and walked to the information board. Glancing at the email every now and then, he drew three circles, and marked #1, #2 and #3 on the margins of the board. Inside each circle, he drew an arrow to indicate the position of the body.

'What's going on?'

Startled, Kadam dropped the marker. 'Ketul! Thanks for scaring me like that. When did you come in?'

'If only they could see you now! The great Prakash Kadam, scared out of his wits!' Ketul grinned. 'I rang the doorbell a couple of times. I guess you were too lost in your own world to notice. So, I used my key.' She glanced at the figures he had drawn on the board. 'So, what's going on? You have that look you get when you're on to something.'

Kadam nodded, scratching his stubble. 'I have an idea. Still working on it.'

'Anything I can do to help?' asked Ketul.

'Well, now that you mention it ...' Kadam trailed off with a chuckle.

Ketul groaned. 'I'm going to regret this, aren't I? Okay, tell me what you want.'

'Do a little digging on the three victims,' said Kadam. 'Find out if there's any link between them—anything. Did their children attend the same school? Did they operate an account at the same bank? Did they share a doctor, dentist or hairdresser? It doesn't matter how remote or silly it may seem.'

'Don't you have Shinde working on that for you already?'

'Yes, and you know how much faith I have in him.' Kadam puffed out a cheek.

'I see. And how do you expect me to access all this "personal" information?'

'Ask the AI geek, no … Your hacker boyfriend.'

Ketul flushed, her fingers reaching for her coral. 'You know that Nirmal and I are just friends. I've told you that before.'

Kadam held up a placatory hand. 'Of course. So, ask your friend, no? He can get into all sorts of records.'

Ketul looked hard at Kadam, trying to figure out his game. 'Fine,' she eventually said. 'If it's so important to you, I'll ask Nirmal.'

Kadam thanked her and turned back to the board, the brief moment of light-hearted banter with his daughter already forgotten.

36

'Saheb, link saapadli,' said Shinde's junior.

Shinde shut the file with a loud thwack. 'You found a link between all three victims?'

'Ho, saheb. Someone called Mangesh Shivalkar. His number was in the phone address book of all three.'

'What does he do?'

'Agent for railway tickets, ration cards, Aadhaar, etcetera.'

'Do you have his address?'

Shivalkar's office was in the basement of an old building located close to St. Michael's Church in Mahim. The road, known as Mahim Causeway, used to be the only artery between Worli and Bandra until a swanky over-sea bridge made it redundant. Mercifully for the residents of the area, the traffic had since reduced.

The basement office consisted of a single hall with one cubicle in a corner for the boss. Three desks were set up in the middle of the room, and some chairs were placed in the area near the door, presumably for customers to wait. Shinde entered, accompanied by a constable.

An elderly man with dyed black hair and a skinny young fellow, who looked barely out of his teens, were the only people present. At the sight of the police, they rose hurriedly to their feet.

'Mangesh Shivalkar?' asked Shinde. For a moment, he wondered if he ought to have informed Kadam, but then he shrugged off the thought. He didn't have to report every little detail to that bugger. *It's not like he's my boss.*

'He's not here, saheb,' said the elderly man. 'May I help you?'

Shinde eyed him quizzically. 'You are?'

'Karthik Rao, his accountant.'

'Where is Shivalkar?'

'Out of town. Hasn't been here the last few days,' said Rao.

'Did he say where he was going?'

'Somewhere in the Chambal valley, saheb. Took the train to Kota. Spiritual retreat. There is bad mobile connectivity, so he calls kabhi-kabhi.'

'When did you last speak with him?'

'Two days ago. He took the business report from me.'

'Any idea when he's back?'

Rao shook his head. 'Should be a week or so.'

'Theek. I have some questions. About three of your customers.' Shinde rattled off the names. 'What work have you done for these three?'

'We record our orders on transaction slips,' Rao said. 'Let me check.' He flipped through the papers in a box file. 'We've only done business with two of them: Suchandra Agarwal and Ravi Mehra. She booked a railway ticket through us two months ago.'

'And Mehra?'

'Needed a PVC version of his Aadhaar card.'

'What about Mangala Shah?'

'No record for that name. Maybe the boss did a side deal in cash—'

'To save GST?' smirked Shinde. 'Check again.'

But the result was the same. Shinde frowned. 'Okay. I'm going to need that file for a few days … I'll have a warrant sent over. And give me your phone number as well, just in case I need to call you.'

As Shinde walked towards his vehicle, he turned to the constable accompanying him. 'Ek kaam kara. Get Shivalkar's mobile number traced. Also, get the call records of this Karthik Rao. Let's see if he was telling us the truth.'

37

'So, what information do you have for me?'

Raju smiled at the young reporter asking the question. 'Arrey deva, deva … If I tell you that right away, there won't be any masala left in the story!'

Raju had disposed of his entire loot and was feeling relaxed. The two were sitting on a bench at Oval Maidan, watching kids play cricket. Located just south of Churchgate, the field, along with Azad Maidan, Cooperage Ground and Cross Maidan, was part of the area that used to be known as the Esplanade. The sun had just started to set, casting an orange glow on the sky. It was a beautiful sight, but neither man was particularly interested.

'I'm just a reporter. I can't promise you any money. Only my editor can take that decision,' said the journalist.

'Theek,' said Raju. 'Then talk to your boss and tell me a price. You know my number.' Raju got up, signalling that the meeting was over.

The reporter grabbed him by the wrist. 'Hold on, Raju bhai. How is my channel supposed to take a call when you won't even tell us what this information is? Kya boloon unko?'

Raju grinned, revealing irregular, stained teeth. 'Just tell them I'm giving you the biggest story of your life—about serial killings in Mumbai that no one is talking about. Now ask yourself: How do I know this?'

Standing a short distance away was a man in his fifties wearing a checked bush shirt. He was the lawyer Aslam had introduced to Raju. Bhagwan Keswani walked over to Raju and said, 'I think it is all falling into place.'

38

'I heard you had a little chat with my son. He was limping for a few days after that.'

Rane tensed at the deputy home minister's words. He looked up at Gaikwad's eyebrows. They were the best indicator of the minister's mood. If they merged, it usually meant trouble. But they were separate now. Gaikwad smiled, reassuring Rane.

'Ho, saheb, I'm sorry I was a little rough with him.'

Gaikwad shrugged. 'Someone should have given him that treatment a long time ago. His mother spoilt him completely, and I was never around. When she died, I tried to reach out. But by then we had become strangers who live under the same roof. Public service takes a toll on your personal life.'

The two men were in the garden of Gaikwad's bungalow on Altamount Road, the poshest and leafiest part of Mumbai. *You've done pretty well for yourself*, thought Rane, looking around. He always found it hypocritical when politicians talked about the sacrifices they had made.

Tea and snacks had been set out on a table under a gorgeous gulmohar tree, but remained untouched. At Gaikwad's prompting, they had left their mobile phones on the table and gone for a stroll. Rane was amused to see that the deputy home minister—someone who routinely ordered wiretaps on others—was worried about his phone being compromised. Yet, as Rane well knew, it was a sensible precaution.

'Do you think Pankaj's problem is sorted out?' asked Gaikwad.

'I'm afraid not, saheb. He's back fully into it. Not just using, but also dealing—at one of the clubs owned by Home Minister Lokhande.'

'Crazy fucker,' muttered Gaikwad.

'I scared the shit out of him that night,' said Rane, sounding particularly nasal as he attempted to reassure the deputy home minister. 'It will stop him for a while, but he needs professional help; else he'll slip again.'

Gaikwad sighed. 'I'll speak to my doctor about it. I tell you, one never stops worrying when it comes to bachchas, no matter how old they become.'

He lapsed into a gloomy silence. The two men walked together quietly for some time. Rane looked longingly at the tea and samosas, wondering whether it would be out of line to suggest they sit down—and partake.

'Any news on that Gorai land matter?' asked Gaikwad suddenly.

'You mean the plot that's been illegally occupied by Momuma and his mad bunch? They've built quite an elaborate structure there,' said Rane.

'One can only do that with some powerful backing. So who's helping Momuma?'

'Bhau Patil.'

'That madarchod? Any time something shady is going on, he's involved somehow. So, what's his game here?'

'It's a very valuable piece of real estate. The cult's illegal occupation is driving down the price. The owner is helpless because the police won't do anything, given the relationship between Bhau Patil and Commissioner Chavan, and if he were to go to court, the case would drag on for decades,' Rane explained. 'When the man becomes desperate, Patil will buy the property at a throwaway price and Momuma's gang will disappear. Then they'll find another plot, and the process will begin all over again. In the meantime, the place is a drug haven—a captive market for Patil's powder.'

Gaikwad frowned, his eyebrows merging together. Rane could almost hear the wheels in his brain turning as he considered various options. Finally, Gaikwad spoke. 'Start preparing for an eviction. We can't allow Patil to squat whenever and wherever he feels like. He needs to be taught a lesson … In more ways than one.'

'Khaatri aahey, saheb? It could get ugly. And Chavan will block me.'

'We'll have to deal with it,' said Gaikwad. 'In the meantime, we'll find a way to take over the home department. When that happens, I'll make sure that you replace Chavan as the commissioner.'

39

'These are difficult times for our little community. All we want is to live in peace and harmony, but the world cannot accept that,' Momuma whispered, looking around at the gathering. All the faces reflected concern and anxiety.

'Salaam, Momuma! Show us the light,' said a person sitting in the front row. Others followed. 'Show us the light! Show us the light!' they cried.

Momuma let the chanting build up to a crescendo, then raised a hand. The crowd fell silent instantly. 'I speak with a heavy heart. I am a firm believer in peace and non-violence. But it is no sin to defend oneself. Our focus so far has only been on building mental and emotional strength, but now we must build our physical strength as well. We need to prepare. Are you with me?'

A loud 'Yes!' resounded across the gathering as the men and women began shaking their heads in earnest.

Momuma nodded, satisfied. 'Then let us get ready,' he said softly into the microphone. 'They hate us and our way of life. But if they try messing with us, they must learn a lesson. Are you with me?'

There was another loud chorus of assent.

'Good. Let us disperse then. We have much to do,' said Momuma.

He made his way back to his luxurious quarters and sank down into his throne-like chair, rubbing his forehead wearily. Two hands gently settled on his shoulders and began kneading them. A little grunt of relief escaped his lips. The hands moved away from his shoulders. 'Don't stop,' he murmured.

'Don't worry, I won't,' said Sarla. She began massaging his forehead. Momuma sighed and leaned back, resting his head against her breasts. Sarla's breathing quickened. She slid her hands under Momuma's robe and began stroking his chest.

'Wait. Not yet. I have some work to do,' said Momuma reluctantly. 'Go to the bedroom. I'll join you after I've made a quick call.'

Sarla pouted. 'Can't it wait?'

Momuma shook his head. 'I won't be long—it's important.' He patted Sarla's bottom as she walked away. Who would have suspected there would be so much passion beneath that demure demeanour? With some effort, he brought his mind back to the task at hand. He picked up his mobile phone and called a number.

'Bola,' said Bhau Patil on the other end through a mouthful of paan.

'Bhau, it's becoming difficult to hang on to this land.'

'Stop whispering to me in the way you address your muttha flock,' said Patil, irritably.

'Yes, Bhau,' said Momuma, switching to his normal voice.

'Stay put. That land is very important to me,' said Patil. 'I've almost got the owner to surrender ... It's just a matter of time.'

'We may not have much time left,' said Momuma urgently. 'I'm getting eviction notices ...'

'Tear them up. No one will dare to move against you.'

'I'm not so sure—'

'Gaandu, *you* don't need to be sure,' said Patil angrily. 'Leave the thinking to me. Sit tight, and keep spouting all that garbage about love and peace.'

'It would help if you would make one or two calls on our behalf.'

'What have you been smoking today, raandichya? You know I can't openly get involved.'

'If our commune gets evicted, you'll lose all the time and money you've invested.'

There was silence as Patil considered Momuma's words. 'I'll speak to Chavan,' he said finally.

'Thank you, Bhau,' said Momuma. 'That will be a big help.'

He was about to hang up when Patil interjected. 'How's my sister?' he asked. 'It's been a while since I spoke to her. I deliberately left her in your care, away from that laundebaaz. She's gone through a lot. I'd better not hear that she's uncomfortable.'

Momuma rose, phone still in hand, and strolled into his bedroom. Sarla was lying on the bed, biting her fingernails. She looked up at him eagerly. Momuma parted Sarla's robe and slipped his hand between her legs.

'Don't worry, Bhau, your sister is in very good hands,' said Momuma into the phone. 'I'm personally taking care of all her needs.'

Fifteen minutes later, Momuma sighed with contentment as he rolled off Sarla. They lay side by side, quietly, waiting to regain their breath. In the past, Momuma would have lit up a cigarette, but he had quit the habit some years ago.

Sarla reached over and began lightly stroking his thigh. But Momuma pushed her away gently. 'We need to talk,' he said, sitting up so that his back was propped against the pillows.

Sarla sat up too, the sheet slipping away as she brought up her hand to bite a fingernail. Momuma forced himself to look away.

'When you first came here, you were running away from your husband,' whispered Momuma. 'He was a policeman and you were fed up with his ways, right?'

Sarla shook her head to indicate assent. Momuma was pleased to note that the habit had become deeply ingrained in her. 'I have left him and that life far behind,' she said. Briefly, a sad look appeared in her eyes. 'The only people I miss are my daughter and my half-brother. He was the one who protected me from that pervert.'

Sarla shut her eyes and briskly shook her head, as though trying to get rid of the thoughts in her head. When she opened her eyes, she saw Momuma staring at her. He reached out for her hand and held it gently. 'You are safe with Momuma. But, there is something that we must do. Listen to me carefully …'

40

Nirmal's one-bedroom flat in Byculla was tiny, but the location was amazing. The building stood near the perimeter of Jijamata Udyan, which housed not only a gorgeous heritage park and the Byculla Zoo, but also Mumbai's oldest museum, a beautiful Victorian building with a pale green façade. The view from the flat's windows was incredible, so much so that that one could almost ignore the desolation that had descended upon parts of the area since the closure of many of its textile mills.

Ketul, though, could not be bothered with the scenery.

'That's almost their whole life stories right here! And we still pretend there's something called privacy.' She shook her head as she looked at the records of the three victims that Nirmal had obtained for her, and which now lay strewn on the living room floor. 'First things first, let's get everything sorted. It's impossible to find anything in this mess,' she said.

She began separating them and soon all the papers were neatly arranged on the dining table. 'That lot is their online searches, that one is their Aadhaar records, that one is phone bills and so on,' she explained. 'Now, instead of just looking at papers randomly and hoping to find something, we can search through them systematically.' In addition to the information obtained by Nirmal, Ketul had managed to get the victims' income tax returns using one of Kadam's old contacts in the Income Tax Department.

'And I thought I was your only shady friend,' said Nirmal.

'Don't flatter yourself. There's a lot about me you don't know,' said Ketul, gathering her hair into a ponytail.

I would love to know everything about you, thought Nirmal. *I would love to know when you wake and when you sleep ... what you like, think, eat and wear. I would love to know what you are like in bed ... how your face looks when you make love. I would love to know ...*

Nirmal realized with a start that Ketul was talking to him. 'Sorry, what did you say?' he asked, forcing himself out of his daydream.

'Help me look through these records and underline anything

that the three victims have in common,' said Ketul as she began poring over a bunch of papers.

Nirmal sighed, his budding erection subsiding like a pricked balloon, and began flipping through another set of records. Every now and then his eyes would stray to Ketul and linger on her.

But a few hours later, they had made scant progress. Ketul groaned tiredly and put her head on the table, using her hands as a pillow. After a while, she lifted her head, rubbed her eyes and stretched her arms on the table. Nirmal reached out and patted her right hand. She nodded gratefully and covered his hand with her left hand. Their eyes met; Ketul's lips parted slightly; Nirmal stared at her, transfixed. Suddenly the phone rang. They both sprang apart. Ketul snatched up her phone and answered it. Nirmal cursed silently. *Damn!*

Ketul had a short conversation and then slumped in her chair, deflated. Nirmal raised his eyebrows inquiringly. 'That was my accountant friend. He hasn't found anything in their credit card statements,' said Ketul.

'Do you want to rest for a while?' asked Nirmal.

She shook her head. 'I've got hold of a few numbers of some of the RWA office-bearers of all three residential societies. I'll talk to them and see if I can come up with anything.'

But their luck didn't improve.

'It's no use,' said Ketul finally, after the ninth call. 'We've hit a dead end.'

Nirmal had reached that conclusion quite some time ago, but had sensibly kept it to himself. He pushed back his chair and rose, stretching his stiff limbs. 'So, what do you want to do now?' he asked. 'Should we go out and get some proper coffee instead of the lousy tea I've been making?'

'Tempting, but I think I should go home now. It's getting late.' She picked up her phone to order an Ola.

'No need for that. I'll drop you,' said Nirmal. 'We've been indoors all day. The drive will do me good.'

The journey from Byculla to Matunga seemed interminable owing to the horrendous evening traffic. The two of them chatted casually along the way, until Ketul abruptly fell silent. Nirmal saw that her face had turned sombre. She was staring at a forbidding-looking building with a signboard that said 'Maharashtra Psychiatric Hospital'.

'Bad memories?' he asked softly.

Ketul nodded. 'This is where they brought Baba after he had his breakdown. He was frantic, yelling at the top of his lungs, beyond reason … It took three ward boys to hold him down. I was so terrified.' She shuddered at the memory.

'That must have been awful for you,' said Nirmal. 'How old were you then?'

'Just a few years younger,' said Ketul. 'Those were the darkest days of my life. My mother had already left us, and I feared I would lose my father too. He had already suffered a heart attack by then. He had no idea who I was—it was a complete break from reality. Thank God, my grandmother was still alive and took me in. I got through that nightmare only because of her. He did come back to us, but I was forced to grow up quickly—very quickly.' She wiped a tear from her eye and fell silent. The rest of the journey was completed in silence.

When they pulled into Ketul's complex, Nirmal noticed that Kadam was sitting outside on the balcony. He got out of the car and stood awkwardly, arms by his side.

Ketul smiled. 'You can hug me, you know. It's okay.'

'Your father makes me uncomfortable,' he blurted out.

Ketul couldn't help laughing. 'Nirmal, you've really got to get over this fear of Baba. I'm telling you, underneath that scary exterior he's a softie.'

'I'll take your word for it,' said Nirmal. 'Good night. Now I must go plan our social media campaign for Shakti.'

Hours later, Nirmal tossed and turned in his bed, then punched the pillow in frustration. He sat up, feeling too wired to sleep. He walked to his refrigerator, pulled out a bottle of water and drank straight from it. Then he sat at his desk and turned on his computer. He opened a password-protected folder. It contained several thumbnails. He clicked on one.

A picture of a blindfolded, naked woman filled the screen. She was tied down with a nylon rope, her body was covered in bruises. Nirmal stared at the picture for a while, then minimized it. He opened another picture, then another and then several more.

After a while, he double-clicked on a video file. Another woman appeared on the screen. She lay spreadeagled on the floor, her hands and legs tied to stakes with rope. A burly man, whose face was not visible, loomed over her. He had a whip in his hands. The man flicked his wrist. The whip danced out. A thin line of blood appeared on the woman's stomach. She jerked in pain, whimpering.

Nirmal reached inside his shorts. On the screen, the man rained blows on the woman, who was writhing in agony. With every lash, Nirmal's hand moved faster. 'Ketul,' he whispered. His words turned into a groan and his back arched as he felt pleasure rush through him.

As the high subsided, Nirmal was wracked with guilt. Too much was wrong with his wiring.

41

The machines at the Finek plant at Ambernath were humming, their rhythmic sounds only punctuated by the loading and unloading of trucks.

Inside one of the soundproofed rooms, Sanjay Bhargava, the assistant logistics manager, announced, 'We have a problem.'

'What problem, sir?' asked the despatch clerk, a mousy-looking individual with thick glasses.

'Deliveries are getting delayed and customers are complaining online. We must increase the buffer stock that we leave with our logistics partners.' He stood up to indicate that the meeting was over. He adjusted his blue bush shirt and began doing head rotations on his beefy neck.

'But, sir …' began the clerk.

Bhargava gave him an irritated look. 'Kya hai? Instructions not clear?'

'Awasthi sir has asked for the delivery error rate to be reduced. Increasing buffer stocks will have the opposite effect, sir,' protested the clerk, recalling the conversation with Akash Awasthi, the logistics manager.

Bhargava stared at the clerk. The man visibly wilted under his hostile glare. 'Who's your immediate boss, Awasthi sir or me?' he asked, stretching his arms.

'Aap, saheb,' squeaked the clerk.

'Then I suggest you do what I tell you, and let me worry about Awasthi sir,' snarled Bhargava, a vein pulsing in his forehead.

'Yes, sir. Of course, sir. I'm sorry, I didn't mean it like that, sir,' the clerk mumbled and scuttled towards the door. Just as he reached it, Bhargava called out.

'One more thing'—the clerk paused, his hand on the doorknob—'I hate snitches and people who break the chain of command. Remember that.' Bhargava was holding a pencil in his meaty, powerful hands. He effortlessly snapped it in two. 'Oh, how careless of me,' he said, a grim look in his eyes.

The clerk went pale. For a moment, it seemed he might pass out. With an effort, he composed himself and made a hasty exit.

Bhargava watched him go. 'That should do it,' he muttered, rolling his shoulders.

42

Nidhi looked around nervously. The basement parking of the mall in Lower Parel was largely deserted. There were just a handful of vehicles, including a black Range Rover, which was idling. She looked at the licence plate, then quickly walked over to it and knocked on the front passenger window. The door opened.

'Get in,' said Pankaj curtly. His curls were concealed under a baseball cap and he was wearing shades, probably to hide the glazed look in his eyes. His beard looked neater than usual. An electric hair trimmer lying in the centre console had obviously been used.

Nidhi handed over an envelope to him. 'It's all there, Punky,' she said. 'You can count it.'

Pankaj pulled out the bundle of notes from the envelope, and quickly flicked through it. 'Well, well,' he said. 'Will wonders never cease. You managed to fucking settle your dues.'

'I told you I would, didn't I?' said Nidhi, a spark of defiance in her voice.

Pankaj gave her a long, appraising look. Nidhi had scrubbed her face and her hair was neatly done. It seemed like she was trying to clean up her act. The thought displeased him. He preferred her dishevelled, begging and pleading. 'I'm curious. How did you manage it?'

'Suchandra had gifted me a pair of earrings. I sold them,' said Nidhi.

'Oh dear. That must have been heartbreaking for you,' said Pankaj, wondering whether Nidhi had bumped off her lover to get her grubby fingers on her jewellery.

Nidhi thought he was mocking her, but the shades made it impossible to tell. 'What's important is that I've got your money,' she said. 'We're all square now, right, Punky?'

Pankaj nodded. 'Absolutely. All dues settled.'

'Great,' said Nidhi. She reached for the handle to open the door.

'Hey, Nidhi, would you like a fix for old times' sake? Don't worry. This one is on the house.'

43

'Ketul! It's good to see you. Dropped in for that long-promised cup of tea, finally, eh?' said Dr Desai, beaming as he held the door open for her to enter.

She held up a bag. 'I've got you some guavas. I know you don't eat sweets. I hope that fruits are okay.'

'Of course. Now you're even more welcome,' chuckled Desai, the restrained laugh making him sound even more English. 'Come in and sit down. I'm so glad you came.'

He bustled about the kitchen, making tea. When it was ready, he brought the mugs and some snacks to the coffee table. Ketul was staring into space, massaging the back of her neck. Desai moved behind her chair and placed his hands on her shoulders. The action startled Ketul and Desai immediately withdrew.

'Sorry, Ketul,' he said. 'Didn't mean to startle you ... I thought I would release the tension in your neck and shoulders.'

'That's not necessary, doc,' she replied, fully alert. The gesture had made her momentarily uncomfortable, but she had now recovered. Desai handed her a mug and sat down with his own.

'You were lost in thought,' he said. 'Frowning. Is everything all right?'

'It's this case I'm handling for an NGO called Shakti.' She tightened her hold around the mug to prevent herself from reaching for her pendant.

'The name sounds familiar, but I can't quite place it,' said Desai.

'They rescue and rehabilitate trafficking victims—'

'Oh yes, of course,' interrupted Desai. 'I've done some free consultations there. Many doctors volunteer from time to time.'

Ketul nodded. 'I saw a photo of you when I visited their headquarters. They showed me what happens to trafficking victims who don't get rescued. I just can't get those sights out of my mind.'

'How are you involved in the case?' asked Desai softly.

'I'm trying to get a complaint booked against the gang that traffics those girls. But nothing is moving. How many more victims must be out there—kidnapped, starved, beaten and raped? What kind of perverted system lets helpless women be treated so badly?'

Desai took a sip of his tea. 'Maybe it's their fate to suffer like that,' he said. 'A person's life is often decided by the stars. Human beings are mere characters in a story that's already been written.'

Ketul was stunned. 'How can you say that? You're a man of science!'

Desai shrugged. 'It's precisely because I've spent my life studying and practising medicine that I realize how little we know about life's mysteries.' He pointed to a print of a Raja Ravi

Varma painting of Hindu deities on the wall. 'Man cannot be more powerful than the stars, Ketul.'

She noticed the plethora of books on astrology, philosophy, religion, science and the esoteric on Desai's bookshelves. It was evident that his views were a reflection of his own study. 'But isn't that fatalistic?'

'It's the simple truth. Once you accept it, life becomes a lot less complicated,' said Desai. He realized that Ketul was getting increasingly agitated and decided to change the subject. 'Those guavas looked good. Let me cut a few.'

'I'll help you,' said Ketul, following him into the kitchen.

She pulled out plates from the cabinet while Desai took a long, sharp knife and began slicing the guavas. His movements were quick and deft.

'You cut like a chef,' observed Ketul.

Desai laughed. 'All doctors know how to wield a scalpel even if they do not become surgeons.' He washed the knife clean, then placed it in a rack. As he did, the star-shaped logo caught Ketul's eye. She look at the brand on the knife rack.

Finek.

44

'*Aaj phir jeene ki tamanna hai, aaj phir marne ka iraada hai …*'

Lata Mangeshkar's magical rendition of Shailendra's soulful lyrics filled the room as Kadam sat on the sofa, brooding. Occasionally, he would take a puff from a cigarette, then he would go back to being perfectly still, almost like a statue. The ashtray next to him was overflowing.

'Baba! The house is full of smoke,' Ketul coughed as she entered the flat. 'Are you determined to turn this place into a gas chamber?' She opened a couple of windows and vigorously fanned the smoke away. The sounds of the aarti that filtered in were a sign that evening prayers were underway at the nearby Kochu Guruvayoor Sree Ram Mandir.

'Back from your visit to Desai? Why did you set him on me?' asked Kadam.

'In the hope that he would drill some sense into you,' snapped Ketul. She had intended to tell Kadam about Desai using Finek knives, but her irritation about the smoke caused it to slip out of her mind.

Wordlessly, she stuck a map of Mumbai on the information board and marked the locations of the three murders. 'Goregaon West, Lower Parel and Thane,' she said. 'Nothing common about the locations. Ravi Mehra was a day trader, Suchandra Agarwal was an ad executive, Mangala Shah was a housewife. One victim was a man, two were women. Two were married, one was single. Two straight, one gay. No common school, bank, tailor, hairdresser or shared employment history,' said Ketul.

'Not a single thing that connects them. We have ghanta!' Kadam agreed irritably.

The doorbell chimed. 'That must be Shinde. I'd asked him to drop by with an update,' he said, getting up and answering the door. 'Any luck? Kahihi? Did we check the address books on the victims' phones for common numbers?'

Shinde nodded. 'Ho, saheb. We found only one number common to all three. Turned out to be an agent who assists with government IDs, train tickets and liaisons. He's the biggest in town, so it's no surprise that many people have his number. I visited his office. His employees said he's in the Chambal valley for a retreat. He's been there for more than a week—so he couldn't have killed Mangala Shah.'

'But has he actually been there all this while?' asked Kadam, scratching his stubble.

'Barobar. I've asked the local cops from Jhalawar—the closest police station—to go meet him and check out his story. He's at some strange tantric retreat,' said Shinde.

Kadam ran a finger along his scar, deep in thought. 'Shri Bhairava Tantra, is it?'

'How … ?' began Shinde. *It's true what they say about him*, he thought, raking his fingers through his hair. *This lauda knows something about everything. And everything about some things.*

'These days, the ordinary and the extraordinary— politicians, businessmen, movie stars, bureaucrats—all flock to Bhairavadas,' said Kadam, shrugging. 'He was once a dacoit. Surrendered his arms, got a pardon and devoted the rest of his life to Bhairava—the fiercest manifestation of Shiva—'

'In any case,' Shinde interrupted, 'we have nothing substantial against the ticket tout. His number was in the mobile phones of all three victims, but that could be pure coincidence.'

'Maybe, maybe not,' said Kadam. He lapsed into a zombie-like state, his body perfectly still, save for the occasional cheek puffing out, while his brain worked furiously.

Shinde coughed a couple of times and cleared his throat loudly, but Kadam didn't notice. He finally turned to Ketul. 'How long does he sit like this?' he asked. 'Should I wait, or should I leave?'

Before Ketul could reply, Kadam spoke. 'Who's the medical examiner?'

'Shirodkar.'

'Call him. Tell him to meet us at the morgue immediately,' he said, snapping his fingers.

'Right now?' asked Shinde, startled.

'Yes, right now.'

'It's late. He must have left for home a couple of hours ago.' Shinde didn't say that he too was tired—and that it was a long drive to the morgue.

'It's important, Shinde. Majhe aaik.'

Shinde sighed and pulled out his phone. Kadam could hear an irate voice at the other end of the call. 'Theek aahey. Sorry to disturb,' said Shinde, cutting the call a few seconds later. 'Shirodkar said to come tomorrow,' he told Kadam.

'Oh, acting stubborn, is he?'

'He's the one acting stubborn?' asked Shinde incredulously, one corner of his mouth twitching.

Kadam ignored him and immediately called Rane, who answered on the second ring. 'Is everything okay, Prakash?' Rane sounded particularly shrill over the phone.

'I need help. I need the medical examiner—Shirodkar— to meet me at the morgue right now. He's saying to come tomorrow,' complained Kadam.

'What's the urgency?'

'Just a thought I had. But I need to check it out taabadtob,' said Kadam.

Rane sighed, knowing he had no choice. 'Give me five minutes.'

Kadam paced up and down restlessly, waiting for Rane to call back. Then his phone rang. He snatched it up hurriedly. 'Oh, he will? Arrey wah! Thanks so much.'

Shinde hauled himself to his feet, stifling a yawn. Kadam punched him on the arm playfully. Now that he had got his way, he was in a very good mood. He blew a kiss at Ketul and headed to the door.

'Crime doesn't sleep, Shinde. Chalo.'

45

'Swagat! We're honoured to have such important visitors.'

Shinde winced at Shirodkar's jibe.

Kadam simply smiled. 'Good to see you after all this while, Shirodkar. I see you're keeping things as spick and span as ever.'

Shinde couldn't help sniggering at that. There was nothing remotely clean about their surroundings. The three men were standing in the mortuary of St. George Hospital near the Chhatrapati Shivaji Maharaj railway station in the crowded Fort area. The mortuary was a mess. Bodies were piled up on top of each other on gurneys. The floor was slippery with body fluids. The whole place stank of death and decay.

'Saala, it's the middle of the night! What do you expect?' Shirodkar rasped testily.

Shinde, who had been taking shallow breaths to avoid the stench, reached into his pocket and pulled out a small bottle of Vicks VapoRub. 'Let's hope this helps mask the smell somewhat,' he said. He offered the bottle to Kadam, who applied some just below his nose.

'Tula kaay havey aahey? And why are we here?' asked Shirodkar.

'To take another look at the bodies of the victims—Ravi Mehra, Suchandra Agarwal and Mangala Shah,' said Kadam, trying valiantly to not gag. 'They haven't been released to the families for cremation yet, have they?'

'I've kept them in the freezer,' rasped Shirodkar. 'Which is more than what most that come here get.'

'Five-star treatment,' muttered Kadam, ignoring a rat that scampered across the floor.

Shirodkar gave him a dirty look. 'Do you know how overloaded we are? Now, follow me and watch your step. If you slip and crack your head, I'll have one more dead body to deal with.'

The three corpses were pulled out and laid side by side on gurneys. Kadam bent over each one to examine them closely. He straightened a few minutes later, wrinkling his nose. Shinde silently offered Kadam some more vapour rub. He nodded gratefully and applied a liberal amount below his nose. 'Did you take X-rays of the knife stabs?' he asked Shirodkar.

The medical examiner walked across to a filing cabinet. Large envelopes with case numbers written on them were arranged chronologically. He pulled out three. Shirodkar held up the first X-ray against the tube light. Kadam took a good, long look at it, then nodded. 'Next please.' The process was repeated after the second one.

'Anything interesting?' asked Shinde, once Kadam had seen all three X-rays.

'Right ventricular stabs that seem consistent across all three victims,' Kadam answered before Shirodkar could respond. He then fell silent, puffing out a cheek. 'Arrey, I used to do this for a living, remember?' Kadam added when he noticed Shirodkar's shocked expression. He would have said more, but a wave of dizziness overwhelmed him. He grabbed the edge of a gurney to steady himself.

'You okay?' asked Shinde.

'Just give me a minute.' Kadam shook his head to clear it and then straightened up. 'Theek, so the pucca location to strike the heart is the left ventricle, the largest chamber. But these are stabs to the right ventricle. I wonder why.'

'Good point,' agreed Shirodkar grudgingly. 'Actually, the heart is rather difficult to stab because it is located behind the ribs and tough connective tissue. It also has a covering, the pericardium. One needs upper body strength to strike there.'

'Barobar,' said Kadam. 'But remember, the victim's right ventricle would be closer to the killer's left.' He walked up to Shirodkar and made a gentle stabbing motion with his left hand against Shirodkar's chest. 'If the killer is left-handed, then a stab to the heart would hit the right ventricle rather than the left one. Our killer is probably a leftie with significant upper body strength.'

'But why specifically target the ventricle?' asked Shinde.

'The heart is a muscle,' replied Kadam. 'It contracts quickly and repetitively. In case of a stab wound, the ventricle will seal the space around the knife—almost like the lips of someone giving a blow job!'

Shinde tittered.

Oblivious to Shinde's train of thought, Kadam continued. 'People can survive for hours with such wounds. Is the aim to make the victim suffer the agony of a long, painful death? But wh—why? Wh—what d—d—does it s—s—symbol—bolize?' Kadam's words slurred; his tongue felt thick and heavy. The room spun around him. He reached for the gurney, but his hand only hit air. Time slowed down. He felt himself falling, sinking through thick sludge, taking forever to hit the ground. *I'm coming to you, Sarla. I'm coming to you, Aryan. I'm coming,* echoed inside his head. All of a sudden, he felt a jolt of pain go through his body. He heard the startled cries of Shinde and Shirodkar as if from a great distance. Then the world went black.

'Kadam? Kadam. Benchod, wake up!'

Kadam awoke with a start. He was lying on Shirodkar's examining table. He saw Shirodkar and Shinde staring at him. He tried to sit up and winced as a bolt of agony shot through his head.

'Easy there. You had a nasty fall,' croaked Shirodkar. 'Want some water?'

Kadam nodded, then winced again. Shirodkar handed him a bottle from which he drank thirstily and then wiped his mouth.

'What happened to you?' asked Shinde, with a subtle reptilian twitch.

'Don't know. Maybe the closed space got to me,' said Kadam.

'Khaliphukat talk! You used to spend hours here and nothing ever happened to you. Let me check your vitals,' said Shirodkar hoarsely.

'You have more experience with corpses than the living,' joked Kadam feebly.

'Very funny,' retorted the medical examiner. 'Now shut up and let me try to find your pulse, gaandu. Assuming you have one, that is.' He checked Kadam's pulse and then his blood pressure. A serious look settled upon his face. Kadam knew the look.

'The good news is that you're alive,' said Shirodkar finally. 'The bad news is that your indicators are off the charts. It so happens that you're in a hospital right now. I am going to have you admitted and get you thoroughly checked right away.'

Kadam shook his head gingerly, taking care not to make any sudden moves. 'At this hour they'll only have interns—no better than you—on duty,' he told Shirodkar.

Shirodkar frowned. 'Stubborn always,' he said. 'Then go home now. Get your physician to give you a proper examination tomorrow. Get a good night's sleep—and let others sleep too.'

'Plenty of time when one is dead,' said Kadam mutinously.

Shirodkar glared at him. 'The way you're going, you'll be there sooner rather than later.'

46

'Sorry I'm late, Ketul. It took longer than expected,' Kadam said as he walked into the flat. 'Ketul?'

There was no response. But the light in her bedroom was still on. The door was open. Kadam knocked on it perfunctorily, then peeked in. Empty. He scratched his stubble.

'Ketul?' he called out loudly, with mounting concern. He went to the bathroom door and knocked on it. 'Ketul, are you there?' A sense of dread filled his heart. He was fearless when it came to his own safety—often to the point of being foolhardy—but was fiercely protective of his only child.

'It's near midnight. Benchod, where is she at this hour?' he muttered, tracing his scar worriedly.

He called her cell phone. It rang until the automated voice took over. Kadam tried again. As he walked into the living room, he heard a faint buzzing sound. He followed the sound and found Ketul's phone on the dining table, vibrating on the wooden top. With a curse, he picked it up, resisting the temptation to hurl it to the floor. That wouldn't solve anything. *Think, Kadam, think,* he told himself.

Adrenaline pumping, he went down to the apartment gates and asked the guards if they'd seen Ketul leave the complex. Both guards shook their heads. Kadam knew they were telling the truth. Ketul always made it a point to greet the society staff respectfully and share mithai with them on festivals, so most of them had a soft spot for her. If she'd left the complex this late at night, they would have instantly noticed. But if she hadn't left the building, then where was she? His mind was racing. She didn't visit too many people inside the complex apart from ... Desai!

Kadam walked to the doctor's flat as fast as he could. At the door, he realized he was wheezing and his heart was pounding. He bent over, hands on knees and took a few deep breaths. Once his breathing had settled somewhat, Kadam rang the doorbell. There was no response. He rang it again and again, keeping his finger pressed on the bell for a long time. He could hear the sound of the ringer through the door, but there was no answer.

Was she was out taking a walk? Why not do a quick round of the complex? Deep down, Kadam knew he was clutching at straws, but he refused to entertain any negative thoughts. He walked around the complex, checking all the benches in case Ketul was sitting on one. There was a small children's play area near the garden. He visited that as well. There was no sign of Ketul.

Kadam finally admitted to himself that he would have to call Rane. But first, he needed to get a fix on her movements after Shinde and he had left the house. Kadam walked back to his flat, forcing his mind to think logically and methodically. When he opened the door, he caught a faint whiff of the floral perfume that Ketul used. Kadam rushed inside, all logic forgotten.

She was sitting at the dining table, sipping a cup of Horlicks.

'There you are, Baba!' she said. 'Why are you panting and sweating like that? Is everything okay?'

Kadam stared at Ketul for a long time, speechless. He was torn between hugging her in relief and screaming at her in anger. Finally, he sputtered, 'Where were you?'

'Oh, I'm so sorry,' said Ketul as realization dawned on her. 'Were you worried about me?'

'Ketul, saala it's past midnight. You wander off without even taking your phone. What am I supposed to think?' said Kadam, his voice rising.

Ketul rushed up to him and gave him a hug. 'I'm really sorry, Baba. That was thoughtless of me.'

Kadam held her close, feeling his tension dissipate. Finally, he released her. 'So, where were you all this while?'

'Well, I'd gone for a post-dinner walk,' explained Ketul. 'As I was returning home, I met Dr Desai in the corridor and we started chatting. And then Sunil Mishra came running out of 2D—you know, the one with the cute six-year-old son? His wife is out of town and the boy had high fever. He begged Dr Desai to check his son right away.'

'And you tagged along as his assistant?' Kadam gave her a wry look.

'Just as well that I did. The poor boy hadn't been able to keep any food down. I made him my special khichdi and he ate it.'

'Good for him,' said Kadam. 'And for all the stress you just caused me, you can make me khichdi tomorrow.'

'Done,' said Ketul, taking her cup into the kitchen.

Kadam noticed an item lying on the couch that he had never seen in the house before. It was a rabbit-shaped toy, made from coloured nylon ropes. He picked it up and looked at it from all angles. The toy had been very skilfully woven, using ropes of different colours.

'Where did this come from?' he asked.

'Oh, Dr Desai made it himself,' said Ketul. 'It's very good, no? He gave one of these to the boy. When I admired it, he insisted on getting one for me too from his flat.'

'Interesting,' said Kadam.

Something in his voice made Ketul look up. 'What's on your mind, Baba?'

'All the victims were found tied with coloured nylon ropes,' he said softly.

'What are you suggesting. Surely you can't be thinking—'

Kadam held up a hand. 'Chalo, let's list the facts. Desai is a doctor, so he will be admitted into people's homes easily. Now, is he linked to any of the victims in any way? Yes, he provided an alibi for Nidhi—Suchandra's lover.'

'But, Baba, Dr Desai is one of the kindest people I know,' protested Ketul. 'He volunteers at Shakti and gives free treatment to the girls.'

'People aren't always what they seem, Ketul. What do we actually know about him?'

'He reads on so many subjects, including astrology and philosophy. I know he has a daughter in Singapore. That's why we hit it off right from the beginning. He says I remind him of her.'

'Touching. But has anyone seen or spoken to this daughter in all these years? Have you?'

'I … No, I haven't.' Ketul shook her head.

'Be careful around him till this case is closed,' said Kadam. 'And avoid being alone with him.'

'That reminds me! When I went to his house for tea the other day, I saw something odd ... I'd meant to tell you then, but it slipped my mind. He uses Finek knives in his kitchen.'

Kadam was silent for a moment. Then: 'We need to find out a little more about this company—Finek.'

'I have a client visit halfway to Ambernath tomorrow,' said Ketul. 'I can check on them first thing in the morning.'

Kadam nodded, running a finger along his scar.

'What are you thinking?' asked Ketul.

'Could the use of Finek knives have some particular significance?'

47

The gates of Shri Bhairava Tantra Mandal in the Mukundara Hills of Chambal creaked open. The cops from Jhalawar exchanged nervous glances inside their Jeep. It had been a bumpy journey on a road that was little better than a dirt track. Thick desert vegetation grew on either side of the path. There was no other dwelling in sight.

'Are you sure, hukum?' asked the head constable. He was speaking for the team: Nothing good could come from messing with the occult.

Assistant Superintendent of Police Shivinder Tomar chewed on his toothpick anxiously. A freshly minted officer, he was as jittery as the constables accompanying him. But he was determined to do his job thoroughly. 'Main kaain karoon?'

he asked in a thick Hadoti dialect. 'Duty karey hai.' Only the slightest quiver in his voice betrayed his edginess. He cleared his throat and spoke more firmly. 'Chalo.'

The policemen looked around as their Jeep entered the settlement. Wild shrubs dotted the otherwise barren landscape along the Chambal riverbank. The only concession to modernity was a set of brick buildings clustered around the old Bhairava temple. A group of men was seated in its shadow, some in dhotis, some in tracksuits. They looked up as the cops approached them.

'Mangesh Shivalkar kathe hai?' asked Tomar.

'In a group meditation session with Bhairavadas. They should be finishing now,' said one of the men, clearly a city boy. He instructed someone to guide Tomar and his men to the meditation hall.

Tomar was about to follow when he noticed smouldering ashes. 'What's that?' he asked.

'Offerings,' replied the man. 'We offer sacrifices to the one greater than us all.'

'What sort of sacrifices?'

'Only symbolic—like gourds or pumpkins.'

'Pick up samples for forensics,' Tomar ordered one of his men before following the guide to the entrance of a large hall. The guide went in and returned with a short, balding individual in glasses. 'I'm Mangesh Shivalkar,' the man said.

Tomar gestured for Shivalkar to walk a few steps with him. The two of them moved out of the others' earshot. 'How long have you been here?'

'Around nine days,' responded Shivalkar.

'Come here often?'

'I've been coming here once a year for the past five years.'

'I see. And you haven't left this place since you arrived?'

Shivalkar shook his head. 'I come here to get away from things for a few days. I'm in no hurry to go anywhere.'

'Okay,' said Tomar. He permitted Shivalkar to return to his group and asked his men to confirm the story. Then he began walking towards the hall.

A burly man with a shaven head blocked his path. 'Where do you think you're going?' he growled.

'To meet Bhairavadas ji,' said Tomar.

'You think you can just stroll in and meet him?' sneered the man. 'Even VIPs wait for days to see him.'

Tomar bristled, but decided not to force a confrontation. 'Well, I'm already here, so can you please ask if he'll see me?' he asked politely.

The man glowered at him, then went in. He returned a couple of minutes later. 'Bhairavadas ji will see you,' he said, reluctantly letting Tomar by.

The police officer stepped from the bright sunlight into a dark hall. The only illumination was provided by some earthen diyas in the corners. He tripped on the edge of a rug and almost fell, regaining his balance in the nick of time.

'Don't worry, it is my task to guide people who are stumbling through life.' The speaker had a deep baritone and sounded amused.

Tomar shut his eyes for a few seconds and then opened them, adjusting to the gloom. He could smell an earthy, smoky odour lingering in the room. Hashish. In the dimness, he made out a figure seated on a platform. On moving closer, Tomar noticed that the man was bearded and had long, waist-length hair that had been left open. He was bare-chested and had an impressive physique; not muscled like a bodybuilder, but lean and lithe. And he had only one working eye. It was rumoured that the former dacoit had lost an eye to a battle splinter many years ago.

'Welcome to Shri Bhairava Tantra. Thhaaro swagat hai. May I know your name?'

'Mharo naam hai ASP Shivinder Tomar. And you?'

The man spread his hands in a disarming gesture. 'I gave up my birth name—Sardar Abdul Gujjar—when I renounced my old life. Now they call me Bhairavadas.' His English was surprisingly good; many of his disciples were from England.

'And you do black magic in this place?' asked Tomar.

The man laughed softly. 'We do tantra. Spiritual wisdom that is derided by people who have no idea what it means.'

The cannabis fumes in the air were starting to make Tomar dizzy. He shook his head to clear it. 'Mangesh Shivalkar is a disciple of yours?'

'I have an extended family of disciples. Mangesh is one of them, yes.'

'And he hasn't left this … this place since he arrived?'

Bhairavadas shrugged. 'I don't keep tabs on what everyone is doing every minute. But those who come here rarely leave until it is time for them to return home.'

Tomar nodded. 'Thank you for your time. I'll leave now.'

'So be it,' replied Bhairavadas. 'Shivinder Tomar, did you say your name was? You have a fire in you. I like it. I'll definitely mention your name to your police commissioner when he comes on his next visit.' For a moment, Bhairavadas's gentle demeanour slipped and a fierce expression settled on his face.

Tomar's stomach lurched and he felt his throat go dry. He spun around on his heels and walked away without saying a word. Behind him, he heard a soft chuckle; Bhairavadas was back to being amused. Outside, the sunlight seemed intolerable. He squinted and raised his hand to shield his eyes. He felt his head starting to throb and took a deep breath. His men hastily gathered around him. 'Did you ask around about Mangesh?' he asked them.

'Hukum. Everyone said the same thing. He's been here for nine days now,' said the head constable.

'Chaal,' said Tomar, pulling out another toothpick from his pocket. 'Get those ashes checked and send the report to that Shinde in Mumbai. Let's get out of here.' The place gave him the creeps.

48

Deva—alias Ekahata—tapped his driver's shoulder. 'Get off the highway and take that stretch,' he said. The SUV continued for about half a kilometre.

'Thamba,' commanded Deva as they came upon a parked container truck. He stepped out, swinging the stub of his right arm. The area was isolated, save for two men who were lying on jute bags on the side of the road. They rose to their feet as Deva approached. Both were unshaven, their eyes were red with lack of sleep.

'Sab maal hai?' asked Deva with a cockeyed stare.

One of the men walked over to the truck and slid open a panel in the back of the container. Deva peered into the hidden compartment. It was a dark, narrow space. A bunch of terrified girls stared out at him. They were hemmed in so tightly that there was barely any room to move. The compartment stank of human waste. In a corner were several cartons. At a nod from Deva, the truck driver pulled the cartons out. One of the girls began wailing and pleading for mercy. Deva stepped back and the driver shut the panel, abruptly cutting off her cries.

Deva opened one of the boxes, took out a pouch and sniffed it. Mephedrone, also known as 'meow meow', was all the rage in town. The boxes were quickly loaded into his SUV.

'Now listen to me carefully,' said Deva to the truckers. 'Drive through check naka three. The chodu there has already been paid off. His shift will end in two hours, so you need to leave immediately. Then go directly to Sonapur.'

'Abhi?' protested the driver. 'But we stopped just ten minutes ago. We've been driving all night and we're both tired—'

His words were cut off by a ringing slap. The driver clutched at his face. His right cheek had turned bright red where Deva had hit him with his all-powerful left hand, leaving the imprint of his fingers.

'My right hand may not work, but my left more than compensates. Never argue with me. Samjha, bhadavya?'

The trucker nodded docilely, still clutching his face.

'Phone me once you have safely deposited the consignment,' said Deva. The two men left without saying another word. As the truck faded into the distance, Deva called a number.

'People and powder have arrived,' he said to Bhau Patil.

49

'Yes, madam, how may I help you?' asked Sanjay Bhargava.

'I am Sujata Waghamare, vigilance officer from GST Mazagaon,' said Ketul. 'We're identifying retailers who may be evading duty while reselling your products.'

Ketul had a fake ID in her hand, courtesy one of her unorthodox contacts, but it turned out to be unnecessary. Bhargava did not ask to see it. He invited her to sit down, and ordered tea and biscuits. He had no desire to be on the wrong side of a revenue official.

As the refreshments were being served, Ketul noticed that the boy who brought the tea was wearing the same blue bush shirt with 'Finek' embroidered on it as Bhargava. 'Everyone here wears this same type of shirt?' she asked.

Bhargava nodded. 'From the CEO down to the youngest trainee. It's part of our culture. We're very proud of it.'

'Tumachi kampani Japaani aahey ka?' asked Ketul, using a little Marathi to appear genuine. 'From your name, it sounds more German or Swedish.'

Bhargava laughed out loud. 'Sorry to disappoint you, madam, but we're hundred per cent Indian. Finek is just an anagram for the word knife. And we don't need any collaborations because we are already the world's third-largest maker of knives.'

'Kithi chhaan! What is the secret?'

'Top quality at low cost for the huge Indian consumer market. We have the lowest retail price owing to economy of scale. And we only sell online, so no commissions.'

'Barobar. We think there are people buying your items online and reselling them without GST. Is there any way to track customers who place orders regularly?'

'What size of orders?' asked Bhargava, cracking his neck. Ketul thought his head would break off if he kept that up.

'Three or four at a time?'

Bhargava laughed. 'Finek knives sell in thousands each day. Someone placing an order for three knives—or even a hundred—would not be odd. Shopkeepers order online just like customers do. Our delivery service is very efficient.'

'Theek,' said Ketul. 'I must try ordering one to understand the system. Thank you for your time. I'll be in touch.'

Bhargava smiled and folded his hands in a namaste. He waited for her to leave and then picked up his phone. 'We may have a problem related to those missing consignments,' he said. 'Someone from the GST department is sniffing around. I'm not sure if there's more to it than meets the eye. We need to be careful.'

Call over, he paced up and down his small office restlessly. 'Shit, that bitch has got me all stressed out. I need to work it off,' he muttered to himself.

The Finek factory complex housed a neat, well-equipped gym on the premises. Bhargava headed towards it now, bag slung over his shoulder. He changed quickly into his tracksuit in the locker room. The gym instructor greeted him as he entered. 'Hello, Sanjay ji. Legs today?'

Bhargava shook his head. 'Chest and arms,' he said.

The instructor frowned. 'You did that last time too. You must work all muscle groups.'

Bhargava began rolling his arms over, warming up. 'I'll do legs next time, Rocky. Right now, I feel like doing some heavy-duty bench presses. Come and help me load up the bar.'

About an hour later, Bhargava exited the gym, sweaty and exhausted, and went straight to the shower. He emerged with a towel wrapped around his waist and strolled over to a full-length mirror in the locker room. His impressive biceps looked bulkier after the workout, and engorged veins stood out in his arms. Bhargava preened a little, flexing his pectoral muscles. 'Not bad,' he said to himself and changed into a fresh blue Finek uniform.

On his way out, the guard stopped him. 'Sir, you have to sign out,' he said, offering a pen. Bhargava took the pen in his left hand and signed the members' register with a flourish. He started towards the office block, but changed his mind and headed for his car, a blue Maruti Dzire, in the parking lot. He drove out of the factory gate a few minutes later, acknowledging the guard's salute with a nod.

It was a good life—and with his neat little side hustle, quite pleasurable too. He would do whatever it took to keep things that way.

50

The small flat at Worli Police Camp was cramped but bearable owing to the sea breeze that wafted in through the open windows. Shinde groaned when he saw the name flashing on his mobile phone screen. Kadam again. The *harami* had no sense of boundaries. Shinde had just settled down to have breakfast with his wife, who was now glaring at him. Reluctantly, he answered the phone. 'I'm putting you on speaker so that my wife can hear that it's you. You call so often, she's convinced I'm having an affair.'

'The only woman willing to tolerate you is your wife,' said Kadam.

'Tu kasa aahes? Slightly better? Hope you saw a doctor?'

'Since when do you care so much about me?' joked Kadam. 'I'm fine, Shinde. Let's get to the case.'

Here we go again. 'Go ahead,' Shinde said sourly, putting the phone off speaker mode and glancing apologetically at his wife.

'Each of the victims had food in their mouths,' said Kadam.

'We've known this for days,' said Shinde, reaching for a slice of toast. He was more concerned about putting breakfast in his own mouth at this point.

'Yes, but was it the same food? Or different stuff each time?'

Shinde paused, his toast forgotten in mid-air. 'I'll have to check my notes. Give me a minute.' He put down the toast and fished out his notebook from his bag. He quickly leafed through it. 'Okay, I have it here. Shirodkar ran tests on all three food samples. The first one contained wheat, the second one had rice and the third had tuar daal—red gram.'

'Cooked or uncooked?'

'Raw,' replied Shinde. 'Some of it had softened from saliva, but there were several hard bits.'

'Why?' asked Kadam. 'Was it some sort of ritual? Some type of symbolic khichdi preparation in which each ingredient was placed in a different mouth? Why only food grains? Why not fruits or vegetables? Why food at all? Why not just a rag?' Kadam lapsed into silence. There was a long pause.

He's zoned out again, thought Shinde and hurriedly shovelled some food into his mouth. He was wondering if he had enough time to eat another slice of toast when Kadam spoke again.

'Was it the same rope in all three cases?'

This time, Shinde didn't need to check his notebook. He had the answer ready. 'Yes. Same nylon, same thickness, weave and quality.'

'And the same knot,' said Kadam. 'It was a left-handed packers' knot, but different colours. The first one golden, the second silver, the third red.'

Shinde looked at the photographs in his file. Kadam was spot on.

'Let's find out about the origin of the rope,' said Kadam.

'Seriously?! It's nylon rope! There must be thousands of manufacturers, wholesalers and retailers in Mumbai alone.'

'True,' Kadam said patiently, 'but the number of manufacturers who make the same thickness and weave in multiple colours will likely be small. Put someone on the job. Could the individual colours come from the fibres of a single intertwined rope? Get that checked too.'

'Theek. Will do,' said Shinde, intrigued despite his irritation with Kadam.

'I'll talk to you again soon,' said Kadam. 'Give my regards to your wife. Eat your breakfast before it goes cold.'

51

Deputy Home Minister Jayant Gaikwad was over twenty minutes late for his next appointment. His PA looked at his watch and wondered whether he should buzz him, but sir had given strict instructions that he was not to be disturbed. He was with a very special guest whom he had known for years.

Just then, there was a burst of laughter from the room in which Gaikwad and his guest were closeted. Inside, Gaikwad chuckled and wiped his eyes. 'Some more chai?' he asked his guest.

'Nahin, beta, I should be leaving now. I have already taken too much of your time.'

'You are always welcome in my home, Bhairavadas ji,' said the minister.

Bhairavadas patted him on the shoulder. 'I know that, but you have other responsibilities too.'

'You have been an immense help with that Shakti matter too,' said Gaikwad. 'Your guidance has assisted so many.'

'Happy to have helped. Does your boy know about all this?'

'Yes, but he can't remember most things in his drugged state.'

'Phir bhi, be careful,' said Bhairavadas.

'I will. One moment please. I have something for you. A small token of my affection and respect.' Gaikwad handed over an envelope bulging with cash.

The former bandit took the envelope and placed his hand on Gaikwad's head in blessing. Then he stroked his long beard that hung down to his bare chest. 'You have been a great support to us,' he said. 'Shri Bhairava Tantra shall always be indebted to you. May your promotion come through soon. We have done the needful.'

52

Ketul was on her way back into town from Ambernath when her phone pinged. It was a message from Nirmal: 'Check your social media.' Ketul quickly opened X on her phone. A picture of a woman's bare back with whip marks appeared on her screen along with the words: 'I am fourteen. I am forced to sell my body each day. Help me. #JusticeforSonapur.'

Ketul had barely read the first post when she saw another image of a girl being yanked by her hair, her face contorted in agony. 'We are human too. The police won't help us. Will you? #JusticeforSonapur', it said. More posts followed in quick succession. Each one contained a picture of a tormented girl and a message ending with #JusticeforSonapur. Ketul watched as the reposts shot up into the hundreds and then into the thousands. She quickly scanned Facebook and Instagram too. Both were buzzing. Many prominent netizens had begun demanding action.

The moment Ketul reached home, she called Nirmal. 'You are a bloody genius,' she said. 'Where did you get all those images?'

'I reached out on your behalf to the people at Shakti,' said Nirmal. 'I specifically asked for the most graphic pictures they could arrange. It took them a while, which is why there was a delay in the campaign.'

'It was totally worth the wait.'

'Oh, hang on. Our posts are now appearing on the evening news.'

Ketul switched on the television. The anchor was pounding his desk. 'Is this callousness, corruption or collusion?' he thundered. 'India demands answers from the police!'

One of the guests on his panel hesitantly raised a hand. The anchor pointed towards her. 'Yes, ma'am. What do you have to say on the matter?'

'The word is that there are powerful people stonewalling any efforts to—' she began.

'Is the police following orders from someone high up? Who could it be?' The anchor took over once again. 'When the system fails, only the media can help. We speak truth to power. We are here to fight battles for those who can't fight for themselves. Go right ahead. We are …'

He trailed off and a look of concentration appeared on his face. 'Wait, I'm getting some breaking news. All right, we can now confirm that Home Minister Lokhande has ordered the police to file FIRs immediately.'

Two days later, Heena, the young woman who had given Ketul a guided tour of the Shakti facility, recorded her statement before a magistrate at the Esplanade Court of Mumbai in a mixture of Hindi and English.

'Pehli baar main baarah saal ki thhee,' she said, recounting the first time she was raped, at twelve. Ketul was seated nearby and listened to her intently.

Heena was born in the village of Alawanpur in the Ballia district of Uttar Pradesh. Her father had sold her to a local thug. It had served the twin purposes of clearing his debts and ridding him of his panauti—bad luck. She had been transported to the nearest town and resold to a pimp. With remarkable composure, Heena described that night when she had been beaten and violated for the first time. She had thought that she would die. In fact, she had earnestly hoped for that. A few days later, she had been taken by car to Mirzapur and loaded into a truck with several other girls. The truck had taken around thirty hours to reach Bhiwandi. From there, the girls had been taken to Sonapur in small groups of two or three.

'When the first customer came, I screamed,' said Heena. 'Kyaa karti? I scratched his face.' The customer had retaliated by punching her in the face, splitting her lip. Then he had gone to the madam and demanded a refund. Heena was beaten, caged and starved for several days before she agreed to fall in line. Used four or five times a day by different customers, Heena had lost the will to live within a few months.

Then, one day, she had been made to bathe, dolled up in new clothes and make-up, and sent to the house of a powerful VIP who had a fetish for young girls. The customer had used her and fallen asleep. Heena had seized the brief opportunity to slip away unnoticed. Terrified of the police, she had avoided the nearby police station. Instead, she had gone to the clinic of a local doctor. It was fortuitous that he happened to be a volunteer at Shakti. He had immediately taken her there. By the end of her narration, Heena's hands were trembling. Sonapur had scarred her for life. Each face that had terrorized her had become part of a montage that played out in her nightmares.

Heena finished recording her statement and turned away. Her demeanour was calm once again, but there was a terrible sadness on her face. Ketul rose from her chair, her eyes filled with tears. She rushed to Heena and gave her a hug. 'You went through hell and now it'll be their turn,' said Ketul, eyes flashing with vehemence.

'Arrey, didi,' said Heena, smiling, 'chhodo yeh sab. Bhaagya badaltey hain yeh harami taare.'

53

'Put dinner on the table. I'll just wash up and come,' said Shinde to his wife. He went to the bathroom, soaped and rinsed his hands, then splashed water on his face. He was just about to walk to the table when his phone rang.

Shinde winced when he saw who it was. For a moment, he considered ignoring the call, but he knew that Kadam would keep calling and his dinner would be ruined. With a sigh, he tapped on the green button.

'You always call just as I'm about to eat,' he complained, wondering if Kadam would take the hint and offer to call back later. No such luck.

'Maybe you're eating too often,' said Kadam, unmoved. 'Did you follow up on that rope lead?'

'Yes, I did,' replied Shinde. 'In fact, that's all I've done since you asked me.'

'And?'

'Well, first we googled rope manufacturers. We were able to narrow it down to four who make nylon ropes in multiple colours. Then we visited them and took samples from each to compare them to the ropes used in the crimes.'

'Any luck?'

'No,' replied Shinde, watching his wife set the table. 'There's a bigger problem. There are many manufacturers *outside* Maharashtra who have distributors here. Each of those distributors has numerous retailers. So, our killer could have bought the rope from literally any one of hundreds of sellers. Khaliphukat time wasted. It's a dead end.'

'Theek. Well, back to the drawing board,' said Kadam, puffing out his cheek. 'I'll call again when I get an idea.'

'Of course you will,' said Shinde. 'Probably right when I'm sitting down for breakfast or lunch.'

54

Pankaj Gaikwad cursed as he tripped and fell flat on his face. Luckily for him, the floor was thickly carpeted. He lay there for a while, catching his breath. Suddenly, he burst into giggles.

A shadow fell over Pankaj. He blinked and saw with glazed eyes that it was his father. Jayant Gaikwad was standing in the hall of their sprawling Altamount Road residence, glaring at him.

'Oh h—h—hello. You're up late,' Pankaj slurred as he staggered to his feet.

'No, I'm up early,' snapped the deputy home minister. 'I'm beginning my day when you're coming home to end yours after dealing drugs at that Maria place. Don't know why Lokhande's people tolerate you.'

'Oh. Good night then. Or sh—should I say, good morning?' smirked Pankaj.

'This is not funny, Pankaj. I've warned you before: Get your act together. Don't think that having an influential father will keep you out of prison.' Gaikwad's eyebrows were tightly merged into one.

The words washed over Pankaj without any effect. He swayed gently from side to side as he stood there, completely stoned. Exasperated, Gaikwad reached out and shook Pankaj hard. 'Are you listening to a word that I'm saying?'

Suddenly, the expression on Pankaj's face changed. The vacant look in his eyes was replaced by one of murderous fury. He shook off his father's hand and punched him square in the face. A stunned Gaikwad fell to the ground on his knees.

Pankaj loomed over him menacingly. 'Mind your own fucking business, asshole,' he growled. 'I'm sick of your nagging.' He stumbled to his bedroom and slammed the door shut behind him.

A red drop of blood fell on the carpet, staining it. With a start, Gaikwad realized that his nose was bleeding. He fumbled for a kerchief and pressed it against his nose to stem the flow. As he rose shakily to his feet, he saw two domestics looking at him, appalled. He flushed with shame. His faithful butler hesitantly reached out to help him, but Gaikwad shook his head. 'Just clean the carpet please, Suresh.' He walked away slowly, his head bowed. He seemed to have aged several years in just a few minutes.

Yet, his face wore an expression of grim determination.

55

Sandra Gomes removed her glasses and wiped them with a cloth—slowly, deliberately. She was not going to play by Kadam's rules today. Looking up at him, she nodded briskly. 'Yes, we've established that you're a killer,' she said, acknowledging his confession. 'Let's move on, shall we?'

Kadam was caught off guard. 'Don't you want to talk about it?' he asked.

Sandra shook her head. 'No. Today, I want you to tell me about your ex-wife.'

'Technically, she's still my wife. We never divorced formally. She just left one day.'

'Things must have built up for her to reach that point. Why don't you tell me what happened?'

Kadam was silent. All his tics played out sequentially. He scratched his stubble, then stroked his scar, then puffed out his cheeks. Sandra smiled inwardly. He was like a fish caught on a hook, struggling to break free. With her pen poised over her thick yellow pad, Sandra waited patiently. She was in no hurry to reel him in.

'She never told me she was Bhau Patil's half-sister,' mumbled Kadam finally.

Sandra's eyebrows shot up. 'Bhau Patil, the underworld guy?' Everyone knew that name.

'That chodu, yes,' hissed Kadam. 'The man with a finger in every illegal pie in the city. I hate the man and everything about him. I'd sworn to bring him down ... And all the while, his own sister was living in my house. What a joke!'

'It must have been a nasty shock.'

Kadam laughed bitterly. 'When I asked her why she hadn't told me, she said that it didn't seem important initially. And by the time she realized she should tell me, she was afraid of how I'd react. So, she kept quiet, hoping I'd never find out.'

'But you did,' said Sandra softly.

Kadam nodded, drumming his fingers on the arm rest. 'We tried to stick together for Ketul's sake, but it was never the same again. We were strangers living under one roof. The ekdum final straw was that poor boy.'

'The one from your nightmares? What happened to him?'

Kadam started to speak, then clamped his mouth shut. He remained silent, shaking his head from side to side. It was as though he was forcibly holding back the words that were trying to escape. When he finally spoke, it was in a whisper. 'I killed that boy. What else is there to know?'

'What happened, Prakash? You can tell me. It will remain strictly confidential.'

But Kadam was stubbornly silent. He turned his head away from Sandra and stared at the wall, arms folded across his chest. A single tear rolled down his face. It glistened on his cheek until he angrily brushed it away with a flick of his hand. 'I am a killer.'

56

The alarm rang shrilly, slicing through the pre-dawn stillness. Akash Awasthi fumbled for the bedside clock and turned it off. His wife woke briefly, mumbled something and rolled over. In a few seconds, she was fast asleep again.

The bed was comfortable and warm. Awasthi was tempted to close his eyes and drift back to sleep. He almost gave in to the impulse before dragging himself out of bed. His job as Finek's logistics manager and added family responsibilities didn't leave much time for exercise. During his last health check-up, the doctor had bluntly told him he needed to be regular with some form of exercise. To make matters worse, that ox, Bhargava, was always showing off his six-pack.

Awasthi quickly changed his clothes and left the house for his morning walk, taking care not to disturb anyone. The fresh air immediately energized him. He took a few deep breaths, then stretched gently, easing out the kinks in his body. 'Right, let's get that blood circulation going,' he muttered to himself as he set off, at a slow pace initially and then picking up momentum.

It was quiet and peaceful in Ambernath at that hour. The road that ran along MPF Sports Ground was empty. As he walked, Awasthi found his mind turning to a problem that had been worrying him. The error rate on missing parcels was not coming down. If anything, it was getting worse and Bhargava seemed unable to fix the issue.

Lost in his thoughts, Awasthi did not notice the car driving some distance behind him. The driver halted momentarily with the engine running and scanned the surroundings, making sure no one else was around. Satisfied, he floored the accelerator and the car shot forward.

A sixth sense made Awasthi turn around, but it was too late. He barely registered a blue blur dashing towards him before the car hit him with a sickening thud. Awasthi sailed through the air and landed on the side of the road. An excruciating wave of pain hit him. Even as he struggled to process the incident, his system shut down and he passed out.

The car stopped a few feet away. The driver got out to take a look at Awasthi. As the heavy rumble of an approaching truck grew louder, he hastily jumped back into the car and sped off.

Two hours later, Akash Awasthi's family was standing in the corridor of Sanjeevani Hospital on Station Road.

Awasthi's wife and fourteen-year-old daughter had managed to stop weeping, but their eyes were still red and swollen. His son, barely seventeen, was trying hard to act mature and keep his emotions in check, but fear and worry were evident on his face. Finek's general manager, Alok Bhushan, had already arrived.

'I came as soon as I heard. How is Awasthi sir?' Sanjay Bhargava asked Bhushan anxiously as he joined the group gathered there.

The doctor attending to Awasthi answered. 'He has multiple fractures and several broken ribs, but no permanent damage as of now. His brain MRI is also clear. He's extremely lucky to be alive.'

'May I see him?' asked Bhargava.

The doctor shook his head firmly. 'There's no point. He's heavily sedated and won't recognize you. Besides, he needs all the rest he can get.'

'How soon can we expect to see him back at work?' Alok Bhushan asked.

The doctor shrugged. 'Hard to predict an exact date, but I'd say not for several months. Recovery and rehab will take a while. Now, if you'll excuse me, I have other patients.'

'Yes, of course. Thank you for your time,' said Bhushan. As the doctor walked away, he turned to Awasthi's family. 'If you need any help at all, I'm just a phone call away. We're all family at Finek—and Akash is important to me … to all of us.'

Bhushan said goodbye to the family and tapped Bhargava on the arm. 'Walk with me, Sanjay,' he muttered. Bhargava hastily bid farewell to Awasthi's wife and followed him. The two men paused near the exit.

'Sanjay, you'll have to step up, and do both your job and Awasthi's for the next few months. Are you up for it?'

'For you and for Awasthi sir? Bilkul, sir. You can count on me,' said Bhargava.

'Good man,' said Bhushan, patting him on the shoulder. 'That's the kind of team spirit that makes Finek great. I'm proud of you.'

Bhargava waited till Bhushan got into his car and left. Then he walked to the parking lot, to where his blue Maruti Dzire was standing. He glanced at the hefty dent in the bumper. 'Better get that attended soon,' he sighed. 'Back to work. Must make up for the drought that Awasthi created.'

57

'So she lives in Singapore? ... And when did she last visit India? ... Hmm ... Interesting. Thanks, you've been a big help,' said Kadam, hanging up the phone.

'Kaay chaalale?' asked Ketul, handing him a cup of tea. She sat down and looked at him inquiringly.

'I was speaking to my contact in immigration. I wanted to check on Desai's story about his daughter living in Singapore,' Kadam explained, pouring the tea from his cup into his saucer.

'Seriously? You're still fixated on Dr Desai?'

Kadam slurped his tea noisily and smacked his lips. 'How come no one has ever met this daughter?'

'Achcha, what did you find?'

'Well, he does have a daughter in Singapore, but'—he hurriedly raised a hand when Ketul smirked knowingly—'*but* she hasn't been to India in ten years.'

'I hope your curiosity is satisfied now?'

'Something is fishy,' Kadam insisted. 'Why hasn't she come back even once in all these years? Is she even alive? Too many unanswered questions. There's only one way to find the truth.'

'Ask Dr Desai?'

'Of course not! Have you learnt nothing from me? If the man is trying to hide something, why tip him off about our suspicion?'

'*Our* suspicion? You mean *your* suspicion!'

Kadam patted his stomach. 'I'm telling you, Ketul, I've learnt over the years to listen to what this tells me.'

'Maybe it should tell you to eat less and move more,' snapped Ketul, toying with her coral pendant.

Kadam scowled. Ignoring her, he picked up his phone and tapped out a number on the keypad from memory. Kadam was probably the last person left on the planet who still remembered people's phone numbers. His encyclopaedic memory always amazed Ketul. 'Hello, Ashok ji? How are you?' asked Kadam. He made small talk for a couple of minutes before getting down to business.

'That's Ashok Pahwa, I'm guessing?' asked Ketul, once Kadam had finished his conversation. Kadam nodded. Pahwa was his contact at the Indian High Commission in Singapore.

'Now we just have to sit tight while he checks on Desai's daughter for me,' said Kadam. 'What if she is staying away from her dad because she knows what sort of twisted person he is?'

Ketul was about to say something when Kadam's phone rang. He peered at the screen. 'Yes, Shinde. Nava kaay aahey?'

'Remember you'd asked me to get that expired credit card of Suchandra Agarwal checked? Saala, there was cocaine residue on it,' said Shinde.

'I knew it!' Kadam punched the air triumphantly.

'Barobar, but there were no traces of drugs anywhere else in the flat. At none of the other crime scenes either.'

'Think through the situation logically. If there is residue on the card, but nowhere else in the flat, then it can mean only one thing. The card was used to sniff a line of coke, but not in the flat. Suchandra had a lesbian lover, no? Some Nidhi?'

'Ho, Nidhi Khanna. But she has an alibi. Your neighbour, Dr Desai.'

'But that alibi may not hold up if the time of death is inaccurate. In any case, it's likely that this Nidhi has a drug habit. Maybe Suchandra did too? But no, autopsy results were clear. Let's bring Nidhi in ... Something interesting may come up.'

'Chaangla.'

'One more thing. Check the nylon ropes from all three crimes. Find out if there were traces of blood inside the knots.'

'Why?'

'Just do it, Shinde,' said Kadam.

'Whatever you say.' Shinde cut the call.

An hour later, Shinde was ushered into Chavan's office. The commissioner beckoned to him to sit. 'Your message said it was urgent, Shinde. This better be good,' he said gruffly, tapping his pen on the table.

Shinde looked around to make sure they were alone in the room. 'Saheb, Kadam is digging into the drugs angle. If you plan to get him taken off the case, do it soon.'

58

'Sarla, there's a courier for you at the reception,' said the young disciple.

Sarla shut the book she had been reading and rose to her feet. She had recently been shifted out of the dormitory and into her own private room. Nothing fancy—just a basic bed, cupboard, table and chair. But it marked a significant rise in her status in the Gorai commune. Not that she spent too much time in the room. Her days were packed with community activities and her nights were usually spent in Momuma's luxurious quarters. The thought of Momuma made her smile. She felt desire rush through her body and hastily shook her head. There would be enough time later. Work came first.

The courier was waiting patiently with a big box. Sarla signed for it and brought it to her room. The box had multiple layers of packaging, and it took some time to remove them all. Inside, were a hundred brand new knives, each one sheathed in plastic packaging. She took one out and checked its sharpness, nodding approvingly, then put it back with the others. All of them were from the same company: Finek.

Sixty kilometres away, in an Irani restaurant located in the Fort district, another parcel was being delivered.

'For you,' said Shinde, handing over a thick envelope to the journalist. 'With regards from Chavan saheb and Bhau Patil.' The woman hefted it in her hand, smiling approvingly at the weight, but didn't open it. 'Do you want to check the contents?' asked Shinde.

She gave him a condescending look. 'Bhau and I go back a long way. You have something else for me, no?'

Shinde nodded and gave her another envelope, much thinner than the last one. This time, the journalist opened it. There were a few photos in it. She pulled them out and examined them, one by one. Her smile widened. 'This will be good,' she smirked. She nodded at Shinde. 'You can tell them it will be done.'

Meanwhile, a young reporter waited nervously near Haji Ali Juice Centre in Worli. Suddenly, a battered old van pulled up next to him and the passenger door opened.

'Get in,' hissed Raju to the reporter.

They took a random route, entering and exiting alleys, stopping every now and then. Raju kept an eye on the rear-view mirror. After about ten minutes, he relaxed when he realized that they were not being followed. Raju parked the vehicle at Worli Sea Face. 'Don't take my extra caution personally. I don't trust anyone. You have something for me?'

'Yes,' said the reporter, reaching into his office bag. Raju tensed. 'Relax. It's only an envelope.'

'It's thin,' Raju remarked, looking at it.

'It's exactly half of the amount we're willing to pay,' said the reporter. 'You'll get the other half when the channel has your recording. We're only doing this because of your lawyer, Bhagwan Keswani.'

Raju laughed and slapped him on the shoulder. 'You're smarter than you look. Don't worry; a reputation for integrity is very important among chors like me.' He guffawed loudly at the irony in his statement.

The reporter smiled politely, but didn't say anything. He peered at Raju, waiting to hear what he would say next.

'Okay,' began Raju, beckoning the reporter closer, 'here's the story ...'

The reporter winced as his senses were assaulted by Raju's foul breath, but he didn't move away.

59

Nidhi Khanna stumbled out of O!Maria angrily. As she lurched away, she turned around to yell and curse at the club—and bumped into a stranger. Abruptly, she dissolved into a fit of giggles, her mood changing dramatically. The stranger gripped her arm tightly. 'I think you should come with me,' he said.

'Kyaa? Benchod, leave me alone. Help, I'll call the po— poliss,' said Nidhi.

Shinde smiled humourlessly. 'Your *poliss* is already here. Chalo.'

The next day, Shinde briefed Kadam. 'She was ekdum high. She has a large bruise on her face. We'll be questioning her now.'

Kadam nodded, frowning, but didn't speak.

Shinde coughed awkwardly. 'Rane sir wants you to be there during the interview. But …'

Kadam held up a hand. 'I know, Shinde. I'm not officially involved. So I won't ask any questions. I'll stay in the background and not draw attention.'

Nidhi sat with her face buried in her hands inside a room at Oshiwara police station. At the sound of the door opening, she looked up. There were dark circles under her eyes, her hair was a mess and there was an ugly bruise on her right cheek.

A woman officer had been talking to her. When Kadam and Shinde entered the room, she started to rise, but Shinde gestured for her to remain seated and pulled up another chair. Kadam noticed a chair by the wall and sat down on it.

'Miss Nidhi, we have some questions for you,' began Shinde. 'Do you want a lawyer?'

'Am I un—under arrest?' she asked.

'Not at all,' replied Shinde. 'We just need your help.'

'Ummm … I spoke to an officer—some Deshmukh—about Suchi … er, Suchandra's … death,' said Nidhi, choking on the last word. 'You can check the records.'

'Barobar,' said Shinde. 'But we have some new ground to cover. Why don't you start by telling us everything you did on the morning of Monday, 10 February?'

'I've already told you,' said Nidhi, twisting her hands. 'I was at Dr Desai's clinic. I reached a little early … ummm … ar—around 9.45 a.m. You can check with the receptionist.'

'True. But what about earlier in the morning? Were you with Suchandra?' asked Shinde.

Nidhi cleared her throat. 'I went for a walk in the park near my place, which is about ten kilometres away from Suchi's. I came out around 8.30 … I think. There's a guy who sells juice right outside the park—I had the … the carrot and turmeric. You can check with him.'

If what she was saying was true, there was no way she could have driven to Suchandra's house, murdered her and then reached Dr Desai's in just over an hour. Not during morning rush hour. Kadam passed him a note. Shinde looked at it, folded it and stashed it in his pocket.

'When was your last conversation with Suchandra? What did you talk about?'

'I … On Sunday night. We had spent the day together. We … As she was leaving, she … she said she was a little concerned about …' Nidhi hesitated.

'About?' Shinde prompted.

Nidhi took a deep breath. 'Drugs. Both Suchi and I used to snort … kabhi-kabhi. It had been a while for her. But in my case, it was taking over my life.'

'So, you had an argument?' asked Shinde.

Distraught, Nidhi shook her head. 'No! Suchi was very loving and concerned. She … she said she would help me if I took the first step. We … we were to talk about it the n—next time we met.' She shut her eyes as tears rolled down her cheeks. 'There was no next time.'

Kadam passed Shinde another note and scratched his stubble. Shinde waited for Nidhi to compose herself, then resumed his questioning. 'You left the ad agency a year ago?'

Nidhi nodded wordlessly.

'Were you fired because of your drug problem?' asked Shinde, the corner of his mouth twitching.

'No, there were layoffs. Business was down.'

'I see. Aur kal raat?'

Nidhi hesitated and looked away.

'Someone obviously hit you. Why protect such a person?' asked Shinde.

'It was my dealer. Punky.'

'You mean Pankaj Gaikwad?'

Nidhi nodded.

Shinde and Kadam briefly exchanged glances. Then Shinde turned back to her. 'What was the fight about?'

Nidhi laughed bitterly, rubbing her hands on her thighs. 'Saala gaandu hai. I tried to clean up my act and cleared all my dues. Then that madarchod gave me a free sample of top-quality stuff to get me g—going again. Last night, after I'd taken a snort, we had an argument and he hit me.'

'Has he hit you before?' asked Shinde.

She nodded. 'He has a violent temper and extreme mood swings. He's beaten oth—others too. We put up with his shit because we need his maal.' She covered her face with her hands. Her shoulders shook as she wept soundlessly.

Kadam and Shinde walked out of the room, leaving the woman officer to comfort Nidhi as best as she could. 'Well?' asked Shinde.

'I believe her,' said Kadam. 'Ti satya saangata aahey.'

'She could also be a convincing liar,' said Shinde.

Kadam shook his head. 'That convincing? She's an unemployed ad exec, not Kangana Ranaut in *Queen*. See her bank statements. She was financially dependent on Suchandra … Why shut off her only source of funds?'

Shinde looked around to make sure no one was within earshot. 'What about Pankaj Gaikwad? Do you think he could have killed Suchandra? She was trying to get Nidhi to clean up her act. Pankaj would have lost a lucrative customer.'

Kadam ran a finger along his scar, lost in thought. Eventually, he said, 'I think it's best to tell Rane about the Gaikwad angle. Let him deal with it. He has an equation with the deputy home minister.'

'Sure, sure,' said Shinde and scuttled away. When he was certain Kadam couldn't see or hear him, he whipped out his cell phone and dialled Chavan's private number. 'Saheb? A really interesting angle has come up …'

60

'We need to take Pankaj in for questioning. Maaf kara, saheb,' said Rane, his nasal twang a tad more pronounced.

Gaikwad unconsciously touched his nose, where a scab had formed. 'What's it about?' he asked.

'The serial murders. Pankaj was dealing drugs to one of the victims and her close associates. We need to explore that line of investigation.'

Gaikwad shut his eyes briefly. When he reopened them, he wore a resigned look. 'Do your job.'

'We'll need to search his room as well,' Rane said in a low voice, his tone apologetic.

Gaikwad nodded. 'Only trusted men should do the search. Make sure they're discreet and won't spread the news.'

'Don't worry, sir. I'll oversee everything personally,' said Rane. He cleared his throat. 'I'll have to interrogate Pankaj. The questioning could be tough.'

Gaikwad hesitated for a moment, sinking deeper into misery and anguish. Then his expression hardened. 'Do whatever you have to,' he said in a determined voice. 'Saala, I've tried to do my best for that moorkh. But Pankaj is an adult. He needs to learn that his actions have consequences.' He gestured to Rane to go ahead. Rane sighed, and walked over to Pankaj's door and knocked loudly.

Inside the room, Pankaj blinked owlishly and raised his head from the pillow. 'Fuck off and lemme sleep,' he shouted. There was a brief pause. Then the knocking resumed. Pankaj pulled the pillow over his head, trying to drown out the sound.

Suddenly, the door flew open and a small posse of policemen burst into the room. Pankaj sat up, bewildered. 'What's this, you motherfuckers? Who the hell … How dare …' he spluttered.

A shadow loomed over Pankaj.

'You bastard!' he snarled when he saw Rane glaring down at him. 'How dare you? I'll have your job, benchod.' He rose from the bed and took a clumsy swing at the other man. Rane blocked the attempted punch easily, then slapped him hard. Reeling from the blow, Pankaj fell back on the bed with a howl. Rane grabbed him by his shirt, pulled him up and slapped him again.

'Don't try any shit with me, madarchod,' growled Rane. 'I won't put up with your crap.'

'Sir, look at this!'

Rane turned around and saw one of his men pointing to a hammock on the private balcony adjoining the room. It was woven using multicoloured nylon threads. He let go of Pankaj, who collapsed in a heap on the bed, and went over to take a closer look. He gestured to his men to take down the hammock.

'Get it sent across to the Directorate of Forensic Laboratories. I'll have a word for priority examination.' He pointed at Pankaj with disgust. 'Aani hyaa moorkhala … Take him to Crime Branch.'

'Where were you at 6 p.m. on 2 February? And 10 a.m. on 10 February? And 3 p.m. on 18 February?'

Rane and Shinde were sitting at the table across from Pankaj, while Kadam watched the proceedings on camera in the observation room.

Pankaj muttered something inaudible.

'Ti kaay manhalas?' asked Rane, cupping his ear.

'Time is fake,' said Pankaj. Having delivered this profound philosophical statement, he put his head on the table and began snoring.

'Should we dump a bucket of cold water on him?' Shinde suggested, standing up and stretching. 'That should do the trick.'

Rane shook his head. 'Looks like he's had a really strong dose. Even if he wakes up, he won't make much sense. Let him sleep. We'll talk to him when he's alert. Meanwhile, send someone to that nightclub where this scumbag hangs out. Get the CCTV footage of all those days when the murders took place. Don't ruffle any feathers though; the last thing we need is Lokhande getting upset.'

The two men exited the interrogation room. Rane left Shinde and walked across to Kadam. 'I'm hungry. Want to grab a snack while we wait for this chutiya to wake up?' he asked. Kadam nodded and the two men strolled out. They ordered sandwiches and coffee at a hole-in-the-wall eatery that was popular with students.

'How's Gaikwad holding up?' asked Kadam.

Rane shrugged. 'As well as any father would. How do things go so wrong in just one generation? Gaikwad, for all his faults, is a man who has worked his way up in life. He's intelligent, hard-working and relatively clean—as much as anyone who's part of the system can be. His businesses—his schools and colleges—are legit. And then you see the son ...'

'Bad parenting,' said Kadam, scratching his stubble.

'And you'd know all about that, wouldn't you?' Rane said sardonically. 'Ketul turned out pretty well in spite of having you for a father.'

Kadam laughed. 'With everything that she's had to see in her life it's a wonder she turned out to be so sorted.' He paused. 'Are you hoping Pankaj is innocent? For his father's sake?'

'If he's a criminal, he should hang,' said Rane, fuming. 'But I owe his father a serious investigation.' He drained his coffee cup and the two of them strolled back to Rane's office. They'd barely sat down when Shinde knocked on the door.

'Saheb, we've got the CCTV footage from the nightclub. Tech is going through it now, but it looks like Pankaj has a solid alibi at least on the day of the first murder. It was a Sunday night and he was at the club,' said Shinde.

'What about the other two dates?' asked Rane.

'Ho, saheb, we're checking, but it could take a while.'

Rane glanced at Kadam. 'Prakash, I suggest you go home for now. We'll give you an update once the team is done with the CCTV footage.'

Kadam nodded. 'Theek. I'm feeling a bit tired anyway. I'll lie down for a bit.'

Rane stared at Kadam's retreating figure as he left the room. Shinde noticed his worried gaze.

'Everything okay, saheb?' he asked with fake concern.

'Prakash never says he's tired or needs rest,' Rane said broodingly. 'Sometimes, I feel he was better off with the whisky. This case must be really wearing him down. I just hope his health doesn't collapse.'

An hour later, the shrill ringing of the phone cut through the silence in the apartment. Kadam muttered and rolled over on his mattress, ignoring the call. The phone rang again. This time, he woke with a start.

'Pankaj is clear.' Kadam winced as Rane's nasal voice cut through the dreamless fog that had enveloped him. Meanwhile, Rane continued, '... footage shows him entering the nightclub around 5 p.m. on 2 February. He stepped out a couple of times for a smoke, but re-entered the club within five minutes. He finally left around 2.30 a.m. The first murder took place at 6 p.m. several kilometres away. There's no way Pankaj could have done it.' The relief in Rane's voice was evident; it would not do to get on Gaikwad's wrong side.

'Well, I guess that rules him out then,' said Kadam. He puffed his cheeks out as he ended the call. But the phone rang again. 'I'm in demand,' he grumbled as he reached for it. It was Ashok Pahwa, Kadam's contact in Singapore. Pahwa came straight to the point.

'That person you'd asked me to check about?' he said. 'Her full name is Malti Desai Raghavan. She's a professor, married to a Tamilian researcher. Alive and well. Never travels—hasn't stepped out of Singapore for the past several years.'

'Thanks, Ashok ji. You're a treasure,' said Kadam. They exchanged a few pleasantries before ending the call. Kadam had a thoughtful look on his face. *Why does Malti never come to Mumbai? Did her father mistreat her in some way?*

61

The blindfolded woman lay on the bed, spreadeagled, face down, handcuffed to the railings. There was a leather collar around her neck. The man approached her from behind and let the whip lash her butt. The woman whimpered as the man continued lashing her. Then he grabbed her by the collar and bit hard into her shoulder, drawing blood. She let out a shriek of pain, which turned into a scream of pleasure.

Nirmal shuddered in the throes of his own release. It took a while for his breathing to return to normal. The BDSM video was still playing on the screen. With a grimace, Nirmal closed it. A notification popped up in a corner of the laptop screen with a pinging sound. Nirmal clicked on it and entered an online chat. It was an anonymous user with similar tastes.

'Still watching videos and jerking off?'

'LOL. Self-service.'

'Just share with her what turns you on,' said the other person.

'Don't have a girlfriend.'

'Seriously?'

'No name to the relationship yet.'

'Tell her what you like. Maybe she likes it too?'

Nirmal thought for a while before he typed out his response. He doubted he would ever be able to share his darkest secrets with Ketul.

62

'Arrey wah, that was quick,' said Ketul. She opened the package that the courier had just handed over. A brand-new Finek knife gleamed in her hand. Ketul turned it over, checking for flaws, and lightly pressed it against her palm. The blade was razor-sharp.

The courier coughed politely, interrupting her examination. 'Madam, please sign here?'

'Oh yes, sorry!' Ketul said with an embarrassed chuckle. 'I got busy examining it.'

'Arrey, madam, khaliphukat worry mat karo. I have delivered hundreds of these. No complaints.'

'Quality is fine,' said Ketul. 'It's just that I'm surprised. I only placed the order online in the morning. I didn't expect same-day delivery. How did you manage such a quick turnaround?'

'Finek has an arrangement with my company,' the courier explained, pointing to the embroidered logo of a speeding motorbike on the uniform. 'They leave buffer stock with us so that no time is wasted in delivery. At the end of every day, they replace all the sold items with fresh stock.'

'Smart,' acknowledged Ketul. 'Well, thank you. Have a nice day.'

She walked towards the kitchen with a thoughtful look. Kadam was sitting in the hall in his vest, leafing through his files. He raised an eyebrow when he saw the knife in Ketul's hand.

'Should I be scared?' he joked.

Ketul scowled at him. 'Te mazedar naahin. Not. At. All.'

'Sorry, sorry, my bad,' said Kadam contritely. 'What are you doing with that, though?'

'Remember when I'd gone to the Finek plant?' said Ketul. 'I met this person called Bhargava. He had bragged to me about how efficient their delivery system is. I thought I'd check it out myself.'

'And?'

'It's impressive. This knife was delivered within hours of my placing an online order. But there is something that's even more interesting about this company,' she said, stacking the knife along with the others on the rack.

'What?'

'I was looking through the company filings with the Registrar of Companies and noticed something.'

'Jaldi se bolo, baba!' Kadam burst out, impatience getting the better of him.

Ketul rolled her eyes. 'The primary shareholder of Finek Metal Ltd. is a front company that owns several other businesses as well—restaurants, pubs, food products and kitchenware. The owner of that front company is Home Minister Omkar Lokhande.'

Kadam's jaw dropped. Politicians owning official businesses—often to launder their unofficial takings—was not new, but no minister would want to be connected with a company whose products were increasingly linked to a crime spree. Before Kadam could say anything, however, his phone rang. He peered at the screen, then answered.

'Yes, Shinde, bolo,' he said. Then his expression changed dramatically. 'What? Where? … Hmm … When? Give me the details.' He hurriedly picked up an old newspaper and scribbled on it with a pencil, oblivious to the small item in the business section that indicated that Finek Metal Ltd. had taken a beating in recent days. It seemed the markets had a way of knowing things that the public did not.

'I'll be right there,' he said and ended the call.

'Everything okay?' asked Ketul.

Kadam pulled on a shirt that had been hanging on his chair and buttoned it up hurriedly. 'Our killer has just struck again.'

63

Wednesday, 26 February, around 9 a.m., Kandivali West, Mumbai

The milk guy is late again! Lakshmi Budhiraja looked at the clock with mounting worry. She should have left for work by now. 'I'm going to find someone else now,' she muttered as she picked up her bag and headed for the door.

Just then the doorbell rang.

The stench of decomposition was everywhere inside the congested Kandivali flat. Kadam opened a window that overlooked the Church of Our Lady of Assumption.

'Lakshmi Budhiraja, forty-eight. Worked as a receptionist at a construction company. Her husband is an engineer. They have one daughter who's doing an MBA at Symbiosis University. She lives in a hostel in Pune.' Shinde paused to take a shallow breath, then continued, 'The husband discovered her body when he returned from Chennai today—after a two-day trip. Milk and newspapers had piled up outside the main door. When he entered the flat, he found her lying dead.'

Kadam looked at his notes again. The woman was murdered on Wednesday morning. Two days ago. 'Any domestic staff?'

Shinde shook his head. 'No one. They took care of all the chores themselves.'

'Do the CCTV cameras work?'

'Yes, but the recording unit overwrites anything older than twenty-four hours. Nothing left from that day's recording,' said Shinde, holding a kerchief to his nose.

'That's helpful,' grunted Kadam. 'Do you believe the husband's story?'

'We've got the name of the Chennai hotel where he stayed and we've noted down his travel details. We're cross-checking.'

Kadam nodded and walked across to the body, scratching his stubble. 'All the usual elements, I see. No sign of a break-in, stabbed in the heart with a Finek, hands tied with nylon rope, mouth stuffed with food—'

'One difference this time,' said Shinde. 'The husband says a box of jewellery is missing.'

Kadam looked up sharply. 'That's interesting. There was no theft in any of the previous killings. Where is he?'

'He said he was feeling unwell. We've sent him to a nearby hospital for a medical check-up. Don't worry; two of my men have gone with him.'

Kadam walked out of earshot. He pulled out his phone and called Ketul. 'Check if there was a life insurance policy on Lakshmi Budhiraja,' he said.

'She was killed for insurance?' asked Ketul.

'Just do it, Ketul. I'll explain later.' Kadam ended the call and walked back to where the body was lying. He stooped a little and pointed towards the floor. 'There's an arc of blood on the floor. The body was moved after death like the others.'

Shinde was about to bend down to inspect the arc when a strange sound emerged, almost like a sigh. Shinde froze, then cried out in horror. The blood drained from his face as the corpse jerked upwards, as though it were trying to sit upright.

'Relax, Shinde. It's just a post-mortem spasm,' chuckled Kadam.

'Aai chi gaand! Wh—what the hell is that?' he asked in a shaky voice, staring at the corpse with suspicion, the corner of his mouth twitching in fear.

'Usually, the body stiffens after death. But if the body has been moved, the rigor mortis will reverse itself for a while before permanent stiffness sets in. Electrical impulses also trigger some movements,' explained Kadam.

'She moved and—benchod—also groaned,' argued Shinde. 'There's black magic in this place.'

'It's all science, Shinde,' said Kadam. 'Decomposition gases cause movement. Air in the lungs escapes, while the bowels and bladder relax. These cause the body to sigh or groan.'

Kadam squatted next to the body. Then his expression suddenly turned serious. He wrinkled his nose and sniffed the foul air. 'What's that smell?' he asked, puffing out one cheek.

'The rotting body,' replied Shinde.

'No … beyond that,' said Kadam. 'It's that same pest-control smell. It was at the third crime scene too. Did we check about pest-control services?'

Standing at a safe distance from the body, despite Kadam's reassurances, Shinde referred to his notes. 'None of the victims engaged any pest-control services in the past four weeks. Building societies usually have annual maintenance contracts, but none of the earlier three crime scene units were due for treatment.'

Kadam opened his diary and quickly drew a sketch. Another circle for the board back home. As he shut his diary, a thought struck him. He leaned closer to the body. 'Why is her facial skin blue?' he asked. He turned to the examiner. 'Was it the same with the other victims?'

The examiner shrugged. 'Mala naahin maheet. Can't say. Didn't check the notes of the previous examiners.'

It's your fucking job to check the files. Even Shirodkar with his irritating raspy voice is better than this. With some effort, Kadam kept his voice cordial. 'Please check whether there was bluish discolouration in the previous cases.'

'Barobar,' replied the examiner. 'You think it could be an important lead?'

'If it is, then it's literally been staring us in the face all this while,' said Kadam shortly.

64

The members of Momuma's cult sat in neat rows, listening to him in sombre silence inside the massive tent in Gorai. As he spoke, volunteers moved down the rows, handing out parcels.

'I have always walked the path of peace, love and non-violence,' whispered Momuma. 'But sadly, the world that surrounds us is different. Examine history and examples abound of peace-loving humans who were killed for their beliefs.'

Momuma's disciples exchanged uneasy glances. Their expressions became increasingly despondent as he continued, 'The world hates free thinkers. Everyone must conform. Anyone who sticks out is hammered into alignment with the rest.'

Momuma looked around at the assembled faces. They were all gazing at him, lost in his words. *Time for a change of pace,* he thought. 'It is only a matter of time before they come for us. It is possible that the law-and-order machinery and the government will try to shut us down. But will we let them do so? I say to you, no! A thousand times, no!' The mood of the gathering altered dramatically. Everyone sat upright.

'Love and peace cannot become an excuse for cowardice. Non-violence does not mean inaction. If it is a sin to oppress others, then it is a bigger sin to let oneself *be* oppressed.' Momuma paused for effect.

A parcel was lying next to Momuma. He picked it up and ripped it open. A Finek knife came into view. Momuma held it up. It gleamed, almost hypnotically, in the light. 'We will not strike the first blow. But if anybody tries to interfere with our way of life, we will not spare them. Are you with me?'

'Salaam, Momuma! Show us the light!' the crowd chanted in unison, brandishing their knives.

Momuma cast his gaze around his flock. He kept his face impassive, gloating inwardly. He had his very own pack of wolves. His eyes stopped on Sarla, who was in the front row. She was screaming hysterically, tears streaming down her face. She wiped them away with her right hand while energetically waving a knife in the other.

65

The dining table in the plush Malabar Hill bungalow could seat twelve. The dining room itself boasted an opulent chandelier that cascaded light upon the grand mahogany table. A massive picture window overlooked a landscaped garden and the sea beyond. Bhau Patil leaned back in his chair and let out a contented burp. Commissioner Chavan, who was having lunch with him, struggled not to let his distaste show.

'Give me normal ghar ka khaana any day. It's better than all the fancy shit that people go crazy about,' said Patil, patting his belly. 'That stuff is good for Instagram pictures, but it does nothing for my stomach and soul.' He pointed to the silver bowls on the dining table. 'See the simplicity of this meal, Chavan? You need the spicy moong beans to eat the wheat rotis, and you need the yellow tuar dal to enjoy the rice. They work together in harmony, a perfect combination.'

As Chavan nodded, Patil leaned forward. 'You and I are like that, Chavan. You keep doing what you must and so will I. Together, we will rule Mumbai.'

Patil helped himself to a paan from a platter. He chewed it contently, the red juice exploding in his mouth. Chavan could feel the acid bubbling inside his stomach. He quickly popped an antacid.

The server brought out a spittoon and Patil released a jet of betel juice into it, along with masticated bits of the paan. 'Whatever we can't chew or swallow, we'll spit out—like that Kadam. The press machinery is in motion. That dog deserves what is coming for him.'

Chavan was about to reply, but Patil spoke first. 'Speaking of Kadam, I haven't forgotten about that over-smart daughter of his. She may have managed to get the FIRs filed, but I want that Shakti case in cold storage. Make sure there's zero progress.'

Chavan nodded. 'Any reason I should be aware of?' he asked.

Patil raised an eyebrow. He was not used to being questioned. He was about to reprimand Chavan when he had a change of heart. 'If you must know, one of the biggest donors to Shakti Trust is Deputy Home Minister Jayant Gaikwad. As you know, I hate that madarchod … and his chodu, Bhairavadas.'

66

Kadam finished scribbling on the board in his Matunga flat and stepped back. He and Shinde examined the list he had prepared, a day after the discovery of Lakshmi Budhiraja's body.

GENDER: ONE MALE. THREE FEMALES.
COMMUNITY: PUNJABI. MARWARI. GUJARATI. TAMILIAN.
GEOGRAPHY: GOREGAON WEST. LOWER PAREL. THANE.
KANDIVALI.
COMMON ELEMENTS: ROPE. FINEK. KNOT. FOOD. BODY
ROTATION. PEST-CONTROL SMELL.

'Arrey deva! Apart from the MO of the killer, there is nothing in common,' observed Shinde.

'Three out of the four victims were female. Is it possible that the first killing was a fluke?' mused Kadam, rubbing his chin.

'You don't break from a pattern before it has even been established,' said Shinde.

'Fair point,' conceded Kadam. 'There's no sexual angle. Nor is any particular community being targeted. And the killings are spread far apart geographically,' said Kadam. Then a thought struck him. 'What food was in the mouth of the fourth victim?'

'Green moong beans, I think,' replied Shinde. 'Let me check with the medical examiner.'

'The rope was green too,' observed Kadam. 'Were earlier foods colour-matched with the ropes used?'

'I'll have to confirm it, but I'm quite sure that was not the case.'

Kadam huffed in annoyance. 'If they weren't matched earlier, why were they matched now?' He puffed out a cheek. What kind of fucking game was the killer playing? 'There must be something we're missing.' He paced up and down the small living room.

'Right now, I'm missing a nice hot meal,' said Shinde as his stomach rumbled loudly.

'There's some bread and jam in the fridge. Let me make you a sandwich,' offered Kadam.

'Please don't bother,' Shinde protested weakly. He just wanted to go home—and eat. He was still trying to figure out a polite way to say it when Kadam opened the fridge. It was almost as ramshackle as its owner. The door made a squeaking sound as it swung open on its hinges.

'The bread looks a bit old,' said Kadam. 'Let me check the expiry date.' As he leaned forward to examine the date on the packet, he suddenly froze.

'Kaay?' asked Shinde.

Kadam abandoned the bread and rushed back to the board. 'Tell me the dates of the killings,' he demanded.

Shinde opened his diary and began reading them out.

Kadam wrote each date against the name of the victims. 'The 2nd, 10th, 18th and 26th of February.'

'Yes, those are the dates I just said. So?' Shinde was getting increasingly infuriated with Kadam's flights of fancy.

'Open your eyes, Shinde! There's a pattern here.'

'Maaf kara, I can't see it ... Oh, wait. These are weekly ...' said Shinde, his mouth twitching.

'There's an eight-day gap between each of the killings,' corrected Kadam. 'Why eight days in particular? Why not six, seven or nine? Why any constant gap at all?' There was a glint in his eye as his mind raced through possibilities.

'Is there anything special about the number eight?'

'Yes,' replied Kadam. 'For Hindus, Krishna was the eighth avatar of Vishnu. The star of Lakshmi is eight-pointed and she has eight forms. In Islam, there are eight angels carrying the throne of Allah. In Christianity, eight represents resurrection. In the Vedas, there are eight solar deities. The science of yoga has eight limbs so it is called ashtanga yoga.'

Shinde gaped open-mouthed as Kadam rattled off facts like a talking encyclopaedia. 'Are we going somewhere?' he asked when Kadam began pulling on shoes.

'I think a visit to the Directorate of Forensic Laboratories is in order,' said Kadam.

'So, inside or outside?' asked Kadam twenty minutes later.

The forensic specialist at the Directorate of Forensic Laboratories was an elegant grey-haired woman named Durga Pandey. She peered over her glasses at Kadam. 'That odd request originated from you? I'm not surprised. Only you have weird ideas like that.' She took a puff from a herbal vape, something that had helped her end her daily consumption of a pack of cigarettes.

'I still haven't got my answer,' said Kadam drily, ignoring the fly that was buzzing around his head. The large but poorly maintained facility in Kalina had the final word in technical and forensic matters.

'Well, you can have the answer now,' said Durga. 'The blood was on the outside of each knot. No traces of blood inside.'

'Can I have an answer too?' asked Shinde, looking pointedly at Kadam. 'How does it matter whether the blood was inside or outside the knots?'

'It means the victims were tied up first and then stabbed. Nylon hardly absorbs anything. Even if the killer wore gloves, there would be blood inside the knot if the victim was tied up *after* stabbing—'

Durga interrupted before Kadam could explain further. 'There was another query. I'm guessing that also came from you?'

'The bluish discolouration? Yes, that was me.'

Durga nodded. 'It was common to all the victims. Facial cyanosis.'

'Cya ... what?' asked Shinde, feeling way out of his depth.

'Reduced blood flow and oxygen,' Durga said.

'Reduced blood flow and oxy—' Kadam suddenly shut his eyes and slapped his forehead. 'I'm so stupid. The spray! The killer uses a spray to incapacitate the victims, then ties their hands before killing them.'

'Pepper spray like Capsaicin?' asked Durga.

'Cockroach-killer spray—like Baygon or Hit—just as effective,' said Kadam, shaking his head. 'That's why there is the smell of pest-control products at each location. Very smart.'

Durga nodded approvingly. 'I see you haven't lost your touch. Always a pleasure to meet an old-timer who knows his stuff.' She powered off the laptop on which she had shown them the magnified photos of the rope knots.

'That blue fibre still pending?' asked Kadam.

'In a few days,' replied Durga. 'Have had to leave other assignments for you.'

Ten kilometres away, in Matunga, Dr Ravikant Desai frowned in concentration as he looked at the chart in front of him. He was in his study, a pile of multicoloured nylon ropes beside him. A couple of nylon rope toys were already complete, but the one he was planning to make next was quite complicated. He studied the chart carefully, paying close attention to the intricate twists and turns that would be required. After a while, he nodded, satisfied. He picked up an apple and a knife kept on a plate on his table, and deftly cut it into precise slices. He ate a couple, then set the plate aside.

'Here goes,' he muttered. He looked at the chart one more time for confirmation, then picked up a length of rope and began tying a complex knot. His hands moved dexterously, almost as though they had a life of their own.

67

Alone at home, Kadam reached for his Caravan radio. As he touched it, he felt a tightening in his chest. He paused, with a frown. Muscle spasm? And then the pain slammed into him, like a sledgehammer. Gasping, he clutched his chest, struggling to breathe. He broke into a cold sweat. The pain bloomed, engulfing his neck, jaw and left arm. It seemed to race through his body like wildfire. Kadam scrabbled for his phone desperately—Ketul had saved Dr Desai's number on the speed dial—but his movements were clumsy and uncoordinated, as though he was swimming in a lake of treacle.

The pain intensified and his vision blurred. The room swam before his eyes. He could feel his senses slipping away. 'Please, please. Just a few seconds more,' he muttered. He jabbed down on the button. Desai's phone seemed to ring forever.

'Hello?'

'Get here … jaldi …' Kadam rasped frantically, struggling to form the words. His tongue seemed to have become too big for his mouth. The lights in the room flickered for a moment, then darkness descended over him.

'Prakash, Prakash! Wake up.'

The voice seemed to be floating down from a distance, as though Kadam was at the bottom of a deep well and someone was calling out to him from above. He tried to open his eyes, but they felt leaden, as if they had been glued shut. He forced them open. Desai's anxious face swam before him. Kadam shut his eyes, took a couple of deep breaths and then reopened them. This time, he saw Desai clearly.

'Hi, doctor sa'ab,' he mumbled. 'I've never been so glad to see you.'

'You're incredibly lucky,' said Desai, with a grim look on his face. 'I just happened to be home. Here, try to sit up.'

Kadam realized that he was lying on the sofa. With a little help from Desai, he struggled into a sitting position. The doctor propped a couple of pillows behind Kadam.

'Have a couple of sips of water.' He handed Kadam a glass. Then he handed over a tablet. 'Just place it in your mouth and let it dissolve.'

'What is this?' asked Kadam.

'Isosorbide Dinitrate—Sorbitrate. It relaxes and widens blood vessels so that blood can flow more easily to the heart. I already forced one into your mouth earlier.'

'You think I had a heart attack?'

'I'm not a cardiac specialist, but it seems like angina. You need to see a specialist and get admitted for a thorough check-up. I can recommend some good places ...'

'Tu veda aahey kaa? I'm not going anywhere. Doctor sa'ab, I have a case to solve.'

Desai glared at Kadam. 'Don't be an idiot, Prakash! You can't solve anything if you keel over and die.' He paused, then pulled out his trump card. 'If you won't go, I'll tell Ketul.'

'Bastard.'

Desai nodded smugly. 'People tell me I can be that. Particularly for a patient who's hell-bent on committing suicide. You got a stent last year—'

'Three years ago!'

'Fine, three years ago, but you had a breakdown a year later. The point is: A stent doesn't just work in isolation. You need to make lifestyle changes, watch your diet, get exercise and monitor your critical parameters. You need to take this seriously—the way you gave up the bottle. And Ketul deserves to know.'

Kadam sighed dejectedly. 'You're right, of course. But Ketul is already so stressed with that whole Shakti matter ... She hardly slept a wink last night.'

Desai's angry expression was replaced by one of concern. 'That girl worries too much,' he muttered.

'Absolutely. And I don't want to add to her stress right now. Let's just keep this between us for now, doctor sa'ab?'

'Only if you promise to get a thorough check-up done at the earliest.'

'I promise,' lied Kadam. 'Meanwhile, could you leave some magic pills with me in case of an emergency?'

Desai nodded and handed over the blister pack to Kadam. 'Only SOS. And get rest. No physical exertion.'

Kadam nodded obediently. After Desai left, he carefully concealed the pack in his underwear drawer. *My body may be failing me, but saala, I still have my mind. Now to catch the killer before my heart kills me.*

68

The morning sunlight streamed into the room through the windows. Kadam blinked and gradually came awake. Through half-open eyes, he saw Ketul open the door and bring in the newspaper. Kadam stretched contentedly, basking in the sunlight. Life was a bitch, but sometimes it still felt good to be alive.

Suddenly, Ketul gasped. Kadam sat bolt upright, the spell shattered. 'What is it?' he demanded. Ketul looked up at him, startled. 'Arrey ... it's nothing,' she mumbled, wishing Kadam had not witnessed her reaction.

Kadam grimly beckoned his daughter over. 'Ketul, whatever you're trying to hide ... I will see it eventually. You might as well show me. Bring the newspaper here.'

Ketul reluctantly handed it over to Kadam, nervously toying with her coral pendant. He looked at the front page and his jaw dropped. 'Benchod!' he exclaimed. There was only one story on the front page: 'SERIAL KILLER ON THE PROWL'. A smaller subhead read 'Suspended Alcoholic Cop Heading Probe' with a picture of Kadam lying on the floor, unconscious, his mouth agape. Any reader would think that he had passed out drunk.

Kadam raced through the article. It provided details of the four murders, including the use of nylon ropes. It then went on to add that the man tasked with catching the killer was a suspended officer with a 'history of alcohol abuse'. The article said, 'According to reliable sources, suspended DCP Prakash Kadam recently ventured into the mortuary to inspect corpses, where, to the great concern of his colleagues, he simply passed out. This begs the question: Could a force as capable as the Mumbai Police not find a better candidate to lead this critical investigation?'

Ketul was reading the article over Kadam's shoulder. 'How dare they!' she said. 'I'll send them a notice for defamation.'

Kadam shook his head. 'Don't bother. It's worded very carefully. It says that I've been suspended and have a history of alcohol abuse. Both are true. It says that I passed out at the mortuary, which is also factually correct. The reader will assume I was drunk, but the article doesn't say that.'

Ketul sighed. 'I hate to admit it, but you're right. By the way, what exactly happened at the mortuary that day? And why didn't you tell me about it?'

'Well, I was fine, but then I started feeling woozy. Luckily, Shirodkar and Shinde were there …' His voice trailed off as something else seemed to dawn on him. He scratched his stubble.

'What are you thinking?'

'There were only three of us there that day. I was out cold, which means this photo must have been taken by either Shirodkar or Shinde. I've known Shirodkar for a long time— he's a pain in the ass, but not sly. That only leaves Shinde.' His brow furrowed in concentration as he tried to recall the events of that evening. 'Shinde gave me Vicks VapoRub to apply under

my nose ... but I never saw him use it. The bastard set me up!'
Kadam paced up and down furiously. 'Shinde didn't do this on
his own. Someone put him up to it. Chavan and that harami
Patil must be involved too.'

Ketul's phone rang. She looked at the screen. It was Nirmal,
so she took the call. 'Yes. We've seen it.' She glanced at Kadam
and then moved to the kitchen, covering her mouth as she gave
short replies to Nirmal.

Kadam phoned Shinde. There was no response.
'Madarchod,' swore Kadam. He called again. Shinde still didn't
pick up. Kadam then called Rane. After a while, a WhatsApp
message appeared from Rane. 'In a meeting. Will call back.'
Kadam swore.

'What was your friend saying?' he asked once Ketul was
done with the call.

Ketul took a deep breath. 'He advised us to stay away from
social media and news channels for a while.'

'I'm not surprised,' said Kadam bitterly. 'Goddamn vultures
... Patil, Chavan and that bastard Shin—'

Kadam's phone rang. It was Rane. 'Sharad, you need to talk
to Shinde. That prick framed me—'

'Hallu kara. Right now, we have bigger problems than
Shinde,' Rane cautioned. 'Chavan just blasted me for involving
you in the case. The chief minister and home minister are
pissed off. The editorial in the Marathi press did not help.'

'What editorial in Marathi? I didn't see it.'

'Just sent it to you on WhatsApp.'

Kadam quickly scanned the clipping. It expressed concern
about deploying a suspended officer with a questionable past

to head such an investigation. And about the larger issues that needed urgent attention such as the soaring crime rate in Mumbai, the city's overworked and unmotivated police, its outdated methods, training and equipment. Mumbaikars deserved better, did they not?

Kadam whistled. 'Strong stuff. Where does that leave me?'

'I'm not sure,' replied Rane. 'I suggest you lie low for a bit while I try to figure things out.'

Kadam frowned as Rane ended the call. Briefly, a debate raged within him. Then he got up decisively. He pulled on a shirt and began buttoning it up.

'Where are you going?' asked Ketul.

'To the scene of the last murder—the Budhiraja house in Kandivali,' said Kadam. 'I want to look at it again.'

'Baba, that's not a good idea.'

'Shinde is trying to sabotage my investigation,' growled Kadam. 'If I stay away, he wins. I can't allow that. Kadhihi nako!'

Never.

69

The taxi driver scrutinized Kadam in his rear-view mirror for the fifth time—in five minutes. It was evident that he had seen Kadam's photograph in the news.

'Why don't you just focus on the road before you get us killed?' snapped Kadam. The cabbie hastily switched his gaze to the road, muttering 'chutiya' under his breath.

For a moment, Kadam wanted to scream at the driver. Then he shrugged. What was the point? The whole world had already made up its mind. *I am the biggest fucking chutiya for getting trapped.* The rest of the journey was completed in silence. The taxi dropped Kadam outside the Kandivali society where Lakshmi Budhiraja, the most recent victim, had lived. The driver nodded brusquely as Kadam paid him, then zoomed off.

Kadam ran a finger along his scar as he entered the complex. Something about this last murder just didn't add up. There had been no theft in any of the earlier cases. So why now? He reached Budhiraja's flat and found it locked. The lock itself was undamaged, which ruled out the possibility of a break-in.

'Why the fuck are you here?'

Kadam swivelled around. Shinde was glowering at him.

'Shinde, you bhadavya,' hissed Kadam. 'You set me up!'

'I have no idea what you're talking about,' said Shinde. He shifted his weight from one foot to another and refused to look Kadam in the eye, but the twitching corner of Shinde's mouth told Kadam how nervous he was.

'Benchod, you knocked me out with the VapoRub, then took a photo of me lying unconscious and leaked it to the press. Now, *you* don't have the brains to think of this. So, tell me, whose idea was it? Chavan's or Patil's? Did they instruct you while you licked their balls?'

Shinde's face flushed bright red. 'You think you're so fucking smart, gaandu! Who's smarter now?'

'So, it *was* you,' said Kadam. 'I knew it.'

'Theek,' said Shinde. 'Now get the fuck away from here, madarchod. And don't come back anywhere near my investigation.' He brought his face near Kadam's as he spoke and aggressively jabbed him in the chest with a finger.

Kadam nodded. Then smiled. Then he took a step back and slammed his fist into Shinde's nose. Shinde let out an anguished cry and stumbled backwards, clutching at his bleeding nose. Furious, he lunged at Kadam, but Kadam grabbed his wrist with one hand and seized Shinde's throat with the other. Shinde struggled to free himself from Kadam's grip, but, despite his age and physical condition, Kadam was surprisingly strong.

They were eventually pulled apart by the constables who came running when they heard the commotion. Kadam's chest was heaving as though he had run a marathon. 'I'll see myself out,' he said to Shinde. 'This isn't over, chodu. We'll meet again. And when we do, I'll make you wish you'd never been born.'

Back home, Kadam sat down, lit a cigarette and took a long, deep drag. He cursed silently as he noticed his hand was shaking. Moodily, he took another puff, then stubbed it out and opened the window. As he fanned the smoke with his hand to clear it, he felt a familiar tightening in his chest. *Fuck, no.* He scrambled for the blister pack concealed in his underwear drawer and hastily popped a Sorbitrate.

After a while, he relaxed. Rubbing his chest, he lay down on the sofa. His mind immediately began racing. There was no sign of a break-in at any of the crime scenes. Who could get inside a house so easily? A locksmith? A servant? A doctor? A repairman? A telephone or cable guy? A security guard? There were so many possibilities.

His phone pinged. It was a WhatsApp message from Rane— no text, just a video. Another ping. This time it was Ketul. She too had sent a video. 'Nirmal shared this with me,' said her message. It seemed like the same video in both cases. With a sense of foreboding, Kadam played it. The video was jerky, but the two men captured in it were unmistakably Kadam and Shinde. They staggered back and forth, with Kadam holding Shinde's neck in a vice-like grip and Shinde struggling to free himself. The video ended with Shinde being rescued by his colleagues. Kadam winced. 'Fuck, this is bad,' he muttered. He called Rane. The phone rang for a long time. Just when Kadam was about to give up and end the call, Rane answered.

'What part of lie low did you not understand?' Rane asked through gritted teeth. Kadam knew he was on the verge of exploding.

'Sharad, lis—' began Kadam.

'No, you listen, Kadam!' Usually, Rane never called him anything other than Prakash. 'This video has gone viral. It's playing on social media and news channels. Te aamachyavar hasat aahey. The whole world is laughing at us. I trusted you, but you've made me look like a chutiya.' In all their years of friendship, Rane had never spoken to Kadam so harshly.

'I'm sorry. I—'

'No, I'm sorry,' interrupted Rane, his nasality more pronounced than ever. 'I have no choice but to take you off this case. Just stay the fuck away from this investigation. For your sake and mine.'

'Sharad, don't do this to me,' pleaded Kadam.

'I haven't done anything to you, Kadam,' Rane said softly. 'You've done it to yourself.'

Kadam kept staring at the phone in his hand long after Rane ended the call. Finally, with a weary sigh, he set it down. *Maybe this is for the best?* He tried very hard to convince himself, but failed miserably.

Kadam paid the delivery boy who had dropped off a bottle of whisky from the neighbourhood wine shop. It had been Kadam's usual brand—McDowell's No. 1—before he ditched the bottle three years ago. He didn't bother with a glass. He opened the bottle and brought it directly to his mouth. He took a gulp, the liquid cascading down his throat. *Fool! Once an alcoholic, always an alcoholic.* Going back to the booze was suicide. He placed the bottle down for a moment and tried to stop himself from picking it up again. But his grip on the bottle remained firm.

A moment later, he was gulping it down like a parched wanderer stumbling upon an oasis in the desert.

Kadam opened his eyes and looked around. The whisky bottle was only half full. He swore. Ketul would never forgive him if she found out. He quickly emptied its contents into the toilet. Then he brushed his teeth, gargled and splashed some cologne on himself. Finally, he wrapped the bottle in newspaper and junked it in the garbage dumpster at the rear of his building.

Back in his flat, he opened the windows to air the room. The accumulated case materials seemed to be mocking him. With an angry grunt, he turned his back on them and shuffled over to his beat-up desktop computer. Ketul often teased Kadam that both he and the blessed machine belonged in a museum. He pressed the power button and waited while it wheezed and sputtered to life. Once it was on, he began playing poker. After winning three games easily, he sat back. 'This is just too easy,' he muttered in disgust. He realized that he had done his best mental work while drinking.

Despite himself, he found his mind wandering towards the murders. He reminded himself sternly to stop focusing on the case, but he could think of nothing else. Eventually, he stopped struggling with himself …

So, if the murders were a poker hand, what kind would they be? Four of a kind? Or a straight flush?

Intrigued, he walked up to the white board and looked at the four murder dates.

Sun, 2 Feb | Mon, 10 Feb | Tue, 18 Feb | Wed, 26 Feb

Four cards of the same rank? Or four cards in numerical order? A gap of eight days each time. Four of a kind? He started to turn away, then suddenly froze. Very slowly, he pivoted back to the board. This time, he underlined each day that a murder had occurred.

Sunday, Monday, Tuesday, Wednesday … Cards in numerical order. It was a straight flush! The killer wasn't trying to keep a gap of eight days, but was choosing successive days of the week! It had been staring him in the face the whole time. 'Shit, shit, shit!' Kadam swore out loud. He picked up his phone and frantically called Rane. The phone rang for a long time, but there was no response.

'Pick up, Sharad. Pick up, dammit! I need to tell you that the next murder will be on a Thursday.'

70

Rane frowned as he ignored Kadam's call. He put the phone in silent mode and placed it on the table.

'Who is it?' asked Gaikwad.

'Kadam. Desperately trying to get in touch,' said Rane. He had barely entered the plush living room of the deputy home minister's Altamount Road bungalow when Kadam's calls had started.

'Stay away from him. He may be good at what he does, but he's also bad news. I've had a hard time protecting you after this latest naatak,' said Gaikwad sternly, his eyebrows merging.

Rane nodded. 'Dhanyavad, saheb. I appreciate it.'

'Rane, you're a good officer, but you need to be careful. People know you're a rising star. They're waiting for an opportunity to pull you down. I depend on *you* to keep Mumbai safe—not that rascal Chavan.'

'Hopefully the state will have a home minister like you one day,' said Rane silkily. He wasn't above deploying a little flattery every now and then.

Gaikwad gave a slight nod of acknowledgement. 'And if I do become home minister, you will have a very bright future as commissioner. Don't do anything to jeopardize your chances. Now, what about Pankaj?'

'His alibi checks out. There's enough evidence to show that he definitely wasn't at the site of the first murder. Plus, he was in police custody when the fourth murder took place. So, he's clear on that count. Apart from the drug link to that Nidhi girl, there's nothing else. What do you want me to do?'

Rane waited patiently while Gaikwad made up his mind.

'Let Pankaj go,' Gaikwad said finally. 'But put the fear of God in him first.'

It wasn't every day that a VIP told Rane to rough up his son. He wondered what was going on. Keeping a straight face, he nodded respectfully and took his leave. As soon as he was outside, he checked his phone. Kadam had called several times. He looked around to make sure he was alone, then called back.

'Sharad, thank God!' said Kadam excitedly.

'I can't talk for long. Make it quick.' Rane was curt.

There was a pause as Kadam absorbed the brusque tone. 'Theek. I just realized that the four murders were committed on a Sunday, Monday, Tuesday and Wednesday. There's a clear pattern.'

'Are you sure?'

'Mala khaatri aahey. Check it out for yourself,' said Kadam. 'The 2nd of February was a Sunday, 10th was a Monday, 18th was a Tuesday and 26th was a Wednesday. If the killer sticks to the pattern, the next murder will be on Thursday.'

'Barobar,' said Rane. 'And what do you think we should do about it?'

Rane's response was like a bucket of ice-cold water on Kadam's enthusiasm. 'What do you mean?' he asked, his voice reflecting hurt.

'Think about it. There are 2.7 crore residents in Mumbai. Should I post a look-out at the home of each one on Thursday?'

'Maybe you could put out an alert.'

'Saying what exactly? That people should be "careful" on Thursday?'

'So, I've given you this pattern and you're not going to do anything about it?'

'It's a good insight, but it's not exactly actionable, is it? Thanks, I've got to go now.'

Kadam blinked in surprise as Rane abruptly ended the call. Rane had never behaved in such a cold and distant manner with him before. He leaned back in his chair with a dejected sigh, looking at random objects around the room. Then his gaze fell on the board, where he had underlined the days when the murders took place.

71

'Bhosdiki, tujhe bola na. Keep your stuff out of my space.'

'Desh ka border hai kya, randi?'

The two young girls, both in their late teens, glared at each other from opposite sides of a dormitory bed. They had been recently rescued and brought to the Shakti rehab centre, and were still getting used to the place. It did not help that they had very different habits. Cussing done, they went for each other's throats. The two girls struggled, clawing at each other and shrieking.

Unexpectedly, a pair of hands grabbed each girl by the hair and yanked hard. The two howled in pain and tried to free themselves. But before they could do that, their heads were banged together. The girls cried out, stunned, all the fight knocked out of them. When their vision cleared, they saw Heena standing before them, hands on her hips. 'Have I got your attention now?' she asked.

'Why did you do that?' asked one of them, gingerly rubbing her head.

'Because the two of you needed to be reminded that you have been given a second chance,' said Heena. 'Aur tum dono kya karte ho? Jhagda and time pass.' She glared at the girls furiously. Both looked down, refusing to meet her angry gaze.

'Ek baar auro karo and I'll report you to the trustees,' warned Heena. She added that the girls could end up being thrown out. Why would they want to do that to themselves?

'Bhaagya badaltey hain yeh harami taare,' she said to them. 'Take control. Socho aur samjho. Don't screw up.'

72

'We're acting on vacating the Gorai property occupied by Momuma. Thought I'd let you know,' Rane told Gaikwad. 'There will be an uproar in the press and on social media.'

The deputy home minister nodded. 'What do I tell the media?'

'Say that Momuma and his disciples have been forcibly squatting on a property and have turned it into a drug haven. Also, that people are being held there against their will. Both statements are true.'

'Theek. Are you planning to go in armed?' asked Gaikwad.

Rane shook his head. 'That could turn into a bloodbath. No, we'll cut off all supplies to the commune. Nothing and no one will be allowed to go in. Hopefully, this will force them to come out peacefully.'

'What happens if they don't?'

'I have a Plan B. But no guarantees, saheb. One more thing—Bhau Patil will put pressure on Chavan to have the operation called off. I'll need you to be firm, saheb.'

'Don't worry about Patil and Chavan,' Gaikwad's tone hardened. 'You do your job, I'll do mine.'

Rane nodded. He picked up his phone and gave his team the go-ahead.

In Gorai, Momuma slammed down his phone in frustration. He had been desperately trying to reach Bhau Patil, but to no avail. All cell phone signals from the commune had been jammed and telephone lines disconnected. The police had taken up positions along the perimeter, cutting off the members' access to the outside world.

A voice rang out over a loudspeaker. 'This is the police. All residents are requested to come out peacefully. No one will be harmed.'

Momuma cursed again, a hunted look in his eyes. After checking that his door was shut, he went to his desk, took out some meow meow and inhaled deeply. He shut his eyes as the drug hit him. When he reopened them, the fearful look was gone, replaced by a manic glint. Moments later, he threw open his door and strode to the hall where his faithful followers were gathered. A few doubters had expressed their desire to leave the premises. They had been herded together and locked up.

'Salaam, Momuma! Show us the light!' chanted his committed followers.

'The day I had warned you about is here,' Momuma announced. 'I had told you that the world will not tolerate us because we do not accept their foolish rules. But we shall not be afraid!' The group raised their hands and roared in response. 'The world wants to get rid of us. But I say to you, it is we who should get rid of them! The world needs to be cleansed completely.' His heart pounded at the answering roar. 'I am the final prophet. I will destroy this world and create a new, better one. Will you help me?' hissed Momuma.

'Salaam Momuma! Show us the light!' the crowd chorused in a frenzy.

As Momuma looked around, he noticed Sarla in the front row, eyes glazed, her voice raised along with others' in chant. He knew that she was his best insurance policy.

73

Ketul had just left the courtroom at Esplanade Court when an attendant informed her that Judge Leila Kaur wanted to see her. Ketul wondered why. She wasn't appearing in any case before her lordship currently. She nodded and followed the attendant to the judge's chambers.

'Ah, Ketul, come in,' beamed the judge. Normally a stern woman, she had a soft spot for Ketul.

'Hello, ma'am. How are you?' asked Ketul, dispensing with the courtroom protocol of 'Your Honour'.

'Not getting any younger,' laughed the judge. 'Great work on the Shakti case. You managed to get the system moving.' Ketul smiled. 'I have a hearing coming up soon, so let me get to the point. You remember Raju? You defended him on charges of burglary and theft in my court last year?'

Ketul nodded. 'I can't have done a very good job considering you found him guilty,' she said dismally. 'I only took the case because he couldn't get any other lawyer and I was asked by the court to represent him. Quite a character. Commit crimes, then go to Trimbakeshwar for spiritual cleansing! But why do you ask?'

'I just learnt that he recently escaped from Arthur Road with the help of a canteen supervisor. I thought I'd let you know because he was your client.'

'I doubt he'll try to contact me, but if he does, I'll certainly inform the police,' said Ketul.

As she left the judge's chambers, a thought gnawed at her. She sat down on a bench and tried to remember Raju's modus operandi. Her fingers toyed with the pendant around her neck as she struggled to remember the facts. From what she could recall, Raju would break into people's homes, knock them unconscious, and bind their hands and feet. He would then steal their valuables and leave. Other than a few bruises and a splitting headache, the victims were unharmed. But there was one important detail that was eluding her. *Something about* ... And then it hit her. Raju would use rope to tie up his victims. Nylon rope! He got the rope from a warehousing unit where he had a day job. It was in Ambernath, very close to the Finek plant.

Ketul rose to her feet, and began pacing up and down. The serial murders had begun shortly after Raju escaped from prison. Could he have graduated from burglary to murder? She called Kadam.

'That's a good lead,' he said when she shared her theory. 'If only I could get Rane to listen ... Are you on your way home?'

'I'll be a while. I have another appointment,' she said, glancing at her watch. She was horribly late.

Thirty minutes later, Nirmal looked up and saw Ketul pulling out the chair opposite him. He hastily closed his phone browser and removed his earphones, anxiously scanning her face for signs that she had noticed what he had been viewing.

'Oh sorry, were you on a call?' she asked as she sat down.

Nirmal heaved a sigh of relief. 'Nothing important. Just passing the time till you arrived.' He put down the phone and allowed his fingers to do a few spider push ups.

'I'm so sorry I'm late. A judge called me to her chambers,' said Ketul.

'No problem. We can order coffee now,' Nirmal replied with a smile. 'So, why did the judge call you?' he asked after their coffee had been served.

'Oh, she wanted to tell me something about an old client of mine. She was full of praise for the Shakti case—I can never thank you enough for your help with that.'

'If you want to thank me, that's easily done. Let me take you out for a celebratory dinner.'

'What? Don't be silly. I should be the one taking you out,' protested Ketul.

'Deal,' said Nirmal, putting out his hand. Ketul shook it firmly. Nirmal held on to her hand longer than necessary, but she made no effort to withdraw it. They sat together, quietly, in perfect contentment.

Desperately, Nirmal tried to wish away the scene in his head. But the harder he tried to banish the thought, the more firmly it lodged in his brain. Ketul on a bed, naked, blindfolded, hands and feet tied with rope, whimpering as two strong hands choked her, crying out as her attacker savagely bit her.

Nirmal could almost taste Ketul's blood in his mouth.

74

Bhau Patil looked up as Ekahata was ushered into his study.

'Namaskar, saheb,' said Deva, saluting Patil with his muscular left hand.

'I want you to write off that loan you'd given to Ravi Mehra,' said Patil. 'His loan is just one among thousands. I don't need you attracting attention.'

'But you have fixed that Kutta Kadam for good,' Deva said with a laugh.

'That chhakka is too smart for his own good,' snarled Patil, baring his paan-stained teeth. 'Even if he's officially out, he will probably keep digging on his own.'

Deva scowled. 'You want me teach that bulli-chokya a lesson? We should have done it long ago.'

'Let me think about it,' said Patil. His phone beeped as a message came in. He looked at it and cursed loudly.

'Problem, saheb?' asked Deva.

'The Gorai situation is bad. Looks like that madarchod Momuma has gone veda. I told him to stay put, not do any heropanti. Instead, the chutiya is preparing his followers for war. And that bastard Rane has the whole place sealed off—including phone signals and internet—so I can't even reach Momuma.'

'What about Chavan? Can't he help?'

Patil shook his head. 'This time Gaikwad and Rane seem to be calling the shots; Chavan is useless.' He picked up the glass of whisky in front of him and downed it in one gulp. 'Keep some of your boys in that area,' he ordered Deva. 'I had placed my sister with Momuma for her own protection. But now she needs protection from him.'

75

Kadam rang the doorbell and waited patiently. There was no response. He frowned and looked at his watch: 6 p.m. Desai was usually back by now. Could he have gone visiting a patient? Kadam was about to walk away when a thought struck him. Wasn't this a golden opportunity to explore Desai's flat uninterrupted? It would only take ten minutes. He vacillated for a while, but his initial instincts won in the end.

Kadam examined Desai's lock. It was a very basic one. He shook his head scornfully. *Why do people even bother with such rubbish?* Having ensured that no one was around, he pulled out a multitool from his pocket, expertly sprung the lock and slipped inside. He tiptoed through the apartment, taking care not to disturb anything. Desai's flat had two bedrooms, one of which had been converted into a study. One wall of the study was covered with nylon rope toys in all shapes, sizes and colours hanging from pegs. Spools of nylon rope lay on the desk. Kadam quickly took small clippings from them.

Next, he walked to the kitchen. A bottle of brandy sat in a corner, but it was the array of Finek knives that caught his eye. He picked up a few and carefully checked the blades. They were razor-sharp. Clearly, Desai maintained them well. In the living room, Kadam lingered over the Raja Ravi Varma print of Hindu deities. 'Quite a character,' he murmured. As he passed the dining table, he noticed Desai's diary lying on it. Kadam flipped it open. Desai's daily appointments were meticulously jotted down. There were multiple entries for almost every date. Kadam used his mobile phone to take pictures of Desai's schedule on each of the dates that a murder had taken place.

As he continued to flip through the dairy, he noticed some random jottings: chest pain, shortness of breath, coughing blood, pooling of blood, discolouration, pulmonary embolism. He frowned as he took pictures of the pages. What sort of macabre notes were these?

Outside, in the parking lot, Desai reversed his car into the space reserved for him, then took a couple of deep breaths. It had been a long day and he was bone tired. He got out of the car and began walking towards his block, stopping to chat with one of the residents who was out for a walk.

Upon entering his block, Desai headed towards the stairs, then changed his mind and went to the lift instead. He pressed the call button a couple of times before the elevator eventually arrived, creaking and groaning.

He stepped out as soon as the lift doors rattled open and almost bumped into Kadam. 'Oh my, watch out!' Desai said worriedly. He looked at Kadam closely. 'Are you all right? You seem a little breathless.'

'Just getting some steps in,' said Kadam.

'I'm glad to see you getting some exercise, but don't overdo it,' cautioned Desai, clapping him on the shoulder. 'And get your medical work-up done, as I had said.' He walked to his apartment and put the key in the lock. He had to struggle as the lock seemed to have jammed a bit. As he pushed the door open, he noticed Kadam standing in the corridor, watching him.

Kadam walked back to his flat, grateful for the creaking, groaning sounds that elevators sometimes made. He stretched out on the sofa. He drifted off to sleep, waking when sunlight streamed into the living room. He blinked and rolled over, trying to shield his face from it. Finally, he surrendered. Rubbing the sleep from his eyes, he sat up and looked out of the window. He reached under his pillow and pulled out a cigarette packet. No treasure hunt today, thankfully. He lit up and took a deep puff.

The guilt of having guzzled half a bottle of whisky was slowly dissipating.

His phone beeped. It was a message from Ketul: 'Check News5'. Puzzled, he turned on the TV and switched to the news. The bottom ticker was flashing the headline 'BREAKING NEWS: COPS CRACK NYLON KILLER CASE'.

Above it, the anchor was breathlessly announcing, 'We can confirm that Mumbai Police has solved the recent serial killings case. The killer has been apprehended thanks to some solid investigative work by officers of the elite Crime Branch.' The camera cut away from the anchor and showed a reporter talking to a grinning Shinde. 'It was a difficult case, no doubt,' he was saying. 'Criminals should remember that the law will eventually catch up with them.'

'Get to the point. Who's the killer?' muttered Kadam impatiently. Almost as though the network had heard him, the camera cut back to the anchor. 'The nylon killer, dubbed so because he ties up his victims with nylon ropes before stabbing them in the heart, is a hardened criminal called Raju Dabhade. Only last year, he was arrested and sentenced for a series of burglaries. His stint in prison, however, seems to have hardened Dabhade further. He recently escaped and has since embarked on a series of brutal killings.'

Kadam recalled what Ketul had said about this man the previous day.

'We have obtained exclusive footage of Raju Dabhade's confession,' said the anchor. The video that appeared on the screen was a little jerky in the beginning before it stabilized. The camera zoomed in on Raju, the thief. He was speaking confidently. 'Ho, mi tyaana maarle. But I have prayed for forgiveness at Trimbakeshwar. Har har Shambho!'

Kadam pressed rewind on his set-top remote and narrowed his eyes, focusing on Raju, and briefly on the man standing behind him: Keswani, the lawyer. Many of the police department's cases had been ripped to shreds by Keswani's tactics. As a seasoned poker player, Kadam always looked for tell-tale tics. People invariably revealed information through involuntary actions. He mentally ran through his checklist of stuff to watch out for—gulping, rapid breathing, sweating, fidgeting, talking fast, blinking ... And then he spotted it: Raju was drumming his fingers on his thighs as he spoke.

'He's lying through his teeth,' muttered Kadam. 'But why?'

76

Three hours later Kadam was no closer to finding the answer to that, or of any of the other questions that were plaguing him. Finally, he decided to occupy his mind with something else. Often, when he stopped consciously thinking about a problem, his subconscious came up a with the solution.

Kadam began channel-surfing. After ignoring the dance shows, the daytime soaps and the news channels, he paused on a documentary. It was about the twelve sacred Jyotirlingas, the columns of light that symbolized Shiva. The narrator covered each location in some detail—Somnath, Mallikarjuna, Mahakaleshwar, Omkareshwar, Baidyanath ...

Nothing new here, Kadam concluded as the camera zoomed in to take a close-up shot of Bhimashankar. He was about to switch the channel again when the image on the screen changed to Trimbakeshwar. Kadam sat bolt upright as a thought struck him. He put the television on mute and phoned Rane.

'Tumhi kase aahat, Prakash?' asked Rane, sounding more cheerful than he had in a while.

'You seem quite happy,' observed Kadam.

'I feel like a load has been taken off my shoulders. I had all the bosses breathing down my neck.'

Kadam felt a pang of guilt. 'I'm sorry to disturb your peace, but you've got the wrong man. Can we meet somewhere?'

Rane sighed. 'Prakash, I know you're upset about this case, but sometimes you need to move on. Why not let Shinde have his victory?'

'Just five minutes. Let me explain. How can that hurt? If I'm wrong, I'll accept it,' said Kadam, scratching his stubble.

There was a long silence. 'Theek. But if you're talking shit—'

'Where should we meet? Ram Ashray?' asked Kadam, cutting him off.

Rane hesitated. 'Naahin. I'll come over to your place.'

Kadam realized that Rane didn't want to be seen with him in public. He never thought that he would become an embarrassment for his friend. For a moment, he bristled with anger. The temptation to tell him to fuck off was immense, but Kadam swallowed his pride. 'Come over any time. I'll be waiting,' he said.

An hour later, Rane walked in. 'The man has signed a full confession,' he said, settling down on the battered old sofa.

'Just tell me one thing. How exactly was Raju caught?' asked Kadam.

'Shinde got a tip-off over the phone. When he raided Raju's hideout in Mazagaon, he found him there. Raju readily confessed his guilt.'

'Barobar,' said Kadam, tracing his scar thoughtfully. 'And within a few minutes of Raju being captured, the footage of his confession was all over television.'

Rane shook his head. 'We didn't shoot that confession video. And it wasn't *all over* anywhere. Only one channel— News5—had it.'

'Exactly. Now do me two favours. One, check if either Raju or that rogue Keswani has a deal with this channel. Two, scan the video surveillance camera footage in and around the Trimbakeshwar temple for 2 February.'

Rane frowned. 'Kadam, what the hell is going on?' he demanded, agitation making him shriller than usual.

'Just do it. You'll thank me later.'

A deflated Rane walked into Kadam's house the next day. He sat down and silently nodded when Kadam offered him a glass of water. 'Gaandu, you were right on both counts,' he said morosely a few minutes later. 'News5 paid Raju a large sum of money for the confession video. They even bought rights for his life story.'

Kadam nodded. 'I'm not surprised. News5 is part of the same media group that printed the Marathi editorial. What about the CCTV footage?'

'Raju was at Trimbakeshwar on 2 February, around the time of the first murder. He had a minor scuffle with someone in the queue. We even questioned the constable on duty that day. He couldn't have killed Ravi Mehra.'

'I was sure that he would go to Trimbakeshwar for darshan after escaping from prison. Ketul had told me about this old habit of his. If he broke out on 1 February, he would definitely visit the temple on 2 February.'

'But why do this then? He has a solid alibi. Why this bogus confession?'

'Money! Raju made chutiyas of all of us. He got himself a big payout. Keswani—that badmash fellow—will also get a cut from the deal. The two of them cooked up this story and sold it to News5 after they learnt that the first murder took place on 2 February. Shinde and Chavan lapped it up. Now, had the case come up for trial, Keswani would have poked holes in it and used the Trimbakeshwar footage to get Raju off. By then Raju would be rich. Pretty solid plan.'

Rane considered Kadam's argument and nodded. 'I need you back on the case. But I'm not sure how to do that.'

'You'll get the chance,' said Kadam. 'The real killer is not going to stop. If the pattern holds, his next strike will come on 5 March. Raju is an escaped convict so he will remain in custody. If I am right and there is another murder, the case against Raju will fall apart completely.'

77

Thursday, 5 March, around 5 p.m., Khar West, Mumbai

'You're back in business,' Rane said when Kadam answered the phone. 'There's been another murder.'

Kadam put Rane on speaker and pulled out a fresh set of clothes. 'Who's the victim?' he asked, unbuttoning his shirt.

'Some fellow called Gururaj Advani.'

'Gururaj Advani? *The* Gururaj Advani?'

'So you know him?'

'He's a playback singer. Also makes viral videos by setting dialogues to melodies. A YouTube sensation. Ketul often listens to him. Who found him and where?'

'A friend who'd gone to pick him up for a recording appointment. Gururaj was a divorcee. He lived in a studio apartment opposite Khar Gymkhana.'

'Signs?'

'The usual. Hands tied with rope, knife in the heart, food in the mouth.'

Kadam exhaled. 'Raju was in custody when this murder took place, so there's no way he could have been the killer.'

'Barobar. Which is why I can bring you back now. Interested?'

'Arrey, ho, baba,' said Kadam. 'Should I come to you or go to the crime scene?'

'Come to your society gate. I'll be there in five—with your yaar Shinde.'

Rane and Shinde were already at the gate when Kadam arrived. He gave Shinde a dirty look. 'No words for me?' he hissed as Shinde looked away, refusing to meet his gaze. 'You sure had a lot to say last time.' Shinde flushed, but kept quiet. Furious, Kadam stepped right up to him, crowding him till they were almost nose to nose.

Rane placed a restraining hand on Kadam's arm. 'Prakash, I need you to calm down. Otherwise, this isn't going to work.'

Kadam gave Shinde one more poisonous glare, then reluctantly stepped back.

'Thank you,' said Rane. 'I was planning to accompany you both to the crime scene, but I have an urgent meeting at Mantralaya. Can I trust you both? I don't want another viral video.'

Kadam nodded tightly. Rane looked at Shinde. 'Yes, sir,' came the terse response.

'Theek,' said Rane. 'We'll talk later. And remember—best behaviour please.'

The two men got into Shinde's car amidst a strained silence. Kadam lit up a cigarette. Shinde opened his mouth to protest, then thought better of it. Instead, he lowered his window slightly so that the smoke would drift out. He coughed deliberately to make a point. Kadam ignored him and kept puffing away—often in Shinde's direction. The journey was completed without a single word being exchanged.

North of Bandra and south of Santacruz, Khar is an affluent suburb with quality schools, hospitals, restaurants, parks and malls at convenient distances. The residential building where

Gururaj Advani lived was one of the new and modern ones near the 13th Road–15th Road junction. A couple of junior officers rushed to greet Shinde as he entered the flat. They looked curiously at Kadam, but kept quiet.

'This building is posh. Any CCTV footage?' asked Shinde.

'Yes, sir,' said one officer. 'We have footage for seventy-two hours. We've taken the hard disk for examination.'

'Finally some luck,' said Shinde.

Kadam, meanwhile, had pulled on a pair of gloves and strolled over to Shirodkar, who was inspecting the body. 'Your date and time estimate is unchanged?' he asked. The examiner nodded.

Kadam bent down to peer at the body. A Finek knife was protruding from the left side of the victim's chest. His hands were tied with yellow nylon rope. 'Any food in the mouth?'

'Yes, I think it's chana—chickpeas,' said Shirodkar in his raspy voice.

Kadam nodded and pulled out his phone. He looked at the pictures of the previous four victims. Then he laid his phone on the ground and used the compass app to understand the orientation of the flat. Taking out his diary, he quickly drew a sketch. As he was putting the diary away, something caught his eye. 'Can I borrow a pair of forceps?'

The examiner silently handed him his pair. Kadam gingerly removed a piece of blue fibre stuck in Gururaj Advani's watch strap. There were two strands, entangled together. He deftly concealed one strand in his palm while placing the other in a specimen bag. 'The killer definitely wears blue,' he said. 'There was a piece of blue fibre at the first crime scene too.'

'But not at any of the other crime scenes,' offered Shinde.

'Absence of evidence is not evidence of absence,' said Kadam. He puffed out a cheek as he paused in thought. 'Speaking of blue, notice the bluish discolouration on his face?' He sniffed the air, then nodded. 'Cockroach spray.' He began walking towards the rear door.

'Where are you going?' asked Shinde.

'To check the dustbin,' replied Kadam. He rummaged through it, then beckoned Shinde over. 'Do we have a list of what was bagged from the dustbins at each of the previous scenes? Send me those lists. Also, go meet Gururaj's ex-wife. Find out her movements too.'

'Theek aahey. And what about you?' asked Shinde.

Kadam smiled humourlessly at him. He held up the specimen bag containing the blue fibre. 'I'm going to the Directorate. Time for another chat with my old friend, Durga Pandey.'

78

'What type of material is it?' asked Kadam. 'Standard or special?'

'Patience, Kadam. Dekhne do,' said Durga Pandey, peering at the fibre under a microscope.

'What type of clothes might be made with it? Fashionable denim? Or repair overalls?'

Durga sighed. After a while, she straightened up and nodded. 'Well, both samples—from the first crime scene and this one—belong to the same source. Both are blue polyester-cotton blend. Standard quality, nothing fancy. Like the sort that would be used in uniforms.'

'Uniforms?' mused Kadam. Suddenly, he sat bolt upright.

'What is it?' asked Pandey, taking a puff from her herbal vape.

'A very interesting idea,' said Kadam. 'Thanks. Aap param hain, Durga maa.'

'You're welcome!' she called out as he dashed out of the lab.

Kadam walked to the car park and called Ketul. 'I need you to find out which security company provide the guards in the residential societies where the five murders have happened. Could it have been the same one?'

'Okay. But what's this about?' asked Ketul.

'The same blue fibre has turned up in two of the crime scenes. It's probably used in uniforms. Who's the one person for whom any resident will unhesitatingly open the door in a gated society? The security guard.'

Kadam hung up.

Half an hour later, Ketul called him back. 'It was the same company at three locations: the first, third and fifth. A firm called Supertop Security. I know the CEO. He's a retired army officer. I met him in court once when he appeared as a witness in a case. I'll go and speak to him.'

An hour later, Ketul arrived at the headquarters of Supertop Security in Worli. Namdeo, the constable for whom Kadam had a soft spot, was waiting for her outside. He saluted her and quietly handed over a small envelope from her father. Ketul thanked him and stashed it in her bag before entering.

Inside, the furniture was simple and functional, but the floors were gleaming and there wasn't a speck of dust in sight. The military background of the CEO was evident. Colonel Vinod Gurung (Retd.) rose to his feet when she was ushered into his office. Though it had been several years since he had left the army, he was still lean and fit, and his back was ramrod straight. His grey hair was cut short, and he sported a neatly trimmed moustache. 'Good afternoon, please have a seat,' he said. 'Right, how can I help you?'

Ketul waited until the assistant left. Then she said, 'I'm sure you're aware that there have been a series of murders in the city.'

Gurung's face darkened. 'Terrible business. I hope the police catch the culprit soon. Your father is part of the investigation, isn't he?'

'Supertop provides security in three of the locations where the murders took place,' said Ketul, sidestepping the reference to her father.

'Ketul ji, we're the largest providers of security guards in Mumbai—hundreds of societies and offices. It's not surprising that some of the locations are serviced by us.'

'Do you rotate guard duties across locations?'

Gurung shook his head. 'We like to let our guards become familiar with places and residents. And we recruit our guards very carefully. Most of them are ex-servicemen, and we do stringent background checks.'

'Still, could you check if one or more guards might have been present at all three locations?'

'Just to set your mind at ease, I'll check and get back to you by EOD.'

'Thank you,' said Ketul. 'Also, if you don't mind, could I get a sample of the fabric that's used in your uniforms?'

'You have no official sanction to be here, but I'm happy to assist informally.'

Ketul put on her most grateful smile. After collecting the sample, she ordered an Uber. She was headed to meet an old school friend of her boss who worked at a textile company's R&D department. In the cab, she reached into her satchel, pulled out the envelope Namdeo had given her and peered inside. It contained the second piece of blue fibre that Kadam had quietly pocketed from Gururaj's watch, but she couldn't tell if it was the same as the Supertop fabric. *Let's hope this contact is able to provide some leads,* she thought as she put the envelope back in her bag.

Ketul was scrolling through her phone when she got a message. Her eyes narrowed as she read it. She called Kadam. 'Baba? Yes, I'm on my way to the textile lab. Listen, I got an update on Lakshmi Budhiraja. I think you'll find it interesting.'

Arun Budhiraja squirmed under Kadam and Shinde's joint scrutiny.

'You took out a life insurance policy on your wife, Lakshmi, a few months ago, right? Quite a hefty amount too,' said Kadam.

'Yes,' he mumbled.

'So we have a motive for a murder right there,' said Shinde, excited.

'But I didn't kill Lakshmi!' protested Arun. 'I wasn't even *in* Mumbai when it happened.'

'You could have got someone else to do it. How much did you pay?' said Shinde, playing bad cop to the hilt.

'Please,' said Arun, on the verge of tears. 'I could never hurt Lakshmi. I loved my wife.'

'Save it for the judge. Chalaa,' said Shinde. He walked across to Arun, who shrank in his seat. Shinde was about to grab his hand when Kadam spoke. 'He's telling the truth.' A look of relief washed over Arun's face.

'Most life insurance policies have something called a two-year contestability period. I'm sure this one does too. Is that right, Arun?' asked Kadam.

Arun nodded, a miserable look on his face.

'What is this fucking contestability period?' asked Shinde.

'It gives insurers some time to investigate if something suspicious happens,' explained Kadam. He turned to Arun. 'I'm going to tell you my theory. It's in your own best interest to cooperate. Otherwise,' he said with a shrug, 'Shinde here is itching to lock you up.'

At Arun's answering nod, Kadam resumed, 'It was a shock for you when you returned and found Lakshmi dead. But then you got thinking. The finger of suspicion would point to you, the beneficiary of the policy. And if there was even a hint of suspicion on you, the insurer wouldn't pay up.'

Kadam paused, searching for a reaction on Arun's face. 'So, you staged a break-in to make it look like a burglary gone wrong. The insurer would then be convinced of your innocence and you would get the full payout.'

Tears were pouring down Arun Budhiraja's face. He dabbed at his cheeks with a kerchief and heaved a deep sigh. 'I returned from Chennai and saw Lakshmi lying there. I knew she would have wanted me to use the insurance money to secure our daughter's future. But if I was implicated in any way, we would never see the money. That's why I staged the burglary. But I had nothing to do with Lakshmi's death. I swear on our daughter.'

Kadam and Shinde walked to one corner of the room. 'I could charge him with obstruction of justice,' said Shinde.

'Yes, you could,' said Kadam. 'And you could also put him through the misery of a prolonged trial. But hasn't the family suffered enough already? Let's not waste time. Our killer is still out there.'

79

'Doctor, come quickly. The patient is waking up.'

The on-duty physician hastily followed the nurse to the bed where Akash Awasthi was stirring. He was checking the patient's vitals when suddenly …

'Stop that car!' Awasthi woke up with a terrified cry. He looked around the room in confusion and lapsed into silence.

'You are in hospital, Mr Awasthi,' said the doctor gently. 'You were in an accident.'

'I … I was out walking and this car came straight at me …' Awasthi spoke haltingly.

The doctor patted him on the shoulder. 'Take it easy for a while. We'll call your family right away. They've been so worried about you.'

'Okay,' said Awasthi as he lay back in bed. 'But, doctor?'

The doctor looked at him inquiringly. Though his voice was shaky, there was a determined look on Awasthi's face. 'I want to talk to the police. It wasn't an accident.'

'It was a blue Maruti Dzire,' Awasthi told the policemen who had come to take his statement. 'It was a wide road. By the time I sensed the danger and turned around, it was too late. The car came straight at me.'

'Did you by any chance catch the licence plate number?' asked the policeman.

Awasthi shut his eyes tightly. 'It all happened so fast …' he said, shuddering, 'but wait … I remember the last three digits. They were 361. Or was it 316?'

The moment he exited the hospital building, the inspector told his constable, 'Ek kaam kara. Check in the Kalyan RTO for all blue Maruti Dzires with licence plates ending in either 361 or 316.'

Sanjay Bhargava smiled flirtatiously at Rosie, the receptionist, as he walked into the main Finek office building. He had been to the gym during his lunch break, and was flush with post-workout endorphins and dopamine. The receptionist gave a hesitant smile in return. 'There are some gentlemen here to see you,' she said uneasily, pointing to two men sitting on a sofa near the entrance. The men noticed her gesture and rose to their feet.

'We're from Ambernath police station,' said one of the men. 'We'd like to question you regarding the attempted murder of Mr Awasthi.'

Bhargava nodded, his mind working furiously. Out of the corner of his eye, he saw Rosie staring at him in shock and disbelief. As he stepped forward, a constable with a paunch put a hand on his arm. Bhargava snapped, his instincts wavering between fight and flight. He roughly shoved the man away and broke into a run.

The two cops charged at him. The one on his left was closer. Bhargava quickly unslung the gym bag from his shoulder and swung it hard. It hit the constable squarely on his face. He grunted in pain and clutched at his nose. The inspector—a toughie who quite enjoyed a brawl—tackled Bhargava. They rolled on the ground, each trying to pin the other down. The injured constable too joined the fray, and eventually the policemen were able to overpower Bhargava and handcuff him. They were about to leave when the inspector's phone rang.

A short, murmured conversation followed. 'Ho, saheb, right away, sir,' he said and then turned to his team. 'Yojana badalne. We have to take him to Mumbai Crime Branch HQ. Our friend may be linked to the serial murders. They also want a sample of Finek's uniform fabric.'

80

'We know that a Finek knife was used in each of the murders. We know that your company's uniform is blue and that blue fibres were discovered at crime scenes. We know that you tried to kill your boss and make it look like a car accident. You are now at the top of our list of murder suspects.'

Shinde slammed his hands on the table and leaned over it, glaring at Bhargava. Handcuffed to the metal table, Bhargava stared back at him, then rotated his head on his thick neck, and flexed his biceps and chest muscles. Even under his shirt, the rippling motion was clearly visible. 'I have nothing to say without my lawyer,' he said defiantly.

'This isn't working,' sighed Kadam. He had been watching the interrogation on a monitor in an adjoining room for the last forty minutes. Despite Shinde's tactics and all the evidence against him, Bhargava refused to speak. Observing his obvious vanity, Kadam was struck by an idea. He suggested it to Rane.

'Why don't you take a break, Shinde?' Rane said a few minutes later, stepping into the interrogation room. Once a mystified Shinde walked out, he turned to Bhargava and said, 'Think of me as a well-wisher. Like you, I'm a fitness buff. But I get my exercise from running, while you obviously do weights.'

'You want to discuss my fitness routine?' asked Bhargava drily.

'I want to discuss what will happen when your lawyer comes into the picture. Trials take a very long time. Meanwhile, your ass will be thrown into a special cell at Taloja Central Jail, awaiting trial and denied bail. Month after month of rotten food, no exercise, three thousand stinking inmates, overflowing toilets, frequent diarrhoea … Tougher men than you have come out from there like skeletons. Answer me truthfully and I'll try to get your bail arranged.'

Bhargava's shoulders slumped and he stared at his handcuffed hands. When he finally looked up, there was a look of resignation on his face. 'What do you want to know?'

Rane switched on a recorder. 'Why don't you tell me exactly what is going on at Finek?' he asked in his nasal voice.

'I'm no murderer.'

'Then why did you want to put Awasthi out of action?'

The gears in Bhargava's mind were turning. 'I was running a side business,' he finally admitted.

'What sort of side business?'

'We leave knives as buffer stock with courier companies. Many are deliberately recorded as misplaced. These are sold unofficially as half-price rejects. Finek generates huge sales volumes every day—and we skim off around five per cent.'

'By "we" you mean your accomplices in courier companies?'

Bhargava nodded.

'But why did you need to knock down Awasthi?'

'He was too suspicious for his own good,' replied Bhargava. 'His investigation into buffer stocks was threatening our scheme.'

'What is your connection to the Mumbai serial killings?' asked Rane. 'Finek knives have been used in five murders till date. The company's share price has tumbled even further due to the bad publicity.'

Bhargava shook his head vigorously. 'I have no idea what you're talking about.'

'That seems unlikely.'

'Thousands of Finek knives are sold every day,' shot back Bhargava. 'I admit to trying to injure Awasthi, but nothing more.'

Rane wanted to probe further, but Kadam called for him.

Ketul was on speakerphone. 'The report from the textile lab came in,' she said. 'The blue fibre from the crime scene only looked similar to the Supertop and Finek uniforms, but the composition turned out to be different.'

Kadam scowled. 'I'm quite sure the fibre came from a uniform of some kind.'

'Baba, blue is the most common colour other than khaki when it comes to uniforms. Everywhere you look, you'll find blue.'

'Who else wears uniforms? Drivers, repairmen, pest-control people, delivery boys, security guards …' Kadam was lost in thought when he noticed a call waiting. It was Sandra Gomes. He had forgotten about his appointment.

81

'Let's talk about what happened to you after your wife left five years ago,' said Sandra.

Kadam shifted uncomfortably in his chair, stroking his scar. 'It's ancient history. Over and done with.'

Sandra shook her head. 'I think we need to explore it. How did you feel? Hurt? Sad? Disappointed? Angry?'

Kadam rubbed his hands over his face. 'All of the above.'

Sandra nodded. 'One can often experience a cocktail of emotions. How did you cope? Come on, Prakash, I really do need you to work with me … Please?'

Kadam sighed. 'I sank deeper into my private work after my suspension. More work meant more stress. I began drinking heavily. I neglected Ketul when she needed me most …'

'Then?' Sandra prompted after a few minutes' silence.

'Two years later, I passed out on the floor one night.' Kadam swallowed uncomfortably. 'I was lying face-down in my vomit when I had a heart attack. Luckily Ketul found me before it was too late. I woke up the next day in an ICU bed with a stent inside me.'

Kadam shut his eyes and shook his head, as though trying to drive away the painful memories. Sandra placed a small bottle of water in front of him. Kadam nodded gratefully, unscrewed the top and took a gulp.

'Ketul was sitting beside me, her eyes red and swollen,' he continued. 'She begged me to get well. She had already lost one parent … she didn't want to lose another.'

'How did you feel?'

'Guilty. So I promised to cut back on the drinking and to pay more attention to her.' The recent whisky relapse was still nagging at him, but he was determined not to discuss it.

'And how did that work out?'

'Without alcohol, the nightmares started. Every night. I went into a downward spiral and had to be admitted to Maharashtra Psychiatric Hospital just a year after my heart attack. Ketul was with her grandmother during that time.'

'And you still get the same nightmare?'

Kadam nodded. 'Every now and then I wake up feeling exhausted—like I've run a marathon.'

'Tell me about the young man in your nightmare. What was his name? Did you hate him? Did you love him? Did you kill him?'

Kadam remained defiantly silent.

'How was your sex life after she left? Any intimacy at all?'

Kadam jerked upright as though she had slapped him. 'Fuck! Why ask me something like that?'

'Nightmares are often our subconscious trying to tell us what the conscious mind is supressing,' she explained calmly. 'The harder we try to push away thoughts, the louder they scream at us.'

'Khaliphukat time waste here,' blurted Kadam before lapsing into silence again.

Sandra stared at him, wondering if Kadam's was a case of repressed sexuality in addition to all his other problems.

Kadam was tense during the cab ride home. The moment he reached, he swallowed a Sorbitrate. He sat at the dining table, drumming his fingers, his mind in turmoil. Still feeling restless, he got up and prowled around the tiny flat. He turned on the Caravan radio and lay down, but even that failed to soothe his agitation. Finally, he got up and strode over to his computer.

The machine wheezed and spluttered, like an old car engine struggling to start. 'Oh, come on!' he muttered, irritated. Usually he found humour in the laboured way his desktop booted up and even joked about it with Ketul. But today, he was on edge. Was it the conversation with Sandra Gomes? Why was that woman intent on discovering whom he slept with?

Kadam went to Google and began entering the terms that he had found noted in Desai's diary. Chest pain … Shortness of breath … Coughing blood … Pooling of blood … Discolouration … Pulmonary embolism.

'What the hell are you keeping track of, doc?' he muttered. 'Some sadistic ritual of collecting data on how your victims died?'

Google threw up millions of possible answers. Kadam quickly read through the first few, then shook his head. He began looking at the photos he'd taken of Desai's diary. Specifically, he examined Desai's appointments on 2, 10, 18 and 26 February. The 5 March murder had occurred after Kadam had broken into the doctor's house. Desai had had several appointments on each of the days, so though he was in Mumbai at the time, would he have had enough time to commit the murders? Kadam made a list of all the gaps in Desai's schedule—times when he didn't have any appointments. Then he consulted his notes for the estimated time of death of each victim. He scratched his stubble and exhaled. Desai had had a clear window of time on every single occasion.

A family doctor would have been welcomed into the house by everybody, without any questions asked … But what about the blue fabric? Kadam's mind struggled to make sense of his thoughts. Didn't Desai wear blue Nehru jackets? And didn't he use Finek knives at home? And wasn't he Nidhi's alibi? And wasn't that crook Keswani his lawyer? And he even made toys with nylon ropes. Every piece of the puzzle seemed to fit except for motive. But then, serial killers often murdered without one. Was Desai one of those nutjobs?

Kadam grabbed his phone and called Rane to discuss his theory.

'Prakash, do you know how many people live in Mumbai? And the killer just happens to live right under your nose? Does that sound plausible to you?'

'Theek, it's a weird coincidence. But the evidence …'

'Circumstantial, all of it! Not to mention the fact that you basically broke into his house to get the diary data. On what grounds do we arrest him?'

'I don't know,' said Kadam. 'But today is 12 March. If he sticks to his schedule, there's going to be another murder tomorrow, Friday the 13th. Can we at least keep an eye on him?'

Kadam groaned and opened his eyes at the insistent ringing of the phone. It had been another restless night. With an effort, he propped himself up on one elbow and picked up the phone.

'We have a problem.' Rane's voice, grim, nasal, broke through the fog that was clouding Kadam's brain. He sat up, drowsiness gone.

'Dr Desai is nowhere to be found,' Rane continued. 'His phone is switched off and his apartment is locked. He never went to his clinic. He has no appointments scheduled for today … so his day is free.'

'Better put out an alert for his car,' said Kadam.

'His car never left the parking. We spoke to the guards in your society. He was spotted leaving the complex early in the morning and hailing a taxi. Hasn't been seen or heard from since.'

'So Desai is basically in the wind. And we have no way of knowing where he is.'

'I've put out an alert for him. Let's see where and when he surfaces.'

'Hopefully not at another crime scene.'

The conversation over, Kadam got out of bed, bathed and changed into a fresh set of clothes. Then he walked over to Desai's flat and checked the door. It was still locked. He was tempted to go in once more and have another dekho. Even as he was mentally debating the pros and cons of the idea, his phone rang. It was Rane again.

Kadam picked up the call. 'Bolo,' he said, his tone a mixture of eagerness and anxiety.

'We got lucky … sort of.'

'What does that mean? Did you find Desai?' asked Kadam, stroking his scar.

'No sign of him yet. But the killer struck again and didn't fully succeed.'

'Was someone killed or not?' asked Kadam, perplexed.

'There was an attempt, but the intended victim is in coma,' explained Rane. 'She's been taken to Bhatia Hospital in Tardeo. Can you get there right away? Shinde will meet you there and brief you.'

82

Friday, 13 March, around 7 p.m., Tardeo, Mumbai

She groped around for her phone with bound hands, but could not reach it. She hoarsely whispered, 'Siri, call Dhruv.' Her iPhone immediately dialled her brother's number. When he came on the line, she could only bring herself to stutter, 'H—h—help,' before passing out.

The voice at the other end was agitated. 'Hello? Hello? Divya? What's happened? Speak to me!'

But Divya lay on the floor, oblivious to the world, blood oozing from the deep wound in her abdomen.

'Divya Shukrapani, twenty-nine, fitness trainer. Was attacked in her flat—opposite Swati Snacks in Tardeo. It seems she managed to fight off her attacker, but sustained serious injuries while defending herself. The killer rushed off in a panic, leaving behind a cloth bag containing black nylon rope, Baygon spray and rajma beans. The victim had her brother on Siri. The brother's phone log shows a call from her at 7.03 p.m.'

Kadam nodded. Shinde and he were standing outside the hospital where they wouldn't be overheard.

Shinde continued, 'The brother rushed to her place and found her lying unconscious on the floor, bleeding. He called an ambulance and brought her here—less than a couple of minutes away.'

'Any fingerprints on the stuff the killer left behind?' asked Kadam.

'Clean. Probably used gloves.'

'Does the brother have an alibi?'

'He was at a pub with friends when she called. They all vouch for him.'

'Is she single or married?'

'Single. But she has a boyfriend. He's waiting outside the ICU with the brother.'

'Theek, let's go talk to them,' said Kadam. His mind was whirring. The killer seemed to be slipping up. *I am missing something*, Kadam thought, frustrated. It was there at the back of his mind, but it kept eluding him. *Think, Kadam, think!*

The two young men outside the ICU were a study in contrast. One was of medium height, slender and bespectacled, with neatly cut hair. The other was tall and beefy, with long hair tied in a ponytail. Both looked up as Shinde and Kadam approached.

'This is Dhruv,' said Shinde, indicating the slender young man. 'He's Divya's brother.' He gestured towards the muscular man. 'And this is Rajat, her boyfriend.'

'What do you do, Dhruv?' asked Kadam.

'I work with a consumer research company,' replied Dhruv. His eyes were red.

'When Divya spoke to you on the phone, did you hear anything in the background? Any sound or noise that seemed out of place?'

Dhruv tried to remember. 'She just gasped that one word: Help. That sent me into a panic. I kept yelling, "Hello? Hello?" into the phone. But there was no response.'

'The attacker must have already fled the scene by then,' said Kadam. 'When you found your sister, was she lying in a certain way? Anything out of the ordinary?'

'I was freaking out. I didn't notice anything,' said Dhruv, raking a hand through his hair. 'Sorry, I'm not being much help.'

'Arrey, not at all. Your priority was to save your sister,' said Kadam. He turned to Rajat. 'How long have you and Divya been together?'

'Two years,' said Rajat. 'We're both fitness trainers.'

'I see. I wonder why Divya called her brother and not you.'

'I was teaching a kickboxing class at that time,' said Rajat, his voice quivering slightly. 'I leave my phone in my locker. Divya knew that.'

'How did you find out about the attack?'

'Dhruv dropped me a voice note. I rushed here as soon as I got the message.'

Just then, a doctor emerged from the ICU and walked over to the small group.

'What's the news, doctor?' asked Dhruv anxiously.

'She's lost a lot of blood because of a wound to the anterior abdomen,' said the doctor. 'She's young and strong, so we hope her body will fight back. It's fifty-fifty because of the impact on her renal structure.' He nodded at the policemen as he was called away.

Kadam and Shinde walked away. 'Does the boyfriend's alibi check out?' asked Kadam.

Shinde nodded. 'There were at least ten people in that class.'

'Chalo, I'm going to her flat, then going home,' said Kadam. 'Flat number 3B, right?' He phoned Rane as he left the hospital. 'Any news of Desai?'

'Not yet.' Rane sounded dismal. 'What's the scene at the hospital?'

'Hanging by a thread,' said Kadam. 'We need security outside the ICU. She's the only one to have survived an attack. This could be our first lucky break.'

'Done,' said Rane.

'We have to get Desai off the streets.'

83

Kadam puffed out his cheeks as he pushed away the plate of half-eaten pav bhaji at Swati Snacks. The no-frills, canteen-style dining room with stainless-steel tabletops was always buzzing. It was Mumbai's favourite snack place, including that of India's richest man, Mukesh Ambani. The eatery was only a couple of minutes away from Divya Shukrapani's building and a short distance from the hospital.

Kadam's visit to Divya's flat had been unremarkable. The killer had tied Divya's hands and injured her, but had left hurriedly without placing food in her mouth. What had made the killer leave so quickly? Had it been someone knocking at the door? Or had something else needed the killer's attention urgently?

With an effort, Kadam rose to his feet and walked out. It was almost 10.30 p.m. He lit a cigarette and headed towards Bhatia Hospital. He wanted to check on the security detail. The hospital was quiet for the night. A lone security guard at the entrance glanced cursorily at Kadam as he walked in.

Kadam made his way to the ICU. The lights had been dimmed and the corridor was peaceful. As he approached the ICU entrance, he heard gentle snoring. It was the police constable, fast asleep. *So much for security*, scoffed Kadam. Even the usual ICU guard was missing. *Probably gone for a pee or tea break.*

He quietly let himself in. The duty nurse was sitting at the console, struggling to stay awake, but nodding off every now and then. Kadam tiptoed over to Divya's bed and checked on her. She seemed stable. As he was walking back to the nurse's console, he saw a shadowy figure near the entrance. In the dim light, the person's face was not visible. Kadam could only discern a silhouette heading towards Divya's bed. He crouched behind the console to remain hidden.

Suddenly, there was a sharp cracking sound. The intruder had stepped on a pen that had fallen from a bed chart. He froze momentarily, then whipped around. Kadam got off his haunches and charged at the trespasser, swinging a roundhouse punch. The stranger warded it off with his left arm and jabbed hard with his right at Kadam's face. Kadam jerked his head to the side and the blow glanced off his shoulder. He lunged for the prowler's throat, but the man grabbed his wrists. The two men struggled for a bit until Kadam heaved with all his might and the figure crashed into a medical tray placed near a bed. It fell to the floor with a clanging noise that shattered the calm of the ICU. The nurse quickly switched on the overhead lights. Kadam looked at the intruder.

Shinde!

'What the fuck are you doing here?' hissed Kadam.

'I could ask you the same thing,' shot back Shinde.

'I came here to check on the security arrangements,' said Kadam angrily.

'Me too.'

Kadam stared at him, unconvinced. But the nurse was scowling at both of them.

'Maaf kara, sister,' said Kadam as the two walked out.

The commotion had roused the constable, who bustled in importantly.

'Arrey wah, tumhi jaagla aahat,' Shinde sniped at the shamefaced constable as they crossed each other. 'If I catch you sleeping on duty again, I'll shove your laathi up your gaand. Understand?'

What was Shinde up to, wondered Kadam. Had he really come to check on Divya? Or had he planned to silence an inconvenient witness?

84

The next morning, Kadam was woken by the ringing of his phone. He reached for it with a muttered curse. It was Rane.

'I want to talk to you about Shin—' Kadam began, but Rane cut him off.

'Ho, baba, he told me about it, but something more urgent has come up. Desai has been picked up and is being brought in for questioning. Can you come over right away?'

'Finally,' mumbled Kadam. 'Let's see what Dr Evil has to say for himself.'

Half an hour later, Kadam was in the observation room, watching the monitor.

'So, Dr Desai, can you tell us where exactly you were all of yesterday and the previous night?' asked Rane. Shinde was with him inside the interrogation room.

Desai stared impassively at Rane, arms folded across his chest. 'My lawyer, Bhagwan Keswani, will be happy to speak to you. He is on his way,' he said.

'Doc, things are not looking good for you,' interrupted Shinde rudely. 'We know all about your nylon rope toys, your Finek knives and the unexplained gaps in your diary. We know the killer wears blue and you're wearing a blue Nehru jacket right now.'

'I strongly suggest you cooperate,' chimed in Rane.

'You're clutching at straws,' said Desai in his Oxford English. 'You have nothing against me that Keswani wouldn't be able to rip apart. Look, why don't you speak to my neighbour, Prakash Kadam? He's a police officer. I'm sure you've heard of him … Maybe even worked with him. He'll vouch for me.'

Shinde burst out laughing. 'Who do you think ratted you out in the first place?'

Rane shot a poisonous glance at Shinde. In the observation room, Kadam groaned and slapped his forehead. Why was Shinde such a chutiya, he wondered. Now there was no hope of playing good cop–bad cop.

Desai looked crestfallen. 'Really? Kadam thinks I'm guilty?' For a moment, he seemed to be at a loss for words. Then, his face hardened. 'Get Kadam in here. Let him be a man and confront me directly. If he does that, I will answer all his questions.'

In the observation room, Kadam sighed. He thought about his next move for a moment, then walked over to the interview room, pushed open the door and entered. Desai and Kadam stared at each other silently for a long time.

Desai was the first to break the silence. 'Do you realize that I probably saved your life by giving you those pills that day? You have a strange way of showing gratitude.'

Kadam shifted uncomfortably in his seat. 'I don't deny that you have been a good neighbour, doctor sa'ab—'

'And you have been a terrible one,' retorted Desai tersely. 'If you had any questions, you could have asked me directly instead of having me brought here. Or have you become so bitter and broken that you have lost all faith in humanity?'

'So, I'm asking you now,' said Kadam. 'Why are there so many unexplained gaps in your diary?'

'Because, every now and then, I like to take time off. I go to a park, or a beach, or a museum … These are my mental health breaks. You should try them sometimes.'

Kadam ignored the jibe. 'Where were you yesterday?'

'My daughter owns an apartment in Navi Mumbai. She doesn't live here, nor does she want to rent it out. I go occasionally and do some basic cleaning. My phone battery died and I didn't have my charger with me.'

'Why didn't you take your own car?'

'The train is faster.'

'You were there alone the whole day? Can anyone support your claim?'

'No, but that doesn't make me a killer.'

'Why doesn't your daughter ever come to India?'

'That's personal. Nothing to do with you.'

'I'm sorry, doctor sa'ab, but there's lots of circumstantial evidence—enough to make any cop suspicious.'

'As you rightly observed, it's all *circumstantial*.'

'I guess we'll just have to see,' said Kadam. Rane left the room to take a call.

'You think you're so smart, Kadam. But your intellectual arrogance will be your downfall. You have nothing concrete on me. According to you, making rope toys, chopping fruit with Finek knives and wearing blue jackets makes me a killer.' Desai shook his head. 'You're crazy if you think that.'

Kadam's phone buzzed. Rane was calling him out. He left Desai with Shinde and walked out. 'What happened?' he asked a grim-looking Rane.

'I sent a sample from Desai's jacket to Durga Pandey and asked her to compare it with the crime scene fibres,' said Rane. 'Also to compare those samples of the ropes found at his house with the ones used to tie up the victims. Normally, it would take a few days, but I asked her to treat this as top priority.'

'And?' asked Kadam, his heart sinking at Rane's expression and tone.

Rane pursed his lips. 'Neither of them match. The doctor's ropes are 10 mm thick, but the ones at the crime scenes were 12 mm. The quality of the blue fibre from his jacket is far superior to the fibres found at the two crime scenes.'

'Fuck, fuck, fuck,' cursed Kadam. 'I unnecessarily suspected an innocent man. Desai is right. Mee veda aahey.'

'Your suspicions were reasonable,' Rane consoled miserably.

Kadam shook his head. 'I'm a chutiya. While we're doing all this khaliphukat stuff, the killer is out there, planning his next move.'

85

Pankaj Gaikwad cursed as his Range Rover scraped against the rear fender of the car parked in front. He had misjudged the distance in his stoned state and nearly rear-ended his father's favourite Mercedes-Benz S350. As his father's driver came rushing, Pankaj got out of his car and perfunctorily checked the dents on both vehicles. The driver silently gave him a reproachful look.

'W—what the fuck are you g—glaring at, benchod?' growled Pankaj. 'Tumhi naukar aahat. Act like one.' The man flushed and lowered his gaze. Pankaj tossed the keys to his Range Rover at him and sauntered into the house.

To his surprise, all the lights were on. Usually, the household was asleep by the time he returned, but today seemed to be an exception. His father was sitting in the living room, waiting.

'All okay? Y—you're still up?'

The deputy home minister looked at his only child sorrowfully. As he took in Pankaj's glazed eyes, unkempt appearance and wobbly gait, his eyebrows merged together as one. 'No, Pankaj, things are not okay. They've not been for a while. I am finally going to do what I should have done a long time ago.'

'What the f—fuck are you going on about, old man?' snapped Pankaj, scratching his scruffy beard with both hands.

'The drugs stashed in your room have been removed,' said Gaikwad. 'Since none of the fancy treatments have worked, we'll do this the old-fashioned way. Go to your room and stay there until you've overcome your craving. Do not try to leave before that.'

Pankaj laughed incredulously. 'Have you gone mad? F—f—forgotten the beating you got last time? Don't forget that I know about that psycho tantrik of yours.' He moved menacingly towards his father. This time Gaikwad was prepared. He calmly raised a finger and immediately three burly guards materialized.

'Take him to his room,' ordered Gaikwad.

'What?! Get your h—hands off me! How dare you t—touch me, motherfuckers!' Pankaj yelled as the guards grabbed his arms and began hauling him away.

Gaikwad stormed across the room and gave Pankaj a stinging slap on his face. 'Who are you, Pankaj?' asked Gaikwad. 'You are the son of Jayant Gaikwad. That's *all* you are. That's *all* you'll ever be. You are nothing without me. Nothing!' He reached into Pankaj's pockets and pulled out both his phones. 'You won't be needing these.'

Outside his bedroom, Pankaj sank to his knees, refusing to budge. 'I won't go in. You can't m—make me,' he shouted. The guards grabbed him by his arms and legs, lifting him like a sack, and tossed him into the room. While he lay on the floor, stunned, one of them locked the door.

Less than a minute later, Pankaj began hammering on the door. 'Let m—me out. You can't do this!'

Gaikwad looked at the household staff who had gathered in the living room. He asked them to go back to work and forbade them from allowing Pankaj out.

Trapped in his room, Pankaj howled like an injured animal. Abruptly, he began hurling foul abuses and threats of horrific violence, interspersed with kicks and punches to the door. After a while, his tone changed. Now, there was fear and desperation as he begged and pleaded to be let out.

Gaikwad stood outside, unmoving. From time to time, his eyes flickered. But there was a combination of sorrow and determination in them. Pankaj finally fell silent and Gaikwad trudged back to his own bedroom.

The pattern of shouting, door-beating and pleading was repeated several times through the night. By dawn, Pankaj's voice was hoarse and his cries were little more than whimpers. Finally, his screams stopped and peace descended over the household. But the stillness had an eerie quality to it.

Gaikwad awoke early the next morning and went into his study to work. No sounds were heard from Pankaj's room. This was not unusual. On weekends, he rarely rose before noon. Around 1 p.m., Gaikwad emerged from his study and sat down at the dining table. 'Tell Pankaj to get cleaned up and come out for lunch,' he instructed his old cook.

The guards unlocked the door and the old man walked in warily. The guards followed him in, just in case Pankaj became violent again.

'Pankaj baba ...?' the cook called out softly, then let out a startled gasp. 'Hey Ram! Yeh kya ho gaya!'

Gaikwad shot out of his chair and raced into Pankaj's bedroom. The cook and the guards were standing at the entrance to the bathroom. He shoved them aside and entered. Pankaj was slumped on the floor, propped up against the tub.

His lifeless form was sitting in a pool of blood that had poured out from his razor-slashed wrists.

86

'I am grieving for my son—and for the many young lives that are needlessly lost every day in our country. My son did not kill himself. He was killed by the menace of drugs and poor policing. A lethal combination that has claimed the lives of many other bright young men and women.' Gaikwad paused to sip from a glass of water as cameras flashed.

An impromptu press conference had been organized in the sprawling lawns of his Altamount Road residence. Cameramen jostled each other, trying to get the best angle.

'Pankaj was my only child, my only immediate family member,' Gaikwad continued. 'But I have a larger family. Every resident of this state is my kin. I must rededicate myself to serving them with all my heart and soul. Jai Maharashtra, Jai Hind!'

Gaikwad removed his spectacles and dabbed his eyes, then turned and walked towards the house. As he neared the porch, he saw Rane standing there, a sympathetic look on his face, with Shinde behind him. Kadam stood a few feet away, engrossed in his phone.

'I've taken care of all the formalities, saheb,' said Rane in a low voice. 'My deepest condolences.'

'Thank you, Rane. I don't know what I would have done without you,' said Gaikwad. He heaved a deep sigh, patted Rane's arm and walked away, his shoulders stooped in grief.

'Kiti bhayanak,' said Rane. 'No parent should have to go through this. He's handling himself with enormous dignity though.'

'I wonder ...' Kadam murmured thoughtfully, scrolling through photographs of the scene that Rane had sent him on his phone.

'Yes?'

'Is he really sad about it?' asked Kadam.

'Prakash! How can you say something like that?' snapped Rane, anger giving his tone a sharper-than-usual edge.

Kadam held up a hand when he saw Rane's irritated expression. 'Look, I'm not denying that he's heartbroken by his son's suicide. But did you hear him talk right now? He sounded more like an election candidate than a grieving father.'

Rane shook his head angrily. 'There's no point arguing with you. We're not going to agree on this.'

'Well, here's something we might agree on,' said Kadam softly, zooming in on a photograph of Pankaj's body. 'Do you see the slits on his wrist? They were neatly done. A bit too neat for someone who's experiencing the beginnings of withdrawal. Something in that room was not quite right.'

'What the fuck are you implying?' asked Rane, his eyes flashing.

'I just think you're being a little too eager to accept everything at face value,' said Kadam. 'Is your cosy equation with Gaikwad blinding you?'

Rane bristled. 'This is not your case—I only brought you here to assist me. Focus on the assignment that you've been given. You are on that case at my invitation, never forget that!' He stalked off, furious.

Kadam shook his head wearily as he watched Rane go. Another relationship that he was jeopardizing. Everything he touched seemed to wither away.

Like Aryan.

87

Kadam rolled uneasily in his sleep. Beads of sweat appeared on his forehead and his face contorted in distress. Occasionally, he whimpered. One part of his brain told him that it was merely a nightmare, while another drew him deeper into his most terrible memories, blurring the distinction between dreams and reality, forcing him to relive the worst days of his life.

'Seriously sir. You're nothing like what I'd imagined.'

Kadam looked at the earnest young man sitting in his living room. Aryan Kamble was a rookie cop who had been recently assigned to Kadam's team. Fair and curly haired, he had a lithe physique. The day he had joined, Kadam had jokingly asked if he was really a cop or an actor preparing for a policeman's role.

'And what did you imagine I was like?' asked Kadam.

'Arrey, saheb, tumchi pratishtha aahey. You're a legend. But you are so approachable. I can't imagine another officer inviting a junior to drink whisky over a case discussion.'

'Here's what you must understand,' replied Kadam. 'I don't suffer fools, lazy chutiyas or corrupt chodus—and I treat them accordingly. Sincere, honest and hardworking people, I like. So far, I like you.'

'Thank you, sir,' said Aryan, smiling.

Kadam's phone rang. It was Sarla. 'Kaay chaalale?' he asked his wife.

'Ketul and I will be late. Don't wait up for dinner,' she said.

'Theek,' said Kadam.

'Not that it matters to you, but we're going to your mother's place for dinner,' said Sarla, obviously spoiling for a fight. 'She wanted you to join, but I told her that you have work.'

'Fine,' said Kadam.

'She's got a coral pendant made for Ketul,' said Sarla. 'Apparently, our daughter is manglik and needs something to counter any misfortune that might cause. But why should you care.'

Kadam took a deep breath. He was not going to get sucked into a fight. 'Anything else?' he asked mildly.

'It's like talking to a wall. You have absolutely no interest in what I say,' fumed Sarla, and hung up.

Kadam picked up his glass and drained it in one swallow. He grabbed the bottle of McDowell's No. 1 and poured a drink for himself and one for Aryan. 'Are you married, Aryan?' he asked.

'No, sir,' said Aryan promptly, a horrified look on his face.

Kadam laughed. 'You're smarter than I thought,' he said. 'Girlfriend?'

Aryan shook his head.

'Come on! A good-looking guy like you? Women must be falling all over you.'

'Maybe I just haven't met the right person yet,' said Aryan.

Kadam finished his drink and made himself another. He was starting to feel pleasantly buzzed. 'Right, enough personal talk. Let's get to work.' He sat down beside Aryan on the sofa., 'Just set out all the photos on the coffee table. Let's review all of them.'

Aryan nodded and pulled out a file from a leather bag lying on the floor next to the sofa. As Kadam reviewed the pictures, he spotted a detail in the background he hadn't noticed before. 'What's that?' he asked. Both of them leaned forward to take a closer look and suddenly found themselves face to face. They sat like that for a few moments, then Aryan slowly cupped Kadam's face in his palms and drew him closer. Kadam made no move no stop him.

An hour later, they were lying on the floor, spent, their clothes crumpled in a pile. In their frenzy, they hadn't even made it to the bedroom.

'Was that your first time with a man?' Aryan asked Kadam.

'There was some experimentation as a boy. But that was years ago. I had never thought about being with a man. I ... I'd never thought I could. The world I grew up in ... This ... us ... It's just not done.'

Aryan nodded in understanding.

Kadam sighed. 'Sarla and I haven't been intimate in a long time. We're trapped in a loveless, sexless marriage.'

'That's sad.'

'Couples drift along because of society. Sometimes people are forced into situations beyond their control. I wish I'd understood the way I was before I married Sarla. Actually, I wish I'd known many things before marriage.'

'Like what?'

'Like the fact that Bhau Patil is her half-brother,' Kadam blurted, unable to hide the bitterness in his voice.

'The don-turned-MLA!'

Kadam nodded. Before he realized it, the words were tumbling out of his mouth, as if he needed to get the story off his chest. 'Patil's father—Gulabrao—was from a small village called Khadke. He left behind a wife and son in the village and came to Mumbai to make his fortune in crime. Here, he had an affair with a nurse. They met when he was injured during a shootout and ended up in hospital for a bit. A daughter was born to them, Sarla. Now Gulabrao had a wife and son in the village—and another wife and a daughter in Mumbai.'

'Two wives?'

'Yes. Neither family knew about the other. Then, one day, fed up with Gulabrao's life of crime, Sarla's mother walked out with her. She told Sarla that her father had died in a car accident and brought her up independently.'

Kadam took a deep breath. A part of him was still reeling from the events of the evening. Something seemed to have shifted between them. He had never spoken about his life to anyone, yet there was something about the way Aryan was with him—attentive, interested—that made him comfortable, enough to unburden himself. 'Gulabrao brought his son to Mumbai and groomed him to take over. That was Bhau Patil. When Sarla and I got married, she had no idea of the existence of a father or half-brother.'

'Then it's not really her fault.'

'Bhau Patil is a madarchod. He got his men to poke around and eventually managed to reach Sarla. Then he tried to use her to get to me.'

'What did you do?'

'I made her promise that she would never see Patil again,' said Kadam. 'I've seen what happens to cops who are bought over by Patil. They're treated no better than bhadwas. His political career is just a front for his real businesses: girls and drugs.'

'You can't hold that against your wife,' observed Aryan.

'Barobar,' said Kadam. 'She's kept her word and stayed away from Patil. But the fact that she's related to him has definitely come between us.'

'You sound like two good people trapped in a bad situation.'

'We lead separate lives under the same roof ... It gets lonely.'

'You don't have to be lonely anymore,' said Aryan, playing with Kadam's hair.

The two men were so engrossed in each other that they did not notice Sarla standing in the doorway, frozen.

88

Furious and bitter with Kadam, Sarla stormed out of the house.

'I thought I'd surprise him—a quiet evening together to resolve our differences,' she said between sobs as she narrated her story to her half-brother. 'I left Ketul with my mother-in-law and went back home. Baap rey, I was the one who got a shock. He has ruined my life. I gave him my best years. I was a dutiful wife, a loving mother and an obedient daughter-in-law. I even stayed away from my own family because of his wishes. I accepted a loveless marriage for years. And then he cheats on me ... in my own house ... that too with a man!'

Bhau Patil waited patiently for her tears to subside, then handed her a glass of water. Sarla nodded gratefully and sipped from it.

'What do you want to do now?' asked Patil as she wiped her face with a tissue.

'I want to go far away from here. I never want to see his face again,' she spat. 'My mother walked out on our father. My turn now. Looks like it runs in the family.' Sarla laughed bitterly at the thought.

'That's easily arranged,' said Patil, spitting out his paan. 'Would you like to take your daughter with you? You don't have to worry about money. I'll take care of both of you.'

Sarla pondered on it and then shook her head. 'No. Ketul adores her father. She'll be unhappy away from him. I want to disappear from his life completely, but I won't be able to do that if she's with me. Let her stay with him. Besides, she's an adult now.'

'Are you sure?'

'I'm done living for other people.'

'Fine,' said Patil, stuffing another paan into his mouth. 'But tell me, Sarla. Do you want me to teach this chhakka a lesson? You can be honest with me. I'm your own blood, after all.'

Sarla nodded slowly, her eyes filling with hate. 'Yes,' she whispered. 'I want him to suffer, just like he's made me suffer.'

Bhau Patil rose to his feet. 'Consider it done,' he said. 'Now, I have a friend in Gorai. Go stay at his commune. Kadam will never know. You will be fully protected and looked after. You'll be safe there.'

After Sarla left, Patil summoned Deva. 'That fifty-fifty harassed my father and me. Now, he has ruined my sister's life. He needs to pay.'

'Just say the word, saheb. I'll break his neck like a murga,' Deva said, making a wringing motion with his hands.

'Killing him is too easy,' said Patil. 'I want the madarchod to live a life that's worse than hell.' His eyes gleamed with sadistic delight as a thought struck him. 'Let's start with that pretty boyfriend of his.'

What followed would haunt Kadam forever. Every little detail would replay in his nightmares.

In his dreams, the room was always freezing, but Kadam could feel the sweat running down his face and stinging his eyes. He blinked furiously and look around, his heart tightening in dread.

He was inside a cold storage facility near the Deonar abattoir, once the largest slaughterhouse in Asia. Huge carcasses hung from massive hooks. The distinctive smell of meat lingered in the air. He found himself struggling to breathe. He coughed, trying to clear his lungs. 'Aryan,' he called out. 'Aryan, are you here?'

There was no response. Kadam felt his vision blur. His eyes were bloodshot and aching from lack of sleep. He rubbed them and tried to focus. He had not slept the night before, searching instead for Sarla, who seemed to have vanished off the face of the earth. Then he had received an urgent call from the police control room. A shopkeeper had reported an accident: a van had crashed into a motorcyclist. It was Aryan. As he lay dazed on the ground, some hooded men had dragged him into the van and driven away.

Kadam had frantically organized a search, which had brought him to the abattoir. In his haste to get there, Kadam had raced ahead of the rest of the party and entered the building alone.

'Aryan?' he called out again.

There was a faint sound from deep within the refrigerated room. Kadam pulled out his revolver and moved cautiously towards it, his nerves on edge.

'P—p—please, please,' a voice whimpered.

Aryan came into view. He was completely naked and tied to a wooden chair with duct tape. It was impossible to discern his features because he had been beaten black and blue. His muscled body had deep bruises. Both his eyes were swollen shut and blood trickled from his split lips. His body and hair were caked in sweat and blood.

'Please,' he whispered. 'S—s—save me.'

Kadam rushed towards Aryan, all caution forgotten. 'Fuck! You're in bad shape. Who did this to you?'

Aryan frantically shook his head, indicating that Kadam should look behind him. Kadam whipped around just in the nick of time. A bullet rang out; the sound deafening in the enclosed space. It grazed Kadam's face, just under his left ear, and sent pain searing through him. Kadam grunted, then instinctively fired back in the direction of the sound. The shooter let out a loud curse as the bullet hit home and he dropped his weapon. Kadam took cover, wiping away the blood from the gash on his face. He strained his ears and heard footsteps running away. There seemed to be two pairs of feet.

Kadam had a split second to make a decision. He could either rush Aryan to hospital or chase the attackers. He turned towards Aryan, but at the sight of the young man's battered and bloodied frame anger surged through him. *I will not let those madarchods get away.* He ran after the retreating footsteps.

As Kadam raced around a bend in the corridor, he saw Deva, Patil's henchman, struggling to unlock the rear exit, hampered by a right arm that was bleeding profusely. Kadam stopped and pointed his gun at him. 'Your game is over, Deva,' he said. Deva let out an exaggerated sigh and raised his hands, taking his time. Kadam stared at him, wondering what the man was playing at. Then he remembered. There were two of them!

Kadam turned around just as a burly man lunged at his neck, meat cleaver in hand. Kadam instinctively raised his left hand in a bid to save himself. The sharp knife cut through his index finger as though it were butter. Kadam howled in pain and pumped bullets into his assailant's body. The man slumped to the ground.

Kadam's severed finger was lying on the floor, but he ignored it and turned to face Deva.

'Your pretty little gaandu boyfriend wailed like a bhosada when I broke his teeth,' Deva taunted him. 'I did it for you. With no teeth, he can blow better now.'

Kadam's jaw tightened. He raised his right arm and pointed the revolver squarely at Deva's chest.

'Go ahead. Shoot me. That's all that a chhakka like you is capable of. Sad that I won't get to die at the hands of a real man.'

'I'm more man than you ever will be,' hissed Kadam through clenched teeth. 'And so is Aryan.'

'Ho kaa?' sneered Deva. 'Then let's settle this the old-fashioned way.'

He's setting you up—don't take his bait, said a small voice inside Kadam's head. But it didn't stand a chance against the anger raging inside him.

89

'Fine. We'll do it your way,' said Kadam. He dropped the revolver to the ground.

Deva charged at him like a bull. Kadam let him come close, then planted a punch on his jaw. It was perfectly timed and would have knocked out an ordinary man. Deva swayed briefly, then shook his head as though clearing it. Feet planted firmly on the ground, he gave Kadam a mocking smile. 'Is that the best you can do?'

He zipped forward and wrapped his arms around Kadam's lower back, hoisting him off the ground. Then he began squeezing hard. His strength, in spite of his injury, was remarkable. Kadam winced, pain shooting through his spine and ribs. Deva would crush his spine if left unchecked. Kadam rained blows on Deva's head, but the ox ignored them and tightened his hold further.

Kadam's eyelids flickered. He started to lose consciousness. He put his hands on Deva's arms and tried to unlock his iron grip. His fingers touched something sticky: Deva's wounded right arm, which was bleeding freely. He dug deep into the wound with his nails. Deva bellowed in pain and loosened his grip. Kadam continued clawing at the wound savagely, until Deva abruptly released him and staggered back. His eyes fell on a carving knife lying on one of the shelves. He hefted it, grinning evilly. Kadam picked up the meat cleaver that Deva's accomplice had dropped. The two men circled each other warily. Deva's eyes flickered towards the ground near Kadam's feet. There was a large patch of blood on the ground. Kadam realized that Deva was hoping he would slip on it. He moved closer to it, and then feigned slipping. Deva fell into the trap. He rushed forward, arm drawn back to strike. But Kadam struck first. His cleaver whipped out, lightning-fast. It struck Deva's right arm just above the wrist, slicing through layers of muscle, bone and tendon.

Deva howled in agony and fell to his knees, blood spurting from his ghastly wound. Kadam loomed over him in triumph. The sight of his foe's distress filled him with savage exultation. He began to laugh, slowly at first, then louder and louder. His maniacal laughter echoed through the abattoir.

'You're done, Deva,' said Kadam.

'Go to hell, laundebaaz,' Deva spat, writhing in agony.

'You're going there first,' said Kadam. He raised the blade to finish him off, when, out of the blue, he felt a blow to the back of his head before someone pushed him. As he fell to the ground, a man jumped on top of him, pinning him down.

'Deva, run,' shouted the man, wrapping an iron hand around Kadam's neck and squeezing. Kadam struggled to free himself from the man's vice-like grip, but was unable to. Abruptly, the fight went out of him and he blacked out.

For the next few minutes, Kadam drifted in and out of consciousness. He detected blurry shapes a few feet from him, but could not tell who this new accomplice was.

The new entrant was telling Deva. 'I'm Bhau's man on the force. A police party is on the way. Chala patkan jauyaa … Let's get you out of here.'

'Kadam… kill him… won't leave him,' said Deva thickly.

'The search party will be here any minute. We must go, right now.' The man grunted as he hoisted Deva to his feet and half dragged, half carried him towards the rear. They had just reached the door when shouts echoed across the abattoir.

The police party had finally arrived. Kadam struggled to sit up. 'Over here!' he croaked. 'Deva's getting away!'

Moments later, several policemen came running to where Kadam lay. 'The rear exit. Deva went out that way,' he pointed. Some men raced to the door and tried to open it, but it would not budge.

'He's bolted it from the outside,' said one of them. There were groans of frustration as they heard a vehicle racing away.

A constable bent over Kadam and examined his wounds. 'You're injured. We'd better get you to a doctor,' he said.

Kadam's left index finger was gone, the bullet wound had left his face bloody and Deva had all but crushed his torso, making every breath painful. But Kadam only said, 'Aryan ... We need to get Aryan medical care.'

He fumbled as he stood up, picking up the meat cleaver in his haste instead of his gun. He was about to walk away, when his eyes fell on a strip of tablets on the floor. Even in his battered state, his investigative instincts kicked in and he stooped to examine it. 'Sir!' someone called just then. Kadam dragged himself over towards the voice, wincing in pain as he moved. The sight before his eyes hit him harder than a physical blow. Aryan was still tied to the chair, his head drooping forward. A policeman was trying to find a pulse, but he gave up after a few seconds. He sighed and straightened up, shaking his head. 'It's too late,' he said.

Kadam was in a daze. *I should have taken him to hospital instead of going after Deva. I am the real benchod here*, he thought. Kadam's despair breached the dam. Cleaver in hand, he began laughing manically, until, moments later, laughter gave way to uncontrollable sobs. A senior officer put his hand on Kadam's shoulder, trying to console him. Kadam brushed his hand away. 'It's my fault, no one else's,' he repeated, tears streaming down his eyes. 'I killed Aryan. I am a killer.'

'Baba,' said the officer. For some reason, he had a woman's voice. 'Baba, wake up.'

'I am a killer,' Kadam shouted angrily.

He opened his eyes and found himself staring at Ketul's anxious face. His heart was hammering. His throat was parched. His vest was soaked with sweat, as though he been swimming in it.

'Baba, it's okay. I'm here,' said Ketul, stroking his brow gently.

Kadam wrapped his arms around his daughter. His shoulders shook as he wept, the pent-up guilt of years pouring out of him.

Saturday, 21 March, around 9.30 a.m., Bandra West, Mumbai

Vincent D'Souza yawned as he looked at the wall clock in the bedroom. His wife, Shania, had let him oversleep. Not that he minded. Sleeping in was one of the few benefits of being a retired bank official. At seventy-two, apart from being stone deaf without his hearing aid, Vincent was in good shape, thanks to Shania who dragged him out to the nearby Bandstand Promenade for a walk on most days.

He smiled fondly as his gaze fell on a picture from their wedding kept on his bedside table. They had been married for almost forty years. The sepia-toned picture showed the couple standing outside Mount Mary Basilica in Bandra, surrounded by family and friends. Shania had added on a few kilos since. And, in the last few years, she had started allowing a few strands of grey to peep through her mane of dyed brown hair. But she remained just as energetic and spirited as the pretty young thing he had successfully courted and wed all those decades ago.

On Saturday mornings, while Vincent slept, Shania would go to the farmer's market in the MHADA ground. She could happily spend her entire morning haggling with sellers. They had all known her for years and adored her, as did the children she tutored. *Some poor fellow must be at the receiving end of hard bargaining today*, thought Vincent as he headed to the bathroom.

He emerged half an hour later, put on his hearing aid and decided to get the kettle going so that he could have tea with Shania once she returned. He had barely stepped out of the bedroom when he saw a sight that would remain etched in his memory forever.

91

'Shania D'Souza. Female. Age sixty-four. Married forty years. One child, a son, aged thirty-five, settled in Australia. Estimated time of death, around 9.30 a.m. All the usual elements: no sign of a break-in, blue discolouration of skin with faint smell of pest spray, Finek knife lodged in the heart, bloody arc, victim's hands tied with nylon rope—this time black—and mouth stuffed with food. Kaala til—black sesame.'

Kadam nodded grimly as Shinde finished reciting the facts. 'Theek. And you say the husband was present in the flat when the murder happened?'

'To mhanato … he was asleep in the bedroom. He's quite deaf and didn't hear anything. We've spoken to his audiologist. His story checks out,' said Shinde. 'We've also spoken to the neighbours. Well-liked couple, friendly and hospitable. The old man is completely shattered.' He looked over at Vincent, who was sitting slumped in a corner. Every now and then, he would start shaking uncontrollably and burst into fresh tears. A constable was trying to calm him down.

Kadam grunted, scratching his stubble. 'Still doesn't rule him out as a suspect. Everybody knows about the modus operandi of the nylon-rope killer by now. The old man could have bumped off his wife and conveniently planted evidence to make it look like a serial-killer job.'

Shinde looked at Kadam in disbelief. How could someone be so suspicious of everyone? 'Theek, but as you yourself said, our killer strikes every eight days,' said Shinde. 'Well, today is the eighth day since the attempt on Divya Shukrapani. No other crime that fits the pattern has been reported. And how would Vincent D'Souza know of the eight-day pattern? That information has not been made public.'

Kadam nodded. *Shinde may be an untrustworthy ass-licker, but he's not dumb*, he thought grudgingly. 'And does the husband have alibis for the other murders?' he asked.

Shinde raised his eyebrows. 'You seriously think Vincent could be our serial killer?'

'I don't assume anything,' said Kadam. 'Let's eliminate every possibility, no matter how ridiculous.'

Shinde nodded. 'I'll get it checked out.'

Kadam shifted his focus back to the body. 'A black rope this time,' he muttered. 'The killer has used a whole goddamn rainbow of ropes—gold, silver, red, green, yellow, white, black. And a pantry of food items—wheat, rice, tuar dal, moong beans, chickpeas, kidney beans and now sesame seeds.' He rattled off the entire list of colours and foods in perfect order, without once needing to refer to his notes. He smiled grimly; at least his brain was still working fine, even if nothing else in his body was.

Kadam did a slow recce of the crime scene to see if he could find any clues. After satisfying himself that the examiner had not missed anything, he took out his diary and quickly drew a rough sketch of the position and angle at which the body was placed.

Shinde walked back to him. 'The neighbours had gone out for a movie on Friday evening when Divya Shukrapani was attacked. They had left their six-year-old daughter with the couple.'

'Seems like a solid alibi,' said Kadam. 'I think we've got everything we're going to get from here. No, wait … I'm missing something.' He frowned in concentration. 'Ho. I had asked you to get the dustbins of all the victims checked. Did you get that done?'

Shinde nodded.

'Anything in common?' asked Kadam.

'Packaging material discarded in each location.'

'Right, so let's see if there's packaging materi—' He was interrupted by the sound of Shinde's phone.

Shinde took the call and his face fell. 'What? When? How did it happen?'

'Bad news?' asked Kadam when Shinde hung up.

'Divya Shukrapani just died, without ever coming out of her

coma. The only person who could have given us a lead to the identity of the killer is dead.'

'Fuck!' said Kadam heavily.

The policewoman whom Shinde had sent to the neighbours' flat came up to them just then. There was an excited look on her face. 'Saheb, I have some news.'

'What?' asked Shinde.

'The neighbour's six-year-old daughter was playing near the entrance to their flat around 9.30 a.m. The wooden main door was open, so she would have had a clear view of the D'Souza flat through the outer grill door.'

'Barobar, but did she see anyone?' asked Kadam impatiently.

'Unfortunately, the child seems to have gone into shock. She's not saying anything at all.'

92

'What's your name, beta? Don't be scared. Talk to us.'

Shinde tried his sweetest tone, but it didn't work. The little girl burrowed deeper into her mother's lap, her mouth resolutely shut. Eyes wide, she stared suspiciously at the strangers who had invaded her home.

Kadam felt a sense of déjà vu as he looked at her. She reminded him of how Ketul used to be when Sarla and he fought. Ketul would withdraw into her shell, refusing to talk to anyone. Sarla would then lose her temper and storm off, while Kadam would be left hugging his daughter. He glanced around the apartment. Several sketches of stick figures were pinned on a cork board. They had obviously been drawn by the child.

'What beautiful drawings,' said Kadam, addressing the mother and pointedly ignoring the child. 'Did your daughter make these?'

The mother nodded. The child looked up at Kadam, a spark of interest in her eyes.

'She's an excellent artist!' exclaimed Kadam. 'What's her name, if I may ask?'

'Aditi,' replied the mother.

'I see. And does Aditi like chocolate?' continued Kadam.

The mother frowned. 'Yes, but she's only allowed to have it on special occasions.'

'Well, I'm sure you'll make an exception if she makes a drawing for me. Would you like that, Aditi?' The child nodded, but didn't speak.

'Could you please get some paper and crayons?' Kadam asked Aditi. The girl rose, went into her room, and returned with a Hello Kitty satchel containing her art supplies. Kadam smiled at her. Then he summoned one of the constables and handed him some cash. 'Please get an Amul milk chocolate for Aditi. Kripya lawkar.'

He sat down next to the child. 'Why don't you draw something that makes you happy?' he suggested. Aditi got to work and drew a fish. Kadam smiled encouragingly. 'Very nice, Aditi. Now tell me, do you have any friends? Would you like to draw them?' Aditi nodded and made a drawing of lots of children holding hands while standing in a circle. The chocolate arrived and Kadam gave it to her. The little girl's eyes lit up as she tore open the wrapper, broke off a piece and put it in her mouth with a smile.

Kadam looked at her approvingly. His gut told him she was ready. Very gently, he asked, 'Would you like to draw the person you saw in the morning?'

Aditi gave him a long look while Kadam held his breath. Then she bent over the paper hesitantly and began drawing.

Kadam tried to look over her shoulder, but Aditi frowned and covered the paper with her hand. He hastily apologized. 'See, Aditi, I'm looking away. Please continue.'

Kadam got up and walked around the room for a while. Aditi remained focused on the chocolate and her drawing. After a while, she straightened up, looked at the paper and nodded in satisfaction. She beckoned to Kadam and handed the sheet to him. She still hadn't uttered a word. Shinde rushed to his side and peered over his shoulder. Aditi had drawn a stick figure with a blue cap and a bag.

'That could be almost anyone,' Shinde said as soon as he and Kadam left the apartment.

'That's all we're going to get from her. Let's see what's the best use we can make of this information. At least she corroborated that the killer wears blue.'

As they neared their vehicle, Kadam suddenly halted. 'What CCTV footage do we have from the various murder locations?'

'We have footage from two locations. A single CCTV camera was operating in the lift lobby of Suchandra Agarwal's building. But the lens was dirty and the picture quality is grainy.

Plus, there's no way of telling who went or came from which flat.'

'I see. And what about the other location?' asked Kadam.

'Gururaj Advani's home. There were CCTV systems on each floor and they retained the feed for seventy-two hours,' said Shinde.

'Good,' said Kadam. 'Aditi's drawing may not have told us much, but it did confirm some important details. Ask your team to look through every frame of both CCTV feeds to see if they can spot someone wearing a blue cap and carrying a bag.'

Back at his flat, Kadam closed his eyes and mumbled, 'Okay, let's summarize whatever we know about the killer so far.' He began listing the points as they occurred to him. Shinde noted them on the whiteboard with a marker.

— THE KILLER HAS UPPER-BODY STRENGTH TO STAB THE VENTRICLE

— PROBABLY LEFT-HANDED

— WEARS BLUE, INCLUDING A CAP, AND CARRIES A BAG

— KNOWN TO THE VICTIMS OR IN SUCH PROFESSION THAT VICTIMS PERMIT ACCESS

— MURDERS TAKE PLACE EVERY EIGHTH DAY

— THE KILLER IS GOOD WITH ROPE KNOTS

— HAS ACCESS TO NYLON ROPE AND FINEK KNIVES — COMPANY BELONGS TO LOKHANDE

— STUNS VICTIMS WITH COCKROACH-KILLER SPRAY, TIES THEM, THEN KILLS

'Any other points that we're missing?' asked Shinde.

'Well, the killer's operational area is not limited by geography. The murders are across Mumbai. So, we can assume that the killer lives in Mumbai, but has easy access to public or private transport,' said Kadam. Shinde jotted it down.

'One thing,' said Kadam, running a finger along his scar. 'The killer operates only during the daytime. None of the murders took place late at night.'

'What about the first one? Ravi Mehra?' argued Shinde.

'His wife found his body late at night, but the murder had taken place a few hours before that,' countered Kadam.

'Okay,' conceded Shinde.

Kadam put a cigarette between his lips and was about to light up when he took it out again. He puffed up one cheek as he slipped into thought. 'We know the when, where, who and how of each killing. But we don't know the why. That's the key to solving this puzzle. *Why* is the killer doing this?'

93

'Run, the police are here!'

Coughing and choking, Sarla stumbled through the corridors filled with tear gas. All around her, panic-stricken members of Momuma's commune ran helter-skelter. Many of them were in their underwear or pyjamas. After a long and uneasy siege, the special squad of the police had moved in without warning at around 4 a.m. Residents who were fast asleep were jolted awake by the raid. Chaos reigned as they tried to flee.

'Momuma! I must get to Momuma,' mumbled Sarla desperately. A stun grenade exploded nearby. Sarla screamed in fear, but the sound was drowned out by the thunderclap. The intense flash of the non-lethal grenade blinded her momentarily and she fell to her knees. When her vision gradually returned, she tried to stand up, but fell down again. The ringing in her ears eclipsed all other sounds. Sarla shook her head, trying to clear her senses. Instead, a wave of nausea hit her. She retched, but nothing came up. She lay flat on the ground and pressed her cheek to the cool floor. The urge to simply lie there and let events unfold around her was overwhelming, but she shook her head grimly. *Momuma needs you*, said a voice in her head.

Sarla crawled through the corridor on all fours, her eyes shut to avoid the tear gas. Luckily she knew the corridor like the back of her hand and turned left instinctively where it branched towards Momuma's suite. Suddenly, she felt strong hands lifting her up. She stiffened in fear, then relaxed as she recognized the familiar aroma of Momuma's cologne. 'Salaam, Momuma! Show me the light,' she pleaded with her eyes shut.

Momuma had found her! They were going to be fi—

'Let me go or the bitch dies.'

Sarla's eyes snapped open. Through her confusion, she realized that Momuma was holding a Finek knife to her throat and using her as a human shield.

Police commandos, clad in body armour and black gas masks, loomed out of the smoke like creatures from a nightmare. Momuma yelled to them, 'Back off now. And nobody will get hurt.' He kept the knife at Sarla's throat as he retreated, dragging her along.

'Momuma, what are you doing? It's me,' said Sarla, bewildered.

'Shut your mouth, whore. I know who you are.'

'Why are you doing this? Don't you love me?' asked Sarla, trying to make sense of what was happening.

'Love you?' spat Momuma scornfully. 'I only took you in because your madarchod brother was supposed to protect me. Now shut the fuck up and do what I say.'

Unbidden, tears pooled in Sarla's eyes and poured down her cheeks; her heart had been shattered yet again. In a daze, she lurched along as Momuma half pulled, half dragged her.

Momuma's attention was focused entirely on the cops in front of him. As a result, he did not notice a figure creeping up stealthily from behind until it was too late. A rifle butt smashed into the back of his head. Momuma groaned and slid to the floor. As he fell, his knife nicked the delicate skin of Sarla's throat. She felt a brief, sharp pain, followed by the warmth of blood trickling from her wound. But she made no effort to stop the flow. She stood there like a statue, staring into space, unblinking, unmoving.

At the other end of town, Ketul looked at the news alert on her phone.

'That raid at the Gorai complex certainly went well. A few broken bones, but no casualties. The police are actually being praised for once.' She looked up from her phone and glanced across the table at Kadam, who nodded and sipped his tea.

'Gaikwad has scored with this one,' continued Ketul. She turned to her phone again as more alerts came in. According to anonymous sources, the cabinet had been split on how to deal with the situation. Some ministers had suggested granting Momuma and his followers amnesty if they came out peacefully. But Deputy Home Minister Gaikwad had pushed for the raid. 'I wonder who these anonymous sources are. They seem to know everything,' Ketul mused. 'Oh hell!' she exclaimed suddenly as she chanced upon a photograph on X.

'Kaay jhaala?' asked Kadam, but she remained quiet. He got up from the sofa and walked over to her. As he peered over her shoulder at the phone, she quickly exited the app she had been browsing. The wallpaper was a picture of Nirmal.

'Shit!' she muttered, covering the phone with her hand.

Why don't you level with me that you like this boy, thought Kadam as he took the phone from her despite her protests, and opened her recent apps. He started to say something when the image on the screen caught his eye.

A blast from the past. Sarla. His brain went into overdrive. All these years, while misleading information about her was surfacing, had she really been in Momuma's Gorai commune?

Just then, Kadam's phone rang. 'Bola, Shinde, kaahi khabar?' he said, returning Ketul's phone to her and answering his own. 'What? When? Are you sure? Fine, I'm on my way.'

Ketul was still staring at the photograph of her mother. It was an eerie sensation. In some ways, Sarla's absence had been comforting. Kadam reached out and placed his hand on his daughter's shoulder. 'I wish I could stay and discuss this,' he said. 'But there's been another murder today—the seventh day after the last one. The killer has broken the eight-day pattern. I must go.'

Ketul nodded, still in a daze. 'I understand, Baba,' she said. As he reached the door, she called out, 'Baba?'

'Yes?'

'I'm grateful that you are my father.'

94

Saturday, 28 March, around 5 p.m., Chembur, Mumbai

'Rahul Singh. Sikh, seventy-one years old. Retired professor. Killed in his Chembur flat. Estimated time of death, 5 p.m. All the usual elements, but the rope was blue and his mouth has been stuffed with urad dal.'

Kadam massaged his temples to get rid of the dull ache that he was feeling. 'I'm getting sick of hearing the same details again and again. Any wife or family?'

Shinde shook his head. 'Widower for the last five years. There's a part-time fellow called Shyam who comes in for two hours every day to do the cooking and cleaning. Lives in the slum nearby. We've contacted him. He's on his way.'

Kadam walked over to the window and looked out. Towards his right was the Bombay Presidency Golf Club and on his left was St. Gregorios High School. Unimpressed by the view, Kadam scratched his stubble, wondering why the killer would break such a distinct pattern.

A constable brought in a thin, nervous-looking young man wearing an old shirt that was at least a couple of sizes too big for him. 'Tu Shyam aahes ka?' asked Shinde.

Shyam nodded. 'Ji, saheb,' he said, his voice barely a whisper.

'Louder, can't hear you,' said Shinde brusquely. 'And where did you get the shirt from?'

'Rahul sir would give me his old clothes,' replied Shyam.

'And this is how you repay him? By killing him?'

Shyam folded his hands. 'Naahin, saheb. He was like an uncle to me. I would never hurt him.'

'When did you see him last?'

'Baara bajey, saheb. I cleaned the house, and made enough food for his lunch and dinner.'

'And where were you around 5 p.m.?'

'I work in four homes in this colony. I was at Jayalakshmi Society, ten minutes from here, making dinner.'

Shinde nodded at the constable. 'Gaitonde, tithey ja. Check out his story.' He looked at Kadam expectantly.

Kadam asked, 'Can you read and write, Shyam?'

'Ho, saheb. I passed class eight.'

'Barobar,' said Kadam, handing him a sheet of paper. 'Write out a statement describing what you did the whole day.' He observed Shyam closely as he complied. Once the young man had finished, he took the paper from him. 'Chalo, go now. But don't leave town.' As Shyam left, Kadam cursorily glanced at the written statement, folded it and put it in his pocket.

'Aren't you going to read what he wrote?' asked Shinde. 'What was the point of that?'

'I just needed to check which hand he used,' said Kadam. 'He wrote with his right hand. Our killer is left-handed. In any case, I think our killer has more upper-body strength than the skinny guy we just saw.'

Shinde punched his fist into his palm in frustration. 'Will we ever make any progress?'

'If anything, we seem to be heading backwards. We knew that the killer struck every eighth day. The last killing was on a Saturday, so the next one should have been on a Sunday. But Rahul Singh is killed on a Saturday, just like Shania D'Souza. My poker straight flush pattern just got destroyed.'

'Your what-flush pattern?' asked Shinde.

Kadam waved his hand dismissively. 'Leave it. Let's focus on what we can do. Has your team made any headway at all on the footage from the other sites?'

'Let me find out,' said Shinde, pulling out his phone. He made a call. After a brief conversation, he nodded in satisfaction and turned to Kadam. 'They've managed to find faces that match the criteria of someone wearing a cap and carrying a bag. Shall we go have a look?'

The two men braved crazy traffic as they drove to the Crime Branch headquarters. As soon as they reached, a member of Shinde's team stepped forward with a folder. 'We froze the frames wherever the pictures were clearest and took enlarged printouts,' he explained. 'They're still grainy, but at least one can see the person's features. There are five people in all. Three are from Suchandra Agarwal's apartment complex. Two are from Gururaj Advani's.'

'Anyone present at both places?' asked Kadam.

The inspector shook his head. Shinde and Kadam exchanged disappointed glances.

'The killer could be two or more people working together,' said Kadam. 'Maybe they take turns? Let's not rule out any possibilities.' He gestured for the folder and examined the printouts, one by one. The location, date and time was neatly written below each picture. 'We should identify each of these people,' said Kadam. 'Find out who they are and why they were in the area on those days—' He abruptly stopped speaking as he came to the last photo. It was of a person standing in the lobby of Gururaj Advani's building.

The man was wearing a blue shirt and black jeans, and his hair was covered with a cap. A backpack was slung on his broad shoulders, which seemed incongruous on his otherwise wiry frame. He was looking straight into the CCTV camera through his John Lennon–style glasses.

Nirmal.

95

Kadam heaved a weary sigh as he walked into his flat. He looked at the wall calendar. Tuesday, 31 March. It had been three days since he had concluded that Nirmal was a suspect in the Gururaj Advani murder case. Since then, he had been grappling with the dilemma of how to break the news to Ketul.

Kadam and Shinde had agreed that their immediate task was to identify all five suspects and bring them in for questioning. Kadam knew it would be better to inform Ketul before summoning Nirmal, but he put off the discussion when he learnt that Nirmal had left for a camping trip early on Sunday and was not expected till Wednesday. It was evident that Ketul had become extremely fond of Nirmal. Kadam was not looking forward to a conversation with her on the possibility of her boyfriend being a suspect in the case.

There was also another angle to consider. What if Ketul was tempted to warn Nirmal beforehand? If he was indeed involved, warning him would amount to aiding and abetting a criminal and impeding an investigation. That would mean serious consequences for both Ketul and Kadam. Usually, she was sensible and could be relied on to keep her counsel, but love could make people behave in strange ways. Kadam knew this first-hand.

He rubbed his scar absently. Too many thoughts were racing through his mind. To distract himself, he switched on the television. An episode of *Kaun Banega Crorepati* was on. He settled down to watch.

The question on the screen was related to Bollywood. An audio clip—a peppy 1970s number composed by Laxmikant–Pyarelal and sung by Kishore Kumar and Sulakshana Pandit—was played. Then Amitabh Bachchan spoke in his deep and resonant voice, 'Aap ka agla savaal. Identify the film from which this song has been taken. Your options are: A: *Nishana*; B: *Apnapan*; C: *Himmatwala*; D: *Mawaali*.'

The Caravan-addict in Kadam had no trouble answering the question. 'It's B: *Apnapan*,' he answered promptly. 'It is a 1977 movie starring Jeetendra.'

Unfortunately, the contestant's interest in Bollywood music did not equal Kadam's. He scratched his head, then asked, 'May I hear the song again, please?'

'Certainly,' said Bachchan. 'Computer ji, kripya gaana dobara baja dijiye.'

'Seriously?' scoffed Kadam, rolling his eyes. 'Chalo, I get to listen to Kishore.' As the song played, he hummed along.

Somvaar ko hum miley
We first met on Monday

Mangalwaar ko nayan
On Tuesday our eyes locked

Budh ko meri neend gayi
On Wednesday I lost sleep over you

Jhume raat ko chain
The next night I lost my serenity

Arrey shukar-shani kaate mushkil se
Friday and Saturday were impossible to get through

Aaj hai etwaar
And today is Sunday

Saat dinon mein ho gaya jaise saat janam ka pyaar...
In just seven days it feels like the love of seven lifetimes...

As the verse ended, Kadam sat up with a jerk, as though he had been given an electric shock. 'Saala chutiya,' he muttered, cursing himself. He had allowed himself to get trapped into thinking of eight-day patterns and successive days of the week. But what were the days of the week called in Hindi? *Somvaar. Mangalvaar. Budhvaar. Guruvaar. Shukravaar. Shanivaar. Ravivaar.* But where did those names come from? There was some astronomical basis to those names, right? Kadam wracked his brains, but, for once, even his formidable knowledge bank failed him. But, Kadam remembered, there was one person in the building who was a walking, talking encyclopaedia on astrology. *Could Desai be the killer after all?* There was only one way to find out. He got to his feet and switched off the television. He would have to eat humble pie and pay Desai a visit.

Desai scowled when he opened the door. 'You've got some nerve coming here,' he said to Kadam.

Kadam held up a quarter of brandy. He knew that the occasional brandy at night was one of the few indulgences Desai permitted himself. 'I've come to apologize from the bottom of my heart,' he said with as much sincerity as he could muster. 'And also to seek your help.'

Desai glared at Kadam, then shrugged. 'You're a bastard, Prakash. Luckily for you, I'm not. Come in.'

As Kadam entered Desai's home, the landline rang. 'Shut the door behind you,' said Desai as he strode to the phone. Placing the brandy on the coffee table in the living room, Kadam sauntered over to admire the framed Raja Ravi Varma print on the wall to his left. The print showed nine Hindu deities, each enclosed within a circle, floating in a sky-blue background.

While Kadam waited for Desai to finish his conversation, he overheard snatches of it. 'Malti, you will need to monitor your DVT closely,' Desai was saying. 'And no travelling until we can find a solution. Yes, I too miss you very much. But we can't take chances with your health. So, no flying to Mumbai—or anywhere for that matter.'

Kadam stared at Desai as the penny finally dropped. It all made sense now. The notes about chest pain, shortness of breath, coughing blood, pooling of blood, discolouration, pulmonary embolism … These were not the macabre jottings of a possible serial killer. Desai's daughter had DVT—deep vein thrombosis! It explained why she never travelled to Mumbai. Kadam had been wrong about him all along—so terribly wrong.

Desai hung up the phone and looked at Kadam quizzically as he settled into a sofa. 'Are you all right? You look as though you've been hit by lightning.'

'Mee khup moorkh aahey' sighed Kadam. 'I have a lot of apologizing to do to you, doctor sa'ab. I'll probably spend the rest of my life trying to make amends for my stupidity. But, right now, I need your expertise on a subject close to your heart.' He pointed at the Raja Ravi Varma artwork. 'What does this print symbolize?'

'Seriously? You've disrupted my evening to ask me silly questions?' snapped Desai.

'Humour me, doctor sa'ab,' said Kadam, ignoring Desai's irritation.

'These are the Navagrahas—the nine celestial bodies that rule our lives,' replied Desai eventually. 'Seven of them are the sun, the moon and five planets. The remaining two are the lunar nodes, Rahu and Ketu.'

'And these nine have some connection to days of the week, right?'

'Yes, Sunday is Ravivaar, named after Ravi, which is another name for the sun god, Surya,' replied Desai, his annoyance fading as he began expounding on his pet subject. 'Monday is Somvaar because of Soma, another name for the moon god, Chandra. Tuesday is Mangalvaar after Mars, or Mangal. Wednesday is Budhvaar because of Mercury, also known as Budh. Thursday is Guruvaar in honour of Jupiter, the "guru" of the devas. Friday is Shukravaar after Venus, or Shukra. Saturday is Shanivaar because of Saturn, called Shani … What's the matter? Why are you slapping your head?'

'Get me a paper and pen, please,' said Kadam. 'Make it fast!'

Grumbling, Desai brought over a loose sheet of paper and a pen. Kadam began jotting down notes, muttering furiously to himself.

— RAVI MEHRA — KILLED SUNDAY — DAY OF RAVI

— SUCHANDRA AGARWAL — KILLED MONDAY — DAY OF SOMA OR CHANDRA

— MANGALA SHAH — KILLED TUESDAY — DAY OF MANGAL

— LAKSHMI BUDHIRAJA — KILLED WEDNESDAY — DAY OF BUDH

— GURURAJ ADVANI — KILLED THURSDAY — DAY OF GURU

— DIVYA SHUKRAPANI — KILLED FRIDAY — DAY OF SHUKRA

— SHANIA D'SOUZA — KILLED SATURDAY — DAY OF SHANI

— RAHUL SINGH — KILLED SATURDAY — DAY OF NORTH LUNAR NODE RAHU

He sat back with a grunt, stroking his scar. He had been looking at the case all wrong. Could it be possible that the motive was something as random as the victim's name? Would the victims be alive today if they had had different names?

'Does this have something to do with the murder investigation that you dragged me into?' asked Desai, reading what Kadam had written over his shoulder.

'Very much so.' Kadam turned to face Desai as another thought struck him. 'Don't each of the Navagrahas have specific colours associated with them?'

'Absolutely,' said Desai, very much in his element now. 'Each celestial body has a colour, food and even a direction associated with it. Shall I tell—'

'Thamba, let me write it down,' said Kadam.

'Right,' said Desai. 'So, Ravi or Surya—the sun—is associated with the colour gold. The food connected to Surya is wheat. And, of course, Surya is linked to the east because of the sun rising in the east.'

Kadam scrambled to keep pace while Desai listed the elements. When they were done, Kadam looked at what he'd added below each victim's name.

— RAVI MEHRA — KILLED SUNDAY — DAY OF RAVI
GOLD ROPE. WHEAT IN MOUTH. HEAD ORIENTED EAST

— SUCHANDRA AGARWAL — KILLED MONDAY — DAY OF
SOMA OR CHANDRA
SILVER ROPE. RICE IN MOUTH. HEAD ORIENTED NORTH-
WEST

— MANGALA SHAH — KILLED TUESDAY — DAY OF
MANGAL
RED ROPE. TUAR DAL IN MOUTH. HEAD ORIENTED SOUTH

— LAKSHMI BUDHIRAJA — KILLED WEDNESDAY — DAY
OF BUDH
GREEN ROPE. MOONG DAL IN MOUTH. HEAD ORIENTED
NORTH

— GURURAJ ADVANI — KILLED THURSDAY — DAY OF
GURU
YELLOW ROPE. CHICKPEAS IN MOUTH. HEAD ORIENTED
NORTH-EAST

— DIVYA SHUKRAPANI — KILLED FRIDAY — DAY OF
SHUKRA
WHITE ROPE. KIDNEY BEANS HEAD ORIENTED SOUTH-
EAST

— *SHANIA D'SOUZA* — KILLED SATURDAY — DAY OF
SHANI
BLACK ROPE. SESAME IN MOUTH. HEAD ORIENTED WEST
— *RAHUL SINGH* — KILLED SATURDAY — DAY OF
NORTH LUNAR NODE RAHU
BLUE ROPE. URAD DAL IN MOUTH. HEAD ORIENTED
SOUTH-WEST

'Benchod!' muttered Kadam. 'That's why the nylon rope used in each case was a different colour! The rope colour was used to symbolically match the victim to the celestial body. So was the food stuffed in the mouths of the victims and the direction in which the body lay. Everything was done to match the particular Navagraha! That was the motive! Eight people lost their lives for no fault of theirs. The fault lay in their names—names that symbolized the stars.'

He shook his head sadly at the waste of eight innocent lives, then suddenly froze. 'Wait. There have been eight murders. But there are nine grahas ... That means there's still one more murder to go.'

Desai looked at Kadam's notes. 'Well, according to this, Ketu is the only Navagraha left. It is the south lunar node. The colour associated with Ketu is grey. Chana daal is the food. South-west direction, like Rahu. Both Mangal and Ketu are associated with Tuesday—'

'But that's today!' said Kadam. 'The killer may be striking even as we speak. And the victim will be someone whose name has Ketu in it ...' His voice trailed off. He stared at Desai, aghast.

The doctor seemed to have had the same notion as Kadam, for his eyes widened in shock.

There weren't too many people with 'Ketu' in their name.

96

'The number you have called is not reachable,' said the automated voice message as Kadam tried Ketul's number. He had been trying to reach her phone continuously, with no luck. He swore and raked his fingers through his hair, his mind conjuring up the most horrific scenarios possible.

'Prakash, calm down,' said Dr Desai. 'Let's try to think this through. Why don't you call the police for help?'

Kadam nodded, annoyed that in his agitation it hadn't occurred to him. He dialled Shinde's number.

'Hello, kaay jhaale?' asked Shinde.

'Shinde, I know our killer's motive. I'll explain later. But abhi, I need your help taabadtob. Ketul might be in danger,' said Kadam frantically.

'Have you tried calling her?'

'Her number is not reachable.'

'When and where did you see her last?'

'At home, this morning, just before she left for court.'

'If she's inside a courtroom, her phone may be switched off.'

'It's past working hours. She can't be in court.'

'Theek, you go to the court,' said Shinde. 'I'll meet you there. If Ketul is fine—as I'm sure she is—no more khaliphukat tension.'

'I'll see you there,' said Kadam, cutting the line.

'Let me know the moment you see Ketul,' said Desai, a worried expression on his face.

'Thanks for everything, doctor sa'ab. You're a good man,' said Kadam as he raced out of Desai's flat.

The drive to Dhobi Talao seemed to take forever. Kadam kept urging the cabbie to go faster, but the traffic near Chhatrapati Shivaji Terminus was horrendous. When he reached the Esplanade Court, Shinde was waiting near the entrance.

The men dispensed with pleasantries. 'Where do we start looking?' asked Shinde. 'Should we check the courtrooms or the library?'

Kadam thought for a minute. 'Ketul and her colleagues often hang out at a chai place nearby when they're not arguing a case. Let's see if she or her friends are there,' he said.

He led the way, walking much faster than usual. As soon as they entered the tea shop, Kadam spotted one of Ketul's friends, Shruti. He waved to her.

'Hello, Prakash Uncle. Long time since I saw you! Care to join us for some chai?' asked the young woman.

'Some other time, beta,' said Kadam. 'I'm trying to reach Ketul for some urgent work, but her phone is not reachable. Do you have any idea where she might be?'

'Oh? She left some time ago with Nirmal.'

'I thought Nirmal was out of town.'

'Yes, he was. But he returned a day early and came here to surprise Ketul. She was ekdum thrilled to see him. Nirmal was

acting a little strange, like he was nervous about something …'
Shruti giggled, then stopped when she saw Kadam's serious
expression. 'Arrey baba, I hope I haven't got Ketul in trouble.'

Kadam shook his head grimly. 'No, that's fine Shruti. Did
they say where they were going?'

Shruti shook her head. 'No. Umm … Uncle … is everything
all right?'

'I … I hope so …' said Kadam, spinning around and walking
over to Shinde. 'Nirmal came back early. Ketul left with him
some time ago.'

'Benchod!' said Shinde. 'Let's get a search going for them
fatafat. Give me their phone numbers. We'll try getting their
locations traced.'

But Kadam was far away, lost in thought. He was jolted out
of his reverie when Shinde put a hand on his shoulder.

'All the victims were killed inside their own homes,' said
Kadam softly. 'If Nirmal plans to harm my daughter, he will first
take her to our home.' The two men stared at each other for a
split second, then, without exchanging a word, they sprinted to
where Shinde's vehicle was parked.

'Get out of my way, gaandu!' snarled Shinde, almost running
over a pedestrian. He was driving as fast as he could, which,
in Mumbai's late evening traffic, was a risky proposition. He
almost caused three accidents. But he grimly kept his foot
pressed on the accelerator, only occasionally slamming on
the brakes.

Kadam didn't notice any of it. He continued trying to reach Ketul's number. A thousand 'what-if' scenarios were playing in his head. He berated himself for not analysing the CCTV feeds sooner. He cursed himself for not warning Ketul. Exasperated, he decided to try Nirmal's number instead. Perhaps a threat that he was on the way would frighten him off? But this call too went unanswered.

Kadam could feel panic and anger building up inside him. His heart was beating so rapidly, he felt as though his chest would explode. In his hurry, he had not even carried any Sorbitrate with him. He sucked in a few deep breaths. *Easy now*, he thought to himself. He wouldn't be able to help Ketul if he dropped dead from a heart attack.

Shinde brought the car to a screeching halt outside Kadam's building. Kadam opened the door, leapt out and rushed up the stairs. Though he was out of breath after the very first flight, waiting for the elevator—or for Shinde—was not an option. His phone fell out of his hand and shattered. He ignored it and continued.

The door to his flat was unlocked. Kadam barged in, his heart pounding. It took him a moment to realize that it was pitch dark. He tried the light switches, but they weren't working. Someone had cut the power.

He bumped into the living room sofa and halted, trying to catch his breath and get his bearings. He had barely taken a few steps in when he tripped over something and fell to the ground. A chill ran through him. Had he tripped over a body?

'Ketul! Ketul!' yelled Kadam, frantically scrambling on all fours and encountering a wet floor. The smell of Baygon spray filled his senses. Tears ran down his cheeks; he had let Ketul down, yet again. He was the worst father anyone could have asked for.

Suddenly, a beam of light zig-zagged around the room. Shinde had entered and sensibly switched on the torch of his phone. 'Over here! Point it this way,' shouted Kadam. As Shinde directed the beam towards him, Kadam looked down at the floor, fearing the worst. A wave of relief washed over him followed rapidly by a sense of puzzlement.

Nirmal was lying on the living room floor. His eyes were glazed and his face was drenched in sweat. He was gasping for breath, clutching his stomach where he had been stabbed.

97

Tuesday, 31 March, around 8 p.m., Matunga, Mumbai

Kadam stared at Nirmal, his mind racing and heart pounding. Wasn't Nirmal supposed to be the killer? Had he been injured while trying to commit murder? And where was Ketul?

'We need to stop the blood,' said Shinde, kneeling beside Nirmal. He looked around for something with which he could staunch the bleeding. He noticed the thin curtain that Kadam used to cordon off a semi-private sleeping space for himself in the living room. Quickly pulling it off the channel, Shinde bunched it together and pushed it down on Nirmal's wound. With his other hand, he called the police control room on his mobile phone. Call done, he handed over his phone to Kadam.

Kadam quickly pulled himself to his feet and checked the kitchen in the light from Shinde's phone. There was no sign of Ketul. That only left her bedroom. He hurried towards it, his legs feeling wobbly from anxiety. He threw open the door and stepped inside the cramped room. A hazy yellow glow streamed into the otherwise dark bedroom from an old sodium-vapour streetlight near the window. As his eyes adjusted, he saw Ketul lying on the floor near her folding bed. Her hands were bound behind her and her mouth was taped shut.

'Ketul! Tu theek aahes ka?' cried Kadam, rushing towards her. He was about to kneel beside her and untie her, when, in the dim light, he noticed her frantically shaking her head and rolling her eyes. It was evident that she was trying to tell him something.

It took Kadam mere seconds to process the scene. Nirmal was wounded—but alive. Ketul was tied up and helpless—but alive. A cloth bag lay next to Ketul with a few bottles and cans around it ... but no knife. Where was the knife? And then he realized how rash he had been. The killer had been unable to complete the job because ... *Kadam had interrupted him*. There was no knife to be seen because it was still in the killer's hands.

And the killer was in the room.

Even as Kadam realized his mistake, he sensed a movement behind him. He whirled around just as a figure leapt at him from a corner, bloody knife poised to strike. Kadam grabbed the killer's wrist in the nick of time, but the killer continued exerting force, attempting to push the knife into Kadam's chest. The two staggered around the room, straining against each other. The killer was shorter than Kadam, but incredibly strong.

Even as they struggled, Kadam's brain was working furiously. He noticed the embroidered logo of a speeding motorbike on the killer's blue jumper suit and cap. *That's it! Everyone opens doors for courier deliveries!* That's why they had found packaging material in dustbins at some crime scenes.

The killer grunted and pressed hard with his left hand, moving the knife closer to Kadam's chest. Kadam could feel his strength fading, while the killer seemed to be gaining strength. Kadam knew he would have to do something different to break the deadlock. He pulled his opponent towards him instead of pushing back, and sidestepped simultaneously. The killer lurched forward, caught off-balance. Kadam swung hard with his right hand, landing a blow on the killer's cheek. The assailant's cap fell off ... and *her* ponytail came loose. Their killer was a woman!

Kadam froze in shock. Sensing her opportunity, the woman lunged with her knife. Kadam stumbled backwards, tripping over a chair as he did so. He fell down flat on his back and lay there stunned. The woman quickly straddled Kadam's chest and raised her knife to strike. As Kadam looked into her eyes, he could sense her madness. So this was how he was going to meet his end—butchered by a psychopath.

All of a sudden, the lights came on in the room, and the next instant the woman let out a howl of pain. Shinde had come charging in and swung his fist at the woman's jaw, making perfect contact. Her eyes rolled back in her head and she keeled over, unconscious even before she hit the ground near Ketul's feet. Her knife slipped out of her hand and clattered noisily to the floor.

Ketul's eyes widened in astonishment as she got a good look at the person who had been trying to kill her. 'I know her!' she cried out when Shinde removed the tape over her mouth. 'She's Heena! She gave me a tour of the Shakti complex and was a witness in the trafficking case.'

Sweaty and panting, Kadam stared at the unconscious Heena. 'We'll only get answers once she wakes up,' he said. 'We should tie her up till then.' He looked around for something to use and his eyes fell on a bundle of rope inside Heena's bag. He quickly bound her limbs, grunting from the effort, as he fastened the knots securely.

Satisfied, he turned to Ketul, who was being untied by Shinde. 'Saala, where were you, Ketul?' he asked, relief mixing with anger. 'I kept trying your phone—again and again.'

'My phone drained while I was in court,' explained Ketul, rubbing her wrists. 'I was about to charge it when Nirmal arrived …' She broke off as she remembered Nirmal. 'Where is he?' she asked anxiously.

'He's in the living room,' said Shinde. 'I left him there when I went to turn on the main circuit breaker to get the lights working. I came rushing here when I heard the commotion.'

Ketul grabbed the phone and stumbled out to the dark living room. 'Oh no! Call an ambulance, quickly,' she yelled, going down on her knees next to Nirmal. She grabbed the bloody curtain and pressed it down on his wound. His skin was cold and clammy, and his eyes seemed to have sunk deeper into his face.

'Stay with me, baby,' Ketul said, her voice shaking. 'H—help is coming. I—I love you. Stay with me.'

'I've already called the control room,' said Shinde. 'They're sending an ambulance along with backup.'

Kadam frowned. 'The ambulance will take too long,' he said. 'Wait! We have a doctor living right next door.'

'You stay here. I'll get Desai,' said Shinde, rushing out the door.

'Baby, stay with me ... you stay ...' Ketul was weeping uncontrollably now.

Kadam sat down next to her. 'What happened after Nirmal came to meet you?' he asked gently.

'We—we went to Blue Tokai for c—coffee,' said Ketul, between sobs. 'He said that the camping trip had ... had cleared his mind. He told me ... He said he loved me. He was worried about telling me because of some of his k—kinks ...'

The door flew open and Desai came charging in with Shinde behind him. He rushed over to Nirmal and knelt next to him. He placed his index and middle fingers on Nirmal's neck to check the pulse from his carotid artery. He looked up at Kadam, shaking his head gently. 'He's gone,' he whispered.

Ketul flinched as though she had been struck. An anguished cry emerged from her, like that of a wounded animal. She continued sobbing as she touched her forehead to his.

'I know how much you loved me, Nirmal,' she whispered. 'I understand everything, baby ... everything. I'm sorry I brought you back here. Her knife was meant for me, not you ...' In her heart, she knew that her grandmother's concerns had come true. She was a manglik ... and she had destroyed the man who loved her.

Kadam gently stroked the back of Ketul's head, his heart breaking for his only child.

98

'Bhaagya badaltey hain yeh harami taare,' said Heena. 'Off karna padta hai.' These rogue planets determine our destinies, so they must be switched off. Heena's voice wavered slightly as she delivered that profound statement. But she sat upright, her posture almost in defiance of the burden that life had piled on her.

The interrogation room was stark, its walls painted in faded green. A harsh fluorescent tube light on the wall illuminated the cramped space and the laminate-topped table. Two metal chairs stood on either side of the table. A lone ceiling fan creaked above, attempting to alleviate the stifling heat. A camera in one corner allowed Rane and Kadam to observe from an adjacent room.

Ketul was also in the observation room. Rane had been concerned about allowing her to be present, particularly after the trauma she had just suffered, but she was determined. Finally, Rane had acquiesced. Kadam knew in his gut why Ketul had insisted. She was desperate to understand why she had lost Nirmal.

'Pehli baar main baarah saal ki thhee,' said Heena, describing the first time she had been raped. She was twelve. Ketul remembered hearing that during Heena's deposition before the magistrate.

'Where are you from?' asked Shinde.

'Village Alawanpur in Ballia district,' said Heena. 'Uttar Pradesh.'

'Kyaa hua tumhein?' asked Shinde.

'Baap ne panauti ko bech daala,' she said. She almost spat out the words, her hands quivering slightly. Her father had sold her off to a pimp to clear his debts. In any case, he had considered her panauti—bad luck. Neither her mother nor her brothers had attempted to intervene. Her ownership had changed hands and she had eventually reached Sonapur via Mirzapur and Bhiwandi. Heena had been beaten and starved for many days before she agreed to sell herself four or five times each day in the brothel.

'Phir?'

'You know the story,' said Heena, a flash of anger on her face. 'I was sent to a VIP's house where he used me. But I was able to escape. Phir Shakti ke paas pahunch gayi.'

Kadam had thought that it would take a while to crack Heena, but she seemed almost eager to share her terrible story with Shinde. He waved off a persistent fly as he continued observing the interrogation on the monitor.

'Which VIP?' asked Shinde.

Heena used her hand to wipe off a thin film of sweat from her forehead. 'It was Bhau Patil, that madarchod,' she said with an expression of disgust. 'I didn't know he was the gaandu who traded us girls from behind the scenes. And that policewalla Chavan was allowing drugs to come in using the very same trucks.'

Shinde squirmed uncomfortably in his chair. Chavan and Patil would not be happy to hear that their names had been mentioned on record.

'Par chalo, main lucky thi. I was saved by Shakti,' said Heena. 'I learnt to read and write. I built my strength and learnt martial arts. And then I became a courier for Shakti. But I felt gandi, like there was sewage on my skin. Sapnon mein, I saw my dead body floating in a gutter of shit. Kitna bhi naha lo, the dirt would not wash off. Main paagal ho gayi thi.'

'Then what happened?' asked Shinde.

'It was Founder's Day,' said Heena. 'One of the trustees spoke to me. He asked me if I needed spiritual guidance.'

'And?'

'I was introduced to Bhairavadas ji.'

In the observation room, Kadam and Rane looked at each other. Bhairavadas was a powerful man with even more influential friends.

'Why?' asked Shinde.

'Bhairavadas ji said that he would give me a ritual to get rid of the feeling of being unclean. He said the planets had cursed my life from the very beginning. I would have to propitiate them, offer sacrifices.'

Ketul was listening to Heena intently as she toyed with the coral pendant around her neck. She tugged, lightly at first. Then a little harder. The chain snapped and she caught the necklace in her hand. She looked at it as though she was seeing it for the first time. Here she was, a product of twenty-first-century Mumbai, and yet, she had been brainwashed by her grandmother into believing she was a manglik—someone who would be unlucky for her partner if his stars were not aligned with hers. How could she blame Heena?

Kadam saw the tears in his daughter's eyes and the pendant in her hand. He put an arm around her protectively.

'What sort of sacrifice?' continued Shinde inside the interrogation room.

'Each graha—Surya, Chandra, Mangal, Budh, Guru, Shukra, Shani, Rahu and Ketu—were to be made offerings on their specific days, unheen ke rang, food aur direction mein,' explained Heena.

'But why kill people?' asked Shinde.

'Tamasic tantra,' replied Heena, making the swishing gesture of a knife with her hand. 'Bhairavadas ji told me that simple Vedic rituals and prayers would not work. Bali…blood offering was needed. Each must be someone beloved of the planet. Who better than people with the grahas in their very names?'

'How did you locate your victims?'

'Delivery lists at the courier office,' she said. 'They were just names to me.'

'Even Ketul?'

Heena sighed. 'I wasn't happy about it. But sacrifices must be made. She did achcha kaam to help us, but for me wo bas ek naam thee.'

'That's all she was? A name?' retorted Shinde.

Heena slammed her fist down on the table hard, eyes burning with anger and hate. 'Tell me if you still care for anyone after you've been raped hundreds of time, madarchod.'

99

Shinde left Heena inside the interrogation room, and joined Kadam and Rane in the observation room. They played back the last part of the recorded interview.

'Where did you get the coloured nylon ropes?' Shinde was asking.

'They were used to bind parcels together at Shakti Couriers. The colour of rope denotes the pin codes to which the parcels are to be delivered. All the girls are trained to use packers' knots. It was easy to get free supply.'

'And the knives?'

'Buffer stock from Finek,' said Heena.

Kadam looked at her face on the screen. Had she just hesitated? Was she hiding something? He couldn't quite shake the feeling that something was off. He ignored it. What he couldn't ignore was the fly that was buzzing around his face.

'Why stab the heart? Easier to slit their throat if a person's hands are tied, no?' asked Shinde in the video.

'Bhairavadas ji told me that it is the heart that connects us to the universe,' shrugged Heena. 'I'm strong and my left hand is even stronger.'

Ketul remembered the time she had visited Shakti and Heena had performed one-handed acrobatics.

'The heart is towards one's left,' said Kadam. 'But that would mean the killer's right side. If Heena was using her left hand, her stab to the heart would hit the right side of the organ—the right ventricle of the heart.'

Kadam puffed his cheek out, deep in thought. 'One thing I cannot understand. Why did Heena not show up on CCTV? We had footage from Suchandra Agarwal's building and Gururaj Advani's home.'

'The team found someone who could be her—blue uniform, delivery bag and cap—in both cases,' explained Rane in his nasal voice. 'But in the first instance, the footage was too grainy. In the Advani footage, the person had deliberately kept their face lowered so that it wouldn't be captured on camera.'

'But why was Nirmal at Advani's building?' asked Shinde.

Ketul looked up sharply at her father. 'Was he a suspect too, Baba?' she asked Kadam, her eyes filling with tears at his silence. She looked at him accusingly. 'It was one of the things Nirmal and I spoke about on our way home. Gururaj was not just a playback singer but also an internet sensation. He had enlisted Nirmal's help to strengthen the security of his website. Nirmal visited him more than once.'

None of the men in the room—including her own father— could offer anything that would come close to an explanation. Rane broke the uncomfortable silence. He looked squarely at Shinde. 'The woman in custody has been psychologically traumatized into doing what she did. She's a minor pawn in this business. None of this would have happened if Bhau Patil was not running his flesh racket.'

Rane lowered his voice and said, 'Police Commissioner Chavan has looked the other way through all this. Time for you to decide which side you're on, Shinde.'

One corner of Shinde's mouth was twitching. He was nervous about being put on the spot. But his survival instinct was telling him that it was time to ditch Chavan.

Kadam picked up a magazine from a stack on the desk and swatted the fly that was pestering him. His gaze fell on an antacid advertisement on the rear cover. Something about that distinctive pink and blue packaging was vaguely familiar. Where had he seen that before?

And then he remembered. It was the night he had tried to save Aryan. He had seen the same pink and blue pack on the floor of the abattoir. But in his hurry to reach Aryan, he had left it lying on the floor. Suddenly, everything seemed crystal clear. The only person he knew who consumed those tablets regularly was the police commissioner! It was Chavan who had pulled Deva out to safety that night!

'I have an idea,' said Kadam, scratching his stubble.

'What?' asked Rane.

Kadam turned to Shinde. 'Remember that reporter you used to screw me over?'

Shinde looked away guiltily. 'Yes?'

'What if you give her exclusive access to Heena? It would be the biggest scoop of her career. More importantly, Bhau Patil and Chavan will be finished.'

Kadam's explanation was forestalled by the ringing of Rane's phone. Rane took the call and listened to the voice at the other end. A few seconds later, he hung up with a sigh and looked at Kadam. He took a deep breath. 'The call was from Gorai Police Station…'

'Kaay chaal le aahey?' asked Kadam.

'Someone managed to slip Sarla a knife while a group of cult members was being taken to court,' said Rane. 'As they got out of the van, there was chaos. She attacked Momuma during that confusion … Stabbed him to death and then fled. There's a lookout for her.'

Kadam remained quiet. He walked over to Ketul and hugged her, desperate for her to unhear what Rane had just told them. Yet, deep within, he knew that a fresh game had just begun.

100

'The swearing-in ceremony at Raj Bhavan, Mumbai, will commence shortly. A major shake-up in the state cabinet is expected following the sensational revelations made by the nylon-rope killer. Bhau Patil, who faces allegations of human trafficking and narcotics trade, may soon be expelled from the party. His absence could result in a paucity of funds for the ruling dispensation, given that he was a major contributor to the coffers.' The news anchor paused for a moment as he got an update, then resumed. 'Reliable sources have just informed us that Jayant Gaikwad, one of the few dynamic and efficient performers in this government, is set to be promoted to home minister in place of Omkar Lokhande. Gaikwad has been the deputy home minister for a while now and is an outspoken advocate for police reforms. Viewers will recall the tragic suicide of his son recently—'

At the bottom of the screen was a scrolling ticker that indicated that Finek Metals Ltd. was a takeover target owing to its share price having crashed. Kadam looked up as Rane walked into the reception area of the police headquarters, where he had been watching the news.

'Any leads on Sarla?' asked Kadam.

Rane shook his head. 'She's still missing,' he said in his nasal voice. 'But we know that Deva was with her. Bhau Patil is likely to be arrested soon. When that happens, we may have some leverage to reach them.'

Kadam scratched his beard. It was not a comfortable feeling to know that someone who hated him with a vengeance, the way Sarla did, was on the loose. His thoughts were interrupted by Rane. 'You can go and meet Heena now,' he said. 'I've had it arranged, though this is highly irregular. Why do you want to meet her anyway?'

'There's one small detail that's nagging me. I want to clear it up,' said Kadam.

Rane smiled. 'Saala chutiya, how much more will you dig? Anyway, just make it fast.'

Kadam nodded and entered the room where Heena was waiting. Somehow, the infamous nylon-rope killer seemed to have shrunk in just a few days. She had lost weight and there were dark circles under her eyes. Despite what she had done, Kadam couldn't help but feel a pang of sympathy for her.

'Maaf karo, Heena, par I need to ask you a question that's been on my mind,' began Kadam. Heena nodded, though her eyes remained averted. 'You said that you were asked by a trustee of Shakti to seek spiritual counselling, right? Who was it?'

Heena looked up at Kadam and stared at him, expressionless. He waited. The silence lengthened. Finally, assuming that he wasn't going to get an answer out of her, he rose to leave.

'It was Gaikwad ji ... Jayant Gaikwad.'

Kadam froze at Heena's words. 'Kya boli?' he said, leaning forward.

'It was Gaikwad ji. He suggested that I talk to Bhairavadas ji who would give me a solution.'

Kadam sat down again, his mind working furiously. Why not recommend a psychiatrist? Or a therapist? Why had Gaikwad been so interested in having Heena meet a tantric? He puffed out his cheek as he thought about it. Then, without saying a word, he rose, thanked Heena for her help and walked to the reception area. Rane was standing there, watching the news. Kadam glanced at the screen. Gaikwad was being sworn in as home minister.

'Ek minute,' said Kadam, tapping Rane on the shoulder. Rane looked at him quizzically, then walked with him to a quiet corner.

'Gaikwad set up the murders,' whispered Kadam. 'He used Bhairavadas to put the idea of a purification ritual in Heena's head. It was done to create panic in Mumbai and bring about his own promotion. Not only did he manage to get Bhau Patil expelled from the party, but he also ruined Finek's reputation—a company owned by Lokhande. Saala, even his son's so-called suicide was probably assisted—how did old-fashioned razor blades land up in the room of a kid who had an electric trimmer in his bathroom?'

Rane's eyes widened in shock. 'It will be Heena's word against his,' he said softly. 'The word of a girl who's clearly not mentally stable against that of the new home minister.'

Both men turned to the screen where the ceremony had concluded. Gaikwad was now addressing a press conference. 'Criminals have had a free run in this state, especially in Mumbai, for far too long. Starting today, all of that will change. I will revamp the entire police department to improve the law-and-order situation in the city. I have a clear goal: To make Mumbai one of the safest cities in the world,' said Gaikwad as bulbs flashed around him. His eyebrows were distinct and separate today.

'He's certainly making all the right noises,' said Rane in his nasal voice. 'Who knows, he may even deliver. Sometimes, one does bad things to achieve good things.'

Kadam looked at his friend closely.

'What?' asked Rane.

'Gopal Chavan's career is finished,' said Kadam, a hint of suspicion in his voice. 'I'm just wondering whether you taking over as the new police commissioner was part of the plan.'

'Surely you don't think…' began Rane. 'My elevation was pure luck.'

Kadam nodded slowly. Then he murmured something under his breath.

'What did you say?' asked Rane.

'Bhaagya badaltey hain yeh harami taare.'

Acknowledgements

My grateful thanks to Ananth Padmanabhan, Poulomi Chatterjee, Shatarupa Ghoshal, Anuj Bahri and Sharvani Pandit. Each one of them was invaluable in the journey of this series and story.

And, as always, I bow my head before Ma Shakti, the fount of all creative expression.

About the Author

Ashwin Sanghi is among India's highest-selling English fiction authors. He has written several bestsellers in the Bharat Series (*The Rozabal Line, Chanakya's Chant, The Krishna Key, The Sialkot Saga, Keepers of the Kalachakra, The Vault of Vishnu*, and *The Magicians of Mazda*) and two *New York Times* bestselling crime thrillers with James Patterson—*Private India* (sold in the US as *City on Fire*) and *Private Delhi* (sold in the US as *Count to Ten*). He has also co-authored several non-fiction titles in the 13 Steps Series on Luck, Wealth, Marks, Health and Parenting.

Ashwin has been included by *Forbes India* in their Celebrity 100 and by *The New Indian Express* in their Culture Power List. He is a winner of the Crossword Popular Choice Award 2012, Atta Galatta Popular Choice Award 2018, WBR Iconic Achievers Award 2018, the Lit-O-Fest Literature Legend Award 2018, the Kalinga Popular Choice Award 2021, and the Deendayal Upadhyaya Recognition 2023.

He was educated at Cathedral and John Connon School, Mumbai, and St Xavier's College, Mumbai. He holds an MBA from Yale University, USA, and a D. Litt. (Honoris Causa) from JECRC University, Rajasthan.

THE BHARAT SERIES
by
ASHWIN SANGHI

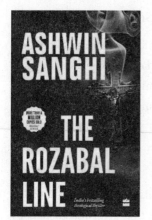

THE ROZABAL LINE

'Sanghi's flair for religion, history and politics is clearly visible as he takes the reader across the world spanning different decades. A mixture of comparative religion, dangerous secrets, and a thrilling plot makes for an esoteric read.'—*The Statesman*

'A provocative, clever and radiant line of theology, Sanghi suggests that the cult of Mary Magdalene has its true inspiration in the trinity of the Indian sacred feminine, thereby out-thinking and out-conspiring Dan Brown.'—*The Hindu*

CHANAKYA'S CHANT

'With internal monologues and descriptions as taut as a-held-by-the-thumb sacred thread, we have Ashwin Sanghi's cracker of a page-turner, *Chanakya's Chant*. Two narratives flow like the Ganga and Yamuna … a brisk technicoloured thriller.'—*Hindustan Times*

'A gripping, fast-paced read, the novel is a true thriller in the tradition set by Dan Brown.' —*People Magazine*

THE KRISHNA KEY

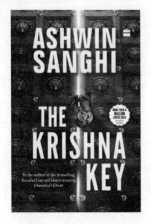

'Why should racy historical thrillers or meaty fantasy sagas come only from the minds of Western writers? Ashwin Sanghi spins his yarns well and leaves you breathless at every cliff-hanger. No wonder his books are bestsellers!'—*Hindustan Times*

'An alternative interpretation of the Vedic Age that will be relished by conspiracy buffs and addicts of thrillers alike.'—*The Hindu*

THE SIALKOT SAGA

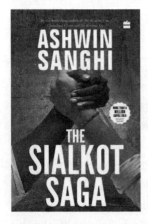

'There are books that take time to develop an interest and then there are books that grip you from the very first page. *The Sialkot Saga* is one such book that hooks you from the start.'—*Hindustan Times*

'There's never a dull moment in the book. In fact, the story takes on such a pace that the overwhelmed reader is compelled to put the book down and take a deep breath on many an occasion.'—*The Financial Express*

KEEPERS OF THE KALACHAKRA

'The author packs a powerful punch ... spicy and saucy, a survey of the past and the present ... without a dull moment, without a dull page.'
—*The Sunday Standard*

'Ashwin Sanghi's *Keepers of the Kalachakra* is as explosive as a time bomb ticking in your hand. Every chapter springs an unpredictable surprise.'—*Deccan Chronicle*

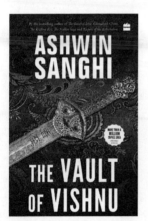

THE VAULT OF VISHNU

'As with all Ashwin's books, the research is meticulous and the technical(ese) leaves one gasping as *The Vault of Vishnu* takes the reader through the highs and lows of history, myth, physics, warfare technology, AI and biochemistry.'
—*The Times of India*

'Sanghi's latest work uses his favourite tool—mythology—and blends it with history to deliver some edge-of-the-seat action.'—*Hindustan Times*

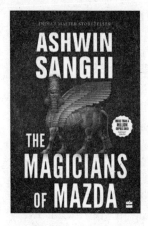

THE MAGICIANS OF MAZDA

'Ashwin Sanghi's *The Magicians of Mazda* is a gripping success story ... Complex and entertaining, informative and intelligently crafted, the latest novel in the Bharat series seamlessly merges fact with fiction.'
—*Hindustan Times*

'A great thriller ... The latest book in the Bharat series is a roller-coaster ride through history, with important lessons for the present times.'—*The New Indian Express*